DESPERATE DECEPTION

BROTHERHOOD PROTECTORS WORLD

DESIREE HOLT

Twisted Page Press LLC

BROTHERHOOD PROTECTORS

ORIGINAL SERIES BY ELLE JAMES

Brotherhood Protectors Series
Montana SEAL (#1)
Bride Protector SEAL (#2)
Montana D-Force (#3)
Cowboy D-Force (#4)
Montana Ranger (#5)
Montana Dog Soldier (#6)
Montana SEAL Daddy (#7)
Montana Ranger's Wedding Vow (#8)
Montana SEAL Undercover Daddy (#9)
Cape Cod SEAL Rescue (#10)
Montana SEAL Friendly Fire (#11)
Montana SEAL's Mail-Order Bride (#12)
Montana Rescue (Sleeper SEAL)
Hot SEAL Salty Dog (SEALs in Paradise)
Brotherhood Protectors Vol 1

Ideas for books come from so many different places, as do my heroes. The genesis for this book began circling my mind when I was privileged to meet and become friends with Jack Carr, former SAL and now an extraordinary best-selling author of *The Terminal List, True Believer* and the upcoming *Savage Son*.

Jack led special operations teams as a Team Leader, Platoon Commander, Troop Commander and Task Unit Commander. Over his 20 years in Naval Special Warfare he transitioned from an enlisted SEAL sniper, to a junior officer leading assault and sniper teams in Iraq and Afghanistan, to a platoon commander practicing counterinsurgency in the southern Philippines, to commanding a Special Operations Task Unit in the most Iranian influenced section of southern Iraq throughout the tumultuous drawdown of U.S. Forces.

In the preface of his second best seller, TRUE BELIEVER, he wrote about veterans of wars in Iraq and Afghanistan who seek to find purpose in their lives after they leave the service. From that line, and from talking to Jack, the idea for *Heroes Rising* was born. Men who deal with the debilitating memories of war, injuries they may have suffered, and a sudden change in their lives. I wanted to tell these stories to show that while the landscape may change, these men are still and always heroes who can be counted on. Thank you, Jack, for your friendship. For putting up with all my questions. And for being a hero who is the embodiment of strength and honor. My heroes are always based on someone. The heroes in this series are based on you.

For all you have done, this series is dedicated to you.

ACKNOWLEDGMENTS

Thank You

To Kate Richards, Margie Hager, and Nan Sipe, who dropped everything to beta read and edit this book so I could meet the deadline. To Frauke Spanath at Croco Designs for her outstanding, incredible cover. Without all of you, this book would never see the light of day. To my excellent resource and advisor, Joseph Trainor, former military officer and current law enforcement specialist.

To all my wonderful readers who travel my journey with me, buy my books, email me and generally make tis such a rewarding experience. I do this all for you.

And to Elle James, for inviting me into her Brotherhood Protectors World.

HEROES RISING

They served their country well, but they had focused for so along on being SEALs that now they are without a purpose or commitment. Their dreams are filled with images of teammates torn and shredded in combat situations. They have learned to live with a mental toughness developed through strict discipline. Those without family to ground them are suddenly facing a new life without direction and purpose. But former SEAL Alex Rossi sees in them the core of the what he wants in the sheriff's staff he is building one block at a time. In the foothills of Montana's Crazy Mountains they will find new purpose, build new lives and open themselves to love.

DESPERATE DECEPTION

She'd only be safe if she got away...

Lainie Taggert needed to break away from her abusive relationship before it killed her, but Sonny Fitzgerald had all the keys to controlling her. Until she landed in the hospital with bruises and broken bones. And her friend, Drea Halstead, convinced her they had to spirit her away.

His life was in limbo...

Zane Halstead was rootless after three tours with the SEALs, medically discharged and not sure what to do with himself. When Sheriff Alex Rossi in Montana reached out to him with an offer to join his staff, he thought, what the hell? A house came with it along with two horses two horses he could work with. But then his sister pleaded with him to take a battered woman with him and keep her safe. How could he say no?

But the best laid plans and all that...

They never expected to fall for each other, Zane with

his determination to stay single and Lainie with her nightmares and a vicious bully after her. And a rich one at that. But chemistry and emotions have their own plans, and when Zane gets word Lainie's ex is on her trail, he realizes he'll do anything to keep her safe…and for himself. With the help of Sheriff Alex Rossi, he is ready to take on the enemy for his woman.

CHAPTER 1

SHE WAS IN A SOFT, warm, comfortable place, cocooned. Happy. She wanted to stay there forever, but a distracting voice kept talking to her.

"Come on, Lainie. Can you open your eyes for me? I want to check your blood pressure again."

The voice was familiar but the last thing Lainie Taggert wanted to do was open her eyes. The pain would come back, along with the feel of *his* fists and *his* voice raging at her. Here, in this darkness, she was safe.

"Please, Lainie?" the soothing voice begged again. "Come on. Open those baby blues. Just for a few minutes. I promise."

The voice was both familiar and nonthreatening, so Lainie gritted her teeth and forced her lids open. Well, at least one. And found herself looking at the face of Drea Halstead. The woman who had once been her friend, eons ago, before *he* had taken over her life and cut her off from everyone.

"There you go." Drea smiled at her. "We have to stop meeting like this."

"Drea?" Lainie tried to blink and realized she could only see out of one eye. "Is that really you?"

"Sure is. I only started here last month. Got a job offer I couldn't refuse."

"Oh god." A tear rolled out of her good eye. "I'm not dreaming, right?"

"Nope. When I got your chart and walked into this room, imagine my surprise to find my friend lying in this bed." Her lips curved in a hint of a smile. "I know we haven't seen each other in a good while, but, really, you didn't have to go to such drastic lengths to make it happen."

Lainie tried to move, but pain surged everywhere in her body, including her left hand. And her left arm seemed to be restrained in some fashion. She wanted to close her eyes again and fall back into the soft place where none of this existed.

"Nope. Uh-uh." Drea's voice was both coaxing and demanding. "You have to wake up so I can talk to you." She paused. "What's going on, Lainie? I pulled up your hospital records. This has become a really bad pattern."

"I know." Lainie tried to hide her embarrassment, but she hurt too much to do anything but lie there. She knew she needed help, but where could she go? Who could she turn to? This time was the worst. Next time he might kill her. "Drea, I—I don't—I'm sorry."

"Stop. Please. You have nothing to apologize to me for. But that asshole you live with, the one whose goon told me to get lost or else, is going to have to answer some questions."

"Oh lord." Lainie closed her good eye. "Please tell me he's not here."

"He's not here. But, Lainie, you can't go back to that house. I'm afraid he'll kill you."

"You're right, but I don't know what to do," she whispered. "I have no one to go to, no one to help me, and I have to get away from him. God, Drea." She closed her eyes for a moment then opened them. "I don't know how a smart woman like me got herself into a situation that looks as if there's no way out."

"I wish I'd insisted you leave him when you had the chance. I've gotten so I can spot the abusers."

"But I didn't see it then," Lainie reminded her. "I still had blinders on." She swallowed back tears that were a combination of pain and humiliation. "I can't believe how stupid I was."

"Not stupid. Men like Sonny Fitzgerald are great con artists." Drea studied her.

"More than that," she whispered. "They're evil."

Something she hadn't discovered until too late.

Drea studied her for a long time, and Lainie wondered if she had bad news to tell her. She wasn't sure she could take any more.

"What?" she asked at last.

"Listen," Drea went on. "I've been thinking about this a lot while you were being treated and lying in here. Lainie, I have a way out for you, if you're willing to take it."

Lainie stared at her. A way out? Was it even possible? "Like what?"

"What if I could make you disappear? Not only from the hospital. I mean from the city. And without Sonny Fitzgerald knowing how or where you'd gone to?"

"I don't know how you could do that." Lainie swallowed, although her throat was so dry it hurt. "He's going to find out where I am. He finds out everything. I had to use my cell phone to call for the ride here. I meant to get rid of it after that, but—" She caught her lower lip between her teeth.

"A cell phone I have in my possession, without a battery or sim card." She grinned. "I watch a lot of television. I'm talking about making you disappear from here."

"You can do that, even with my injuries?" Lainie was almost afraid to hear the answer.

"It's not as bad as it could have been. Your right eye is swollen shut, your face looks like a painter's palette fell on it, your left shoulder is sprained, which is why it's in a sling, and two fingers of your left hand are broken. The doctor taped them together to stabilize them." She paused. "And the rest of your body is sprouting brises like flowers in a garden, but all that will heal. We've got to get you out of here so this doesn't happen again."

"When Sonny comes to pick me up, which you know he will, if I'm not here he'll pitch a fit." She closed her eyes for a moment. "Drea, I learned something I wasn't supposed to know. That's part of the reason he went berserk last night. Teaching me what would happen if I opened my mouth. He'll be insane to find me. What will you tell him?"

"We'll get to that in a minute. Look. We've been friends for a long time. We're still friends, despite the fact that asshole has cut you off from everyone but him and his people."

"I know, and I'm so sorry." She felt like crying, but this was no time for tears. She had to be strong.

"Forget that. This is your fourth visit here this year," Drea went on. "Honey, why didn't you ever reach out to the medical staff? They would have called the police and taken you to safety."

She wiped away a stupid tear with her good hand. This was no time for that. "He'd have found me, Drea. It wouldn't have been pretty for me or the people shielding me."

"But the police—"

"Can't always do what you want them to."

"He won't find out anything. I promise you. But, according to Rick, the other times Sonny brought you, he insisted that you fell, or some other half-assed answer. It was obvious he got you to go along with it or the police would have been called."

"You have no idea how angry that made him, that they wanted to report my injuries. If not for Geoff Miller, his driver/bodyguard, pointing out to him that if he made things worse, he'd be all over the news and possibly be arrested, he might have killed me when we got home."

Lainie could still remember the rage.

"But this time," Drea pointed out, "however you managed it, you got here by yourself. It's the perfect time for you to do a disappearing act."

"I know." The nausea came roiling back, and she swallowed again. "Could I have some water, please?"

"Of course." Drea held the paper cup with a straw up for her to sip. "Slowly, please."

"Thank you."

"It's a damn good thing you aren't married yet." She stopped and looked at Lainie. "You aren't, right?"

"No. I just—"

"Never mind. I've been thinking about this while you were getting patched up and drugged to make the pain a little easier to bear. I have a way out for you, and you need to take it if you want to stay alive."

Lainie tried to shift in bed, only everything hurt even worse whenever she moved.

"But what? How? I'm desperate enough at this moment to do anything, but what? Where can I go? No one will take me in, knowing what Sonny would do if he found out. I don't want to endanger them, anyway."

"Got it taken care of. I have someone who won't be afraid of Sonny and can get you out of here before that man even knows you're gone."

Lainie was almost afraid to hope. "Who would that be?"

"Remember I mentioned my brother, Zane, when we were still able to spend time together?"

"I do. The SEAL, right?"

Drea nodded. "Former SEAL. He's been medically discharged because of injuries from his last mission, but he's still in pretty good shape. Well, he's going to Montana to some rural area to get his act together. I'm going to get him to take you with him."

"What?" Lainie gasped. "But he doesn't even know me. Why would he do that? And what happens when we get there. Is he just going to leave me on my own? I can't—"

"Don't panic." Drea took her uninjured hand. "He'll make sure you're set up there, and he'll protect you, at least until you can make some decisions for yourself."

"He's not going to want to take a basket case like me with him." But god, on its own, a little hope wriggled through her.

"He will," Drea assured her. "I promise you he will. SEALs are big into protecting people. US Navy SEALs are the most elite combat unit in the world, and they carry it into their personal lives."

"And what about when Sonny comes looking for me here, like he always does?"

"Rick will handle it while I make myself scarce. As far as that asshole Sonny Fitzgerald is concerned, you merely walked out of the hospital and no one saw you leave. Rick and I have it all worked out."

"You don't know Sonny," she protested. "He can turn on the charm one minute and cut your throat the next." She grimaced. "Too bad I saw only the charm until it was too late."

"We all do stupid things," Drea assured her. "Sadly, yours turned out to have danger attached to it. But you don't worry about Sonny Fitzgerald. Dr. Carvallo can more than handle him and give him plenty of misdirection. And he made sure my name doesn't appear anywhere on your treatment chart, in case he remembers we're friends."

"Drea?"

"Yes, Lainie?"

"Listen." How could she phrase this? "You should be aware of this. Sonny did something really terrible. Worse than just hitting me because he feels like it. If he finds me, I know he'll kill me." She stopped to take a breath. "And he could easily kill anyone who helps me."

"What did he do?"

Lainie squeezed her eyes shut. She couldn't tell Drea. It would put her in jeopardy, too.

"I can't tell you. But if it gets out—Anyway, I had a tiny window of opportunity, and I took it. But I have to get away. This is way more than his usual stuff."

Drea's mouth tightened, but then she squeezed Lainie's hand.

"Then it's a good thing I have a fearless SEAL for a brother to take care of my friends."

"Are we?" she asked. "Still friends?"

"Honey, we will always be friends, no matter what. So. How about resting here for a few. I'm going to call Zane."

"He won't want to get involved with this," she protested. "I'm a stranger."

"Not to me. Now lie there and rest while I work things out."

"I—I don't know how to thank you."

"Letting me get you out of here is thanks enough. When I come back from my phone call, we have to get your stuff together. Then I want to give you a pill for the pain so you can handle the shifting around and walking out of here."

"I can pay him," Lainie said quickly. "I've been hoarding money, and before I managed to get out of the house this morning, I stuffed all of it into the pocket of my jeans. Will you check—"

"Already got it." Drea pulled an envelope thick with bills from her pocket. "And I can tell you he won't take a dime. But Jesus, Lainie. How long have you been squirreling this away? And how did you do it?"

"Six months." Lainie closed her good eye. "Pretty pathetic, right? Sonny didn't stop me from going to the grocery store, and I always got cash back. Not enough to raise his eyebrows when he checked the account."

"Lord, Lainie. Why didn't you drive to a police station? Or come to me?"

Lainie sighed, the effort hurting her chest. "He always had someone following me. And do you think the cops in this city would go against the great Sonny Fitzgerald? He's an icon. People fall all over themselves to curry favor with him. I still don't know how you're going to pull this off, even if your brother is stupid enough to agree to it."

"My brother is far from stupid, and, like I said, he's a former SEAL. Protecting people is their first order of business." She let go of Lainie's hand, placing it on the sheet. "Let me go make that call. Then I'll be back to get things rolling."

"W-What are you going to tell Sonny? I know he'll show up here when he discovers I'm gone."

"We're going to tell him you walked out of here and we have no idea where you went. Period." She handed Lainie a gel pack. "Meanwhile, hold this on your bad eye."

Lainie lay back against the pillows, trying not to think about the pain and her dangerous situation. After his temper tantrum last night, Sonny had left her alone to crawl upstairs to their room. He hadn't even bothered to ask how she was in the morning, just told her she'd better heal herself because no more hospital visits. Then he dressed and left for his office. Thank the lord she was able to call an Uber and get out of the house before he came back to check on her.

When she'd first gone to work as Sonny Fitzgerald's paralegal, she couldn't believe her luck. She'd spent ten years at two law firms making herself the best paralegal possible, looking for a big break. And the same amount of time looking for her dream man. She'd been drawn to Sonny like a magnet. He seemed to have it all, the things she'd been searching for all her life—big successful law firm, money, a place at the top of society, good looks. She basked in his attention, thrilled when he offered her a job working for him, and even more excited when he started asking her out.

Before she knew it, he'd asked her to marry him and insisted she move into his house. She was ecstatic, thinking she'd plucked the gold ring from the merry-go-round. But when her new role turned into a tool for him to woo clients and polish his image, she realized that once again her antenna had been off and she'd made a mistake. If only she'd known what was hiding behind that public mask and the hell she was descending into. By that time, however, she'd been trapped, desperate to find a way out.

Especially when she discovered his anger had a brutal side to it.

Of course, it wasn't as if she had the best history when it came to picking men. She'd begun to think there was something wrong with her, that men who either cheated on her or left her hanging were the ones she seemed drawn to. Good looks, smooth personalities, a sense of power—those had been on her unconscious to-do list. At least the others hadn't had anger issues.

Now here she was, lucky she wasn't already dead, and wondering how Drea thought someone could sneak her out of the city without a trace. And then what? Sonny had a history of getting rid of people who could do damage to him. Could Drea's brother protect her from that?

She was lying there trying to will the pain away and ignore the swelling in her left eye when Drea came back into the room with something folded under one arm and slid the glass door closed. She set a little pill cup on the nightstand, pulled the lone chair up to the bed, and leaned close.

"Okay, my friend, it's all set. Zane will be here in fifteen minutes. In a second I'm going to give you this pill to help the pain. Rick won't give you a shot because it would knock you out too much, but he's getting enough meds to take with you for the next couple of days."

Lainie tried not to get too excited. She might actually be getting out of here and away without Sonny's knowledge?

"Your brother will do it?"

Drea nodded. "He's a very good guy, and he'll keep you safe. This is going to work, Lainie. I want you to listen to me. I cleared it with Rick and Maggie. As far as anyone will know, you said you were leaving and that was that. We can't prevent you from doing that. The only way we could stop you is if you had psychiatric problems."

Lainie sighed. "Some people might say that's my problem. Otherwise ,why would I have stayed with Sonny all this time?" She looked up at Drea. "And thank you for not asking."

"That's because in my illustrious career as a nurse, I have too often seen how one person can exert control over another so insidiously the chance to leave is gone before the person realizes it."

"So, you *do* understand. Thank god."

nodded and held up a pair of scrubs. "This is your exit wardrobe. You'll merely be another ED employee to anyone who sees you. We keep extras of these around here in case patients' clothes get ruined or whatever. And I managed to snag a set. We're so busy today no one's going to give you a second look anyway." She held up an employee badge and waved it in front of Lainie. "One of the idiot orderlies dropped this somewhere so, lucky me, I found it and can attach it to your clothing."

Lainie looked at her friend. "I don't know how to thank you. Even after I walked away from our friendship—"

"As far as anyone up here will know, you got up and walked out of here. You weren't forced. Period. Sonny Fitzgerald won't be able to prove any different. And speaking of walking, you'll have to move semi-decently until we get out of here. Can you do that?"

"I'll make myself do it," Lainie answered, her voice fierce. She wasn't going to blow this one chance.

"Good. Take this pill first. It usually starts to work at once and will dull the pain enough to help you move. Come on. Let's get you into scrubs. Then we're going to get you to a back entrance where my brother will pick you up. I know where all the security cameras are to avoid them. We only have to get to a rear door. Can you do it?"

Lainie nodded. "I can do anything to get me away from him."

"All right, girlfriend. Let's get it done. Here. Take this pill."

Lainie swallowed the meds then let Drea help her into the scrubs. Was this really going to work?

WHEN HIS CELL PHONE RANG, Zane Halstead was standing in the living room of his month-to-month apartment, checking to make sure he hadn't left anything behind. The furniture was rented, so nothing to worry about there. This morning he'd packed up the truck with everything he owned, which wasn't all that much, and he was in the middle of doing one last check.

Renting a place in Tampa near his sister hadn't been a much better idea than going home to the horse farm his folks owned in Ocala. He'd been far from ready to leave the SEALs, and dealing with the injuries that forced him out wasn't helping. He'd gone to the VA hospital here like the doctors at Walter Reed had ordered and tried to do what he was supposed to. After weeks of physical therapy, his arm and hip were as good as they were going to get, but that wasn't enough to keep him with the Teams. When that last mission had gone to shit, and he'd been badly wounded, he'd known his days in the service were numbered. But knowing it and dealing with it were two different things.

Dr. Andrew Ryan, the shrink they'd sent him to, wasn't half bad. He'd recently transferred to the VA hospital in Tampa from another posting and seemed to know more than most what Zane was going through.

"You need a new purpose," he kept telling him. "There are plenty out there."

Yeah, right. The problem was finding one that was the right fit.

He really had no idea what he was going to do next. He'd never developed a serious relationship, so he had no woman waiting to help him rebuild his life. His most marketable skill was identifying and killing bad guys. He knew some former SEALs had gone to work for security agencies but, for whatever reason, that hadn't appealed to him. So, he'd hung around doing not much of anything, driving himself nuts and wondering what he was going to do with the rest of his life and how he'd fit into society. And then he got *The Email*, from Alex Rossi, sheriff of a small county at the foothills of the Crazy Mountains.

The only thing he knew about that area was that another former SEAL, Hank Patterson, had built a security agency out there called Brotherhood Protectors. All the agents were former military, mostly SEAL. Despite the fact that a friend had highly recommended them, he still had no interest in that kind of situation. So, what did the local sheriff want with him?

He clicked on the link to open the email.

Don't delete this before you read it. I'm a former SEAL myself, and rebuilding the sheriff's office here. Long story. Like you, I wasn't sure what to do with myself after the Teams, and I was lucky to land this job, even though the place is a mess. I'm hoping I can talk you into at least a trip out here to look the area over. You might find a new purpose, even if it's nothing more than raising horses, which are in high demand. I hear you're very good with horseflesh. There's a house on six acres you can use rent-free while you look the place over. It comes with two horses that need a caretaker soon. If you're interested, my phone number's beneath my signature. Give me a call. It's my cell, so I answer all the time.

Alex Rossi.

Zane thought it was the craziest thing he'd ever seen or heard. This guy contacting him out of the blue like this? But the more he looked at the email, the more he thought, why the fuck not? He wasn't doing himself or anyone else much good hanging around in his own private pity party. Maybe a change of scenery would do him some good. If he didn't like it, he didn't have to stay. Right? And maybe, away from his family who tiptoed around him, and his friends who treated him as damaged goods, he might actually find a life again. Maybe.

The first thing he did was an Internet search for the man, stunned at what he saw. Alex Rossi had been appointed sheriff by the county commissions when the previous sheriff had been sent to prison, and for a horrendous reason. A group of uberwealthy men for twenty years had made a game of raping young teenage girls, always approaching from behind so their identity was concealed. Threatening death if they reported it, on the chance that a victim might have some clue as to who they were.

Apparently the former sheriff had been paid off to overlook things. Worse than that, to let the men know when a girl had enough courage to report it. It seemed Sheriff Alex Rossi had cleaned up the mess and made sure the men were punished. But what really stuck out was the fact that Bill Schroeder, Rossi's father-in-law, was a member of the wealthy elite participating over the years in the rapes. A situation in which Micki, unbeknownst to her father, had been a victim when she was fifteen. And that her father had been killed to shut him up. It had been Alex's big case right after he came on the job.

The information that made his head spin was the fact that after the killer was arrested and half the sheriff's deputies fired, Alex turned around and married Micki Schroeder. Knowing all of this, he couldn't wait to meet this woman who had survived a rape, the knowledge that her father belonged to the group, was murdered by them, and survived it all to marry the sheriff. Apparently she'd also supported him in the restructuring of his office and setting a new tone for it. A man certainly couldn't ask for a better leader.

The thirty-minute phone call gave him a good feeling about the man and, an hour, later he had agreed to the crazy idea—crazy like the mountains?— said he'd stay in the house, and set about informing his family. It was a testament to how concerned they were about him that neither his parents nor his sister tried to talk him out of it. Well, maybe he'd figure out the rest of his life in Montana and everyone, including himself, could breathe again.

He was getting ready to walk out for the last time when his phone rang. The readout had his sister's name on it.

"Drea? What's up? Aren't you at work?"

"I am, but, Zane? I really, really need your help. And please don't say no until you hear it all. Okay?"

"Jesus, girl. What have you gotten yourself into now?"

He listened while she laid out her story for him, especially Lainie Taggert's condition and why her fear of Sonny Fitzgerald was so intense. As she outlined the plan, his stomach knotted, and his fingers tightened their hold on the phone.

"You're kidding me, right? This is a joke to yank my chain."

"No, it isn't." Her voice was low. "I'm dead serious. Dead, by the way, being what this woman will be if we don't pull this deception off and sneak her out of Tampa. Please, Zane. She has no place else to turn."

He wanted more than anything to say no, but it wasn't who he was. He knew this last-minute call from Drea might screw up his plans. He also knew she wouldn't ask unless she was desperate. Take a strange woman to Montana with him to a situation he wasn't even sure would work? What the hell?

What was he supposed to do with her when he got there? If she was as banged up as Drea said, she'd need medical care, and he had no idea what kind was available in the sparsely populated area where he was headed.

And what about her? If she was running from an abusive relationship, she was probably terrified of men. He'd seen that before. It always made his blood boil, wondering how a man could treat a woman that way. But she had to be scared shitless, and what would make her trust him? Did she know Drea well enough for that?

Plus, he'd have to find a way to take care of her on the trip. Then, when they got to Montana, he'd have to figure out what to do with her. Hopefully, Drea would have some kind of update for him by then. He needed to know things like how long he was expected to hide Lainie away. Where she would go from there. How she'd get her life together.

Fuck. This wasn't what he needed. He could hardly keep himself together, just taking things one day at a time. But he knew in his heart he'd do that. He was a protector by nature.

"Anything else I should know?"

"Yes. This guy is one mean bastard, and Lainie says she knows something he'd kill her to keep secret."

Fucking great.

He swallowed a sigh.

"You know I can't turn you down, but I'm leaving in five minutes. Can you get her to that exit by the time I get there?"

"Yes. Yes, yes, yes. Oh, and you'd better bring plenty of cash. If he somehow finds out she's with you, he can track your credit cards."

Jesus! What next?

"Okay. No sweat."

"And, Zane? Thank you so much."

He carried the last of his bags down to the truck and stowed them in the back seat. Then he placed his Glock .9mm in the console along with a box of ammo. Finally, he made sure the knife he always carried was securely strapped to his ankle. He didn't know if this asshole would suddenly show up or what, but, like every other

SEAL, he wanted to always be prepared. Then he climbed into the driver's seat and pulled out of his parking space.

What the fuck have I gotten myself into?

He talked to himself all the way to the bank where he pulled out a wad of cash, and then all the way to the hospital, calling himself ten kinds of fool for getting mixed up in this. He could barely take care of himself, let alone someone else who probably needed constant attention.

Fifteen minutes later, Zane pulled up to the delivery door at the hospital, hopped out of his truck, and opened the passenger door. In a moment, a back door to the hospital opened and Drea stepped out, looking both ways before motioning to someone. A guy in scrubs and a white coat, probably the doctor she'd told him about, exited carrying a woman in his arms. As he placed her gently in the passenger seat and buckled her in, Zane took a good look at her, and acid washed in his throat at what he saw.

"We managed to get her dressed and got her out of there without anyone asking questions," Drea told him, "and I also gave her a pain pill, so she's a little out of it."

"What's with the scrubs?"

"So we could walk her through the department and down here without anyone asking questions. I think, though, she's done for. The meds will pretty much knock her out for a while."

Drea had been right about the bruises, the black eye, everything, only she hadn't been quite descriptive enough. Sonny Fitzgerald had most definitely used this woman as a punching bag. Her auburn hair hung limp, and her delicate features were pinched with pain, but even beneath all that he saw a delicate beauty. He wanted to find the man and show him what SEALs did to abusers.

He was sure without the damage she was a knockout. Not that it mattered right now. She was in desperate need, and he hadn't been with a woman in nearly a year. Wasn't even sure he'd know how to deal with one under normal circumstances.

"Jesus, Drea. She's a mess. Can she even do anything for herself? I don't—"

"It will be fine," Drea insisted. "She's stronger than she looks. I trust you to do whatever is necessary. Figure it out, or she's a dead woman."

"Who is this guy, anyway?"

"Rich and powerful. Do a search on him when you stop for the night." She leaned into the truck and shook the woman gently. "Lainie? Lainie, this is my brother, Zane. He's going to take good care of you, like I said. He's getting you out of here before you can get hurt again."

Lainie's eyes had a wild, frightened look in them as she scanned the area, taking everything in. "S-Sonny?"

"Not here," Drea assured her. "But we want to get you out of here before he decides to show up. This is my brother, Zane. Remember? He's going to take good care of you. He's the best protection you can get. I promise."

Zane thought he could only hope that would be the truth. He stood close to Lainie but didn't touch her, noticing how she shrank away from him. All he wanted was for her to become familiar with his presence.

Lainie wet her lips and stared a moment, as if trying to absorb it all. "Drea's brother?"

He nodded. "And I'll be doing my best to keep you safe."

She swallowed. "And thank you."

"We're gonna get going in a second here, Lainie." He pitched his voice low, hoping it sounded reassuring. "I want to make sure you're comfortable in the seat and that your seat belt is fastened."

She nodded, not saying a word, but he saw pain etched on her face.

He had to bite down on the pain in his arm when he moved her at a bad angle and did his best not to groan as he settled her. Maybe he should double up on his exercises if he was going to be carting this woman around. She didn't need some gimp for a protector. He swallowed the bitterness, closed the door, and turned to Drea.

"I'm fine," he assured his sister when he saw the look of concern on her face. "It's the truth. I can take good care of her."

"I know you can. I—" She shook her head. "Yes, you're fine. And thank you again for doing this."

"You're welcome."

Drea handed him a plastic bag with some meds in it plus a plain envelope.

"What's this?" He frowned as he looked at them.

"Her medications for a couple of days plus instructions on how to care for her injuries. There's money in the envelope. She had it with her when she got to the hospital. Apparently, she's been hiding it away for a while. She asked me to give it to you to help pay for the trip."

Zane tried to give it back. "I don't want or need her money."

Drea nodded. "I told her that, but she's going to need some clothing and personal items, since she has nothing with her. You can use some of it for that. I put a note in to let you know what. You can grit your teeth and do it," she insisted when he frowned. "She's in no condition to shop."

"Jesus, Drea." He put the meds inside the truck console and stuffed the envelope into his pocket. "Anything else?"

"One more thing." Drea took a cell phone from her pocket and handed it to him along with the sim card. "It's Lainie's. I turned it off and pulled the sim card and the battery, but you need to get rid of it. I didn't want to do it here at the hospital. You know, just in case. I never know how these things can be traced."

"Will do." He nodded. "I'll text you from the road and let you know how it's going."

"Thank you again, Zane." She gave him a tight hug. "Thank you, thank you, thank you. You're the best brother in the world."

"Yeah, thanks for being a lifesaver," the doctor added.

Zane nodded once, climbed into the truck, and pulled away from the building. Evasion was one of the many things he'd learned as a SEAL, and he didn't trust that this Sonny Fitzgerald asshole wasn't already lurking someplace with his henchmen waiting to see if this woman made a break for it. She certainly couldn't do it without help, so he might be scoping out the area already, despite what Drea said.

He didn't hit Interstate 75 right away, on the off chance someone was on their tail, although he didn't see how that was possible. Drea had accomplished the whole process slick as grease. He drove a few miles on Interstate

4, doubled back, and drove through a couple of busy neighborhoods before he actually headed out of town. When he was satisfied there was no one on his tail, he drove to a street with many warehouses, some of them vacant. Behind one of them, he got out of the car, dropped her cell to the ground, and crushed it beneath his heel. Next was the battery. The remnants went into a trash barrel. Then he headed out of the city, north on Interstate 75 toward Chattanooga. From there he'd head west.

He glanced over at Lainie, bundled into a hospital blanket and scrunched against the door. Somehow, he'd have to find a way for her to trust him, even for a little while.

CHAPTER 2

"LIFE IS ten percent what happens to you and ninety percent how you respond to it."
  Charles Swindoll

LAINIE HAD CLOSED her eyes as soon as he'd settled her in the truck, and they were still closed. Zane was sure her meds had a lot to do with it, but he had a feeling she wasn't sleeping so much as shutting out the world. He couldn't say he blamed her. Drea had told him this was the woman's fourth visit to this hospital, but there could have been others at other facilities. Yeah, she was damned lucky to be alive.

He realized with a shock that in the short time since they'd left the hospital, he'd felt a change in himself. For the first time since his discharge, he had a real purpose. He wasn't aimlessly twisting in the wind. He had a responsibility. A woman to protect.

Of course, he had better figure out what to do with her when they got to Montana. He had no idea what Sheriff Alex Rossi would say when he showed up with an abused female. Well, he was in it now, for sure, but he had to sort out the answers to the questions racing around in his brain. First thing when he got there, he'd have to scope out a doctor. He'd had some medical training, all SEALs did, basic stuff to be used when necessary in battle. But her injuries were severe enough a medical practitioner needed to follow them. And he had to learn what kind of day-to-day care she'd need.

He had planned to deadhead to Billings, the closest city to Alex Rossi's area, catching a nap here and there and eating as he drove. Well, that plan was out the window. Checking the time, he figured they could find a motel somewhere outside Columbia, South Carolina, camp for the night, and get moving in the morning. He hoped she'd understand when he only rented one motel room, it was because he didn't want to leave her alone.

Of course, sleeping in the same room with her presented its own challenges. What if he had one of his nightmares? What if he did something that scared the shit out of her? He tried not to tense up as the thought ran through him.

He was moving along at the top of the speed limit when Lainie shifted slightly in the seat next to him. He glanced over and saw she was sitting up straight rather than huddled against the door the way she'd been.

"Zane?"

Her voice was so soft, he had to strain to hear it.

"Hey, Lainie. What can I do for you?" He worked to make his tone as nonthreatening as possible. "You okay? You need something?"

"Not right this minute. I—" She stopped. "First of all, you can't know how grateful I am to you for doing this. I know I'm a mess and not something you need hanging around your neck."

"No problem." He deliberately made his voice soft and calm. "I like having a beautiful woman hanging around my neck."

"Beautiful?" She made a noise. "Please. I know what I look like. Anyway, I, uh, need to stop at a restroom. Is that possible?"

"Sure is. In fact, there's an exit coming up right ahead of us."

He cut into the right-hand lane and took the exit ramp. Right where the service road hit a highway was a stoplight and a big service station/convenience store. Zane pulled into the parking lot and found a spot not far from the entrance. He didn't want her to have to walk too far. As a matter of fact, he wondered if she could walk at all or if she needed help. And how did that take care of her restroom situation?

Swallowing a sigh, he shut off the engine, walked around to the other side of the truck, and opened the passenger door. When Lainie looked at him, it was hard not to see the fear in her eyes, and it was up to him to assure her she had nothing to be afraid of with him.

Looking down at her lap, she said in a soft voice, "I think I need some help here."

It was obvious she didn't like asking him. For

anything. He needed to make it plain to her that his help was part of the deal. No problem. In fact, this was probably the first time in months he'd thought of someone besides himself.

"Okay, then. I'm your helper for whatever you need."

He unbuckled the seat belt, being careful where and how he touched her. Then, giving her a smile and gritting his teeth against his own pain, he lifted her down from the seat and set her on her feet. He kept his hand on her free elbow until he was sure she was steady. Again doing his best to minimize his limp, he had started them toward the entrance of the store when she stumbled a little.

Zane wrapped his fingers around her uninjured arm as gently as possible.

"I'm sorry," she whispered again. "I guess I need some help again."

"No problem. I love being your helper. Here we go. We'll just move slowly."

He cursed the fact that his body wasn't at full steam and wondered again what the hell he was doing serving as a protector for this woman when he was far from the man he used to be. Damn! He maneuvered her into the store, hand still cupping her elbow. There were a fair number of customers in there, and all of whom stopped and stared as they entered. It was hard not to look, as banged up as she was. He spotted the signs for the restrooms and guided her over to the appropriate door.

"You okay by yourself?"

She actually managed a little smile. "Let's hope so. But if not, I'll scream. Okay?"

"Sure thing. Be sure to walk slowly and take it easy."

It hurt Zane to watch her, moving like a very old lady because she was so racked with pain from her bruises and injuries. He saw her glance at the cashier who was watching them with a stern look on her face, and knew exactly what the other woman was thinking. He started to say something when Lainie halted her progress for a moment and spoke up.

"He's not the one who did this," she told the woman. "He's the one who's saving me."

Then, with slow, careful steps, she disappeared into the ladies' room.

Zane took a moment to text Drea.

"Making a pit stop. So far so good."

"Lainie doing okay?"

"As well as you'd expect. Don't worry. I'm on it."

"She's scared to death, Zane."

"I know. We'll work on that. Later."

He disconnected and wandered up and down the aisles, looking for easy snacks to take with him. He had no idea when Lainie had last eaten, and his own stomach was grumbling a little. He trolled for provisions for the ride, gathering a variety of snacks then carrying them over to the cashier who was still watching him with a stern look.

"That right, what she said? It wasn't you? Or is she so afraid of you she'd say that."

"I'd never do that to a woman," he assured her. "Take my word for it."

"I'd like to take a bat to whoever he is," she told him as she rang up his purchases.

Zane snorted. "I think you'd have to get in line."

He added a cup of coffee for himself and tea for Lainie,

figuring that would go better with the meds still in her system. He also asked the woman if she could put some ice in a plastic bag for him. Lainie's eye needed something to work on that swelling. She pointed him toward a miniature cooler for sale on the endcap of a display unit, and they dumped the ice in that. He added a couple more items before paying the cashier.

By the time he had everything bagged and ready, Lainie was slowly making her way from the ladies' room. She looked at the cashier who was still glaring at Zane and shook her head.

"I promise you, he's not the one. He's helping me. You have my word."

"If you say so, but you'd better take good care of her," the woman warned.

Zane nodded. He managed to juggle everything including the drinks and still be able to help Lainie back outside and to the truck. Without spilling or dropping anything, including her, he got it all into the truck.

When he climbed back into the driver's seat, he glanced over at Lainie. The trip into the store and back seemed to have used up all her energy, cutting deep lines of exhaustion into her face.

"You okay?"

"I'm good. Thank you for your help." She wet her lower lip with the tip of her tongue.

If they both hadn't been in such bad shape, that little gesture would have turned him on. But he was far from the appealing male he used to be, and she was a terrified, injured victim under his protection. That was good. Complications weren't needed.

"I thought you might like some hot tea." He lifted the cup from the holder where he'd placed it. "I figured it would be better than coffee. I added some sweetener, but I've got more if you need it."

"I'm sure it's fine. Thank you." Despite her broken fingers and the difficulty of the sling, she managed to lift the lid and blew on the hot liquid. "You're very kind."

Zane shrugged. "Not a problem. You're pretty good at handling that."

"It's not my first rodeo." Before he could comment, she added, "Forget I said that. I don't want you to think I'm some poor pathetic idiot who—Never mind."

He took that as his cue not to comment. "I got you some sunglasses back at the store. They have oversized lenses, and the frames, I think, are bigger than you might be used to. But they'll cover your eyes and part of the bruising on your cheek. And you won't get blinded staring into the sun."

"Thank you." Her voice was so soft he barely could hear her. "I appreciate it."

She sat quietly while he pulled off the sticker and tag and slipped them onto her face as gently as he could.

"How about meds before we start off again? Drea gave me enough for a couple of days. We'll figure out what to do about more when we get to Montana, but do you need anything at the moment?"

She shook her head. "No. I'm good for the moment. Really."

But he could see from the deep lines pain had carved into her face that she was far from fine. "How about a couple of Tylenol? I bought some in the store just in case. Being brave can get you only more trouble."

"Um, yeah. That would be good. The other stuff makes me nauseous sometimes."

He nodded. "Tylenol it is."

He handed her two and held her tea while she popped them into her mouth with her uninjured hand.

"Thanks. That'll help. A lot." She swallowed some more tea. Then, bitterness edging her voice, she added, "I seem to have developed a high threshold for pain."

Zane didn't want to get into that with her right then so he lifted the bag of munchies from the floor where he'd placed it, opening it so she could see inside.

"I had no idea what you like, and you need something to keep you going until we stop for supper. Take your pick."

She paused in the process of sipping her tea and looked over at him, her face paler, if possible. "Stop? You mean, not keep going?"

Zane forced himself to be calm in the face of her obvious fear. She didn't need anger. He was sure she'd seen enough of that.

"If you're worried that the man who did this to you will find us if we stop, you can put that out of your mind. I did some fancy driving before we hit the interstate, and I've been keeping an eye out since then."

"But—"

He held up a hand. "I spent eighteen years as a SEAL, Lainie. I learned how to know if anyone's tracking me. But okay, how about this. When we stop for the night, I'll hit a drive-through and get some food to take with us to the motel. We'll eat where no one can see us."

Her relief was palpable. "Thank you."

"Meanwhile, I think these chocolate chip cookies would go really good with that tea."

He opened the package, took out both cookies, and set them on the console on a napkin.

She looked at the cookies then at him. "Thank you."

"No problem."

From the corner of his eyes, he watched as she took a dainty bite of the cookie then set it down so she could sip her tea. He wanted to pull the truck over and feed her the cookie bit by bit, but he knew she'd shy away from that. Again, his blood boiled at the thought of a man who could do this to a woman. Sonny Fitzgerald should be glad he wasn't standing in front of Zane at the moment.

By the time he finished his coffee and a Danish, Lainie had managed to consume two cookies and most of the tea. He bagged the trash, took the ice from the cooler, and wrapped it in a T-shirt he'd had lying on the back seat.

"You okay to hold that on your eye for a while?"

"Uh-huh. At least it's on the opposite side from my sling so I can use my good hand."

He helped her get it in place and arrange herself as comfortably as possible then started the truck.

"Think this will hold you for a while? I thought we'd get in some mileage."

Lainie gave him one of those sideways glances. "Whatever you want," she answered in a dull voice.

Zane didn't know whether to rage or cry at what had been done to this woman.

"Let's make a deal, okay? You promise to answer a question truthfully when I ask you. Not just what you think I want to hear. And I promise not to get even the least little bit upset. Can we try that?"

She took so long to answer him, he was afraid she might not say anything at all.

Finally, in a small voice, she said, "Okay. I'll try."

He let out a breath. "Good. That's good. That's all I ask. By the way, Drea gave me your phone to get rid of. I smashed it all to hell before we left Tampa and dumped it behind a deserted warehouse. I don't know if it's still trackable, but I figured best to get rid of it before we left town."

"That's fine," she told him in a monotone. "I have no one to call anyway."

He kept his speed steady at seventy as they rolled along the interstate. His plan was to make Chattanooga before they stopped for the night, but he was keeping a careful eye on Lainie to see how she was holding up. If she looked as if she was in pain or otherwise distressed, he'd stop earlier.

He also needed to update Alex Rossi. He'd wanted to scope out the situation and get Lainie out of town before he communicated with the man and gave him a heads-up on his change in situation. He'd surprised himself when he realized, he was actually looking forward to the move. He hoped to hell this didn't screw things up, but the man he was at his core wouldn't have turned away from Drea's plea and Lainie's situation. He hoped Rossi would understand.

He was about to turn the radio on, volume down low,

when Lainie shifted in her seat, cried out, and tried to flail at the air with the arm in the sling. At least he had some experience with this, having sat with wounded teammates through nightmares far too often. Afraid she'd do harm to herself, he reached over and lightly touched her leg.

"Lainie? Lainie, wake up."

He lifted his hand, slowed down, and eased into the right-hand lane. An accident was the last thing he needed. Then he touched her knee again, making the contact as light as possible while keeping his eyes on the road.

"I'll do it." The voice was thin and quivery. "Whatever you want. You don't have to hit me again."

Rage shot through Zane, and he had to tamp it down. What had the bastard wanted her to do that he had to beat her to get compliance?

"Lainie? Come on. Wake up for me."

Abruptly she stilled, her entire body tense. He waited to see what she did next, relieved when she didn't start trying to wave her arm again. Instead, she tried to inch closer to the door.

"You awake?" he asked.

"Yes." She cleared her throat. "Sorry. I'll try to keep from falling asleep again."

"No problem. You probably need it. All I want is to make sure you don't do any damage to yourself."

There was a long moment of silence. Zane stayed in the right-hand lane, just in case, until he was sure she had it together again.

"Okay."

"I want you to know that I'm not going to do anything to hurt you, physically or otherwise. You're safe with me."

From the corner of his eye, he saw her tense.

"You probably think I'm a nutcase," she told him in a quiet voice.

"I try not to judge anyone," he assured her. "We all have reasons for doing or not doing things."

"Mine probably weren't very good." She paused. "And it seems not very smart."

"Yeah, well, it would be nice if we all made only smart decisions, but we don't seem to be wired that way."

More silence. He waited, determined to let her lead the conversation.

"I want you to know something. I wasn't some idiot floozy who was willing to put up with anything for his money."

He chuckled. "Lainie, the last word I'd use to describe you is floozy."

"Just idiot, right?"

From the corner of his eye, he saw her turn to look out the passenger window. She was silent for a long time again, but, also again, he let her take the lead.

"That's okay," she told him. "You don't have to answer." A pause. "I worked for him as a paralegal. He has so many people in his office, I was thrilled when he chose me to work on his particular clients with him."

"I think I'd be happy about it, too," he agreed. When she didn't say anything else, he added, "Lainie, I don't want you to feel you have to give me any kind of details or share anything with me, especially if it makes you uncomfortable."

The silence was longer this time.

"Thanks for doing this for me," she said at last.

"It's fine. Don't worry about it. Okay?"

Yeah, he'd do the worrying for both of them. Checking to make sure he was clear, he edged back into the center lane and upped his speed. He had a feeling Lainie Taggert was going to need food and a bed sooner rather than later.

CHAPTER 3

"The path to success is to take massive, determined action."
  Tony Robbins

Taking action—or having others do it for you—had long been the motto by which Sonny Fitzgerald lived. Those actions had always been well thought out and well planned. Today, however, he was too enraged to plan. Usually when his plans took a turn for the worse or a predicted outcome turned around, he had a handy object on which to take out his rage. Currently it was his fiancée, who should have been his wife by this time, all neatly wrapped up in a bunch of legal ties that kept her bound to him.

He looked exactly like what he was, although he had deliberately cultivated this image. A couple of inches over six feet, he had a well-toned body, thanks to almost daily workouts. His hair was midnight black, swept back from his forehead, his eyes a startling blue in a face with an aristocratic chin and high cheekbones. There were people who whispered he'd had surgery to create the face he wanted, and he never argued with them, but no one knew if it was rumor or truth, and he sure wasn't telling.

He was a man who had worked his ass off to get where he was, who had without conscience destroyed anyone in his way. Those who fell into line with him fared well, as long as they never stepped across that line. And those few he considered his equal, like his two law partners, knew exactly what they could and could not do. People came to him to litigate their claims, for which he got enormous fees and shares in the largest businesses. They knew if Sonny Fitzgerald was in charge, they could not lose.

Lainie Taggart was a nobody when she fell into his orbit. A college graduate like a zillion others with a degree and ten years at a small law firm. He'd checked her out. No family in the area, no significant other or anything close to it. A few friends she spent time with. But mostly she put a lot of effort into achieving senior paralegal status. She had a real thirst to find her place in the world.

Well, he'd given her that place, ten times over. He'd chosen her carefully, for her looks and her brains as well as her ability to acknowledge the chain of command. Too bad she didn't accept it in her personal as well as her professional life. All he wanted, goddammit, was for her to do whatever he told her, whether it was in the living room or in the bedroom. Couldn't she just manage that? He was prepared to spend a lot of money on her to accomplish it.

But no, she had to go and get all independent on him. Spark the temper he did his best to control professionally, but at home he could be his goddamn self, right? How many episodes would it take to get that across to her? You'd think four trips to the hospital in a year would have gotten the message across.

The other times he'd driven her there himself so he could explain how unfortunate it was that his fiancée was clumsy and fell down a lot. But this time he hadn't wanted to put up with the questions, the know-it-all looks, all that crap. Besides, it might be time to get rid of her. After last night, she had knowledge that could cripple him.

He'd had an unusually unsatisfactory meeting the night before, with a woman whose company he was dead set on acquiring, and it ended in disaster. He'd said as much to Geoff Miller, who had driven him. Killing the woman had been an accident but shit! She wouldn't sign the deal with the Calabreses he'd put together for her, and it was a key piece of a new structure he was building. He hadn't meant to slap her, except she got all mouthy and made threats about suing him. Him! The star of the legal community. That would never do. And it wasn't his fault she fell and hit her head against the coffee table.

Geoff had cleaned away any trace he was there, and they left the woman for her housekeeper to find. As soon as they got back to his house, he'd knocked back two quick shots of whiskey to try and cool himself down. He and Geoff were discussing possible fallout from the situation when he heard movement in the kitchen. The staff didn't live in, so it had to be Lainie.

What was she doing downstairs? She had started going to bed early. Had she heard the conversation? How much of it?

When she stood there stammering at him, he'd lost it and belted her. Not his best move, but then the rage engulfed him. She'd had the nerve to tell him if he hit her again she was walking out, even if she took nothing with her. He'd thought they were long past that stage, that he'd made her understand how things were. That made him see red, and his anger flared again. By the time Geoff came in and pulled him away, she was a mess. Good. Maybe she'd learned something.

Watching her move slowly up the stairs, he'd hollered, "Sleep in a guest room tonight. I don't want you in my bed in that condition."

He hadn't bothered to check on her before he left for the office that morning. He'd set both security alarms and told the housekeeper to leave her alone for the day. Maybe by tonight she'd be ready to do anything he wanted, including keeping her mouth shut and follow orders. That was all he wanted. Not too much to ask, right? A smart, pretty woman on his arm who knew how and what to say? How to keep secrets? Great in bed? All that? He gave her plenty of money, for chrissake. Well, charge cards, at least.

He'd left her alone most of the day, waiting until he was sure she was in enough residual pain to have learned her lesson before he went home. But when he got home, the first thing he realized was the alarm system was off. The second was Lainie was gone. No, the housekeeper hadn't seen or heard her leave. Had she gone to a hospital? He couldn't exactly call around to see if she had and which one she went to without raising questions he didn't want to answer.

He was shocked she could do that in her condition and was torn between anger and panic. What if she'd blabbed about last night's fiasco?

Her phone. Maybe she'd called someone. He had the password to her account, of course. He dialed the last number listed and when he discovered it was Uber, he demanded the direct number of the driver who had picked up a fare at his house that day. Okay, Uber made sense. He'd cut her off from anyone who would get in the way of their situation. But when he called the number, all the driver could tell him was he had delivered her to the emergency entrance of the big hospital downtown.

He was seething by the time he learned where the asshat had taken her. One of the last places he wanted to go. He was tempted to leave her there and knock her out of his life, but she knew too many things. He couldn't leave her out there to flap her gums at people who'd love to destroy him.

He had an idea of how long it would be before Lainie was through being examined, x-rayed, and patched up. He looked at his watch, checking how long he should wait before going to pick her up. It was four o'clock. She'd been gone since about ten, according to the time stamp on her phone call. Based on the previous visits, he figured she'd be about finished right now. Time to show up and play the loving and concerned fiancé, and also subtly remind everyone he was a high-powered attorney who could sue the hospital if they gave him any shit.

He decided to try calling her directly, but the call wouldn't go through. What the hell was going on? After three tries, he dialed the service provider. Some snotty kid told him the sim card must have been removed because the phone was no longer connected to the network. What the fuck? He hadn't imagined she would do anything like that. He'd better get his ass to the hospital and put on a good show.

Geoff Miller, his driver/bodyguard/right-hand man, had been hanging out all day waiting to see if he was needed, but Sonny decided to drive by himself to the hospital. He figured he'd look less threatening that way. God only knew what Lainie had told the staff there, and he needed to put on a good show.

As he made his way through the traffic, he mulled over what he'd say. Lainie was having some emotional problems, he'd tell them. Sometimes her confusion caused her to fall and hurt herself. Sometimes she hit herself. Yeah, that would explain the bruises on her stomach and chest. Yeah, that would satisfy them. He'd make sure it did.

He was a master litigator, for god's sake. He'd faced many people across a conference room table and pushed them into a corner, demanding and getting exorbitant settlements for his clients. He was especially talented when it came to squeezing out every nickel for one of his clients buying another business. Not his problem if the other guy went away feeling he got screwed.

By the time he reached the hospital, he was actually in a pretty good mood, believing he had everything in hand. The good mood lasted while he parked in the emergency department parking area and went inside. But it all evaporated, replaced by anger when the nurse running the ED told him she had left.

"What the hell do you mean, she left?" He glared at the woman. "Don't you keep better track of your patients?"

"Of course we do." Sonny vaguely remembered Maggie Churchill from previous visits. He had no idea, however, that she'd been running the ED for longer than many of the current doctors and nurses had been working at the hospital.

"Well, then. How did—"

"But we don't chain them to the bed. If they want to leave, they have the right to."

Sonny bit back an immediate reply. He wanted to ask them how they could misplace a woman in Lainie's battered condition, but then he might have to answer questions best left alone.

"I want to speak with the doctor who treated her," he demanded. "And the nurse."

"Of course. Let me page them, although they might be busy with other patients at the moment."

"I certainly hope they pay better attention to them than they did to my fiancée."

He waited with scarcely concealed impatience, shoving his hands into the pockets of his slacks so no one would see them curled into fists. While Maggie paged the two people he wanted to speak with, he scanned the busy ED. It seemed there wasn't an empty cubicle. Personnel moved swiftly from one patient to another, assisted by orderlies and nurse assistants. He had a hard time believing that with all these people around, Lainie had been able to somehow walk out of here and no one noticed.

"You wanted to speak to me?"

43

Sonny turned to see a man as tall as he was dressed in hospital scrubs over which he wore a typical white doctor's coat. The pin on the pocket read Richard Carvallo, M.D.

"I do if you're the one who treated Lainie Taggert. I want to know where the hell she is?"

Rick frowned. "Let me check."

"You don't remember a patient you treated earlier today? A hell of a way to operate."

"I'm sorry, Mr.—" He raised an eyebrow.

"Fitzgerald. Sonny Fitzgerald. I'm her fiancé, and I'm here to take her home." He shook his head. "She's so damn independent, she didn't even call me at the office to tell me she hurt herself. I don't know what I'll do if she's really bad off."

He hoped this bastard believed his caring fiancé act. As an attorney, he'd developed enough skills to make people believe anything, but this was a chancy situation. No telling what Lainie had told these people.

"Let me check her chart. Maggie, let me have one of those tablets, please." He reached out for a digital tablet like those everyone used these days. "Okay, let's see. Lainie Taggert." He swiped through some records, searching. "Okay, here it is. Mr. Fitzgerald, it says she left before we could complete treatment."

"Left? By herself?"

Maggie looked at the notes on the chart again. "That's what it says here."

"Look again." Sonny clenched his jaw. "I don't believe she would have left like that. She wouldn't want to worry me."

Maggie stared at him, an expression in her eyes that made him want to smack her.

"How badly did you say she was hurt?" she asked. "Would it have been bad enough to prevent her from leaving here alone? What kind of injuries are we talking about here?"

Sonny wanted to hit someone, starting with the obnoxious charge nurse.

"Listen. She took a bad fall early today, and she wasn't moving too easily. I'm not sure she could leave here without help of some kind."

Lainie disappearing was one thing, but, until recently, she'd worked as his primary paralegal. She had information stored in her eidetic memory that could severely damage him and his clients if anyone got hold of it.

Shit.

The doctor handed the tablet back to Maggie.

"Perhaps she was better off than you thought. I'll be happy to ask some of the other staff if they spoke to her. If she said anything to them."

"Please understand," Maggie told him in an irritatingly patient voice. "It's not uncommon for patients to decide for whatever reason to get dressed when no one's looking and walk out the door."

"Without anyone seeing them?" Sonny could hardly believe what he was hearing. "Or finishing their treatment?"

"We're not a jail," Maggie told him, irritation edging her voice. "People are free to leave any time they want to. We can't make them accept treatment. Perhaps she's already home. In fact, you may have missed her if you

DESIREE HOLT

were on your way here while she was headed there. Why don't you check and see?"

"What about your security cameras?" he demanded. "I bet you have them all over the place. I want to see the video."

"I'm sorry, but you'd have to get permission from the director of the hospital for that." Her voice was polite and formal. "There are a number of rules in place that would prevent us from showing that information to anyone. Perhaps she caught a cab or Uber and is on her way home as we speak."

Sonny wanted to smash something. He moved away from her station but only to keep himself from strangling her.

"Maggie's right," Carvallo told him. "If she could get around under her own power, she could easily have walked out. Maybe she was just tired of being poked and prodded."

Not bloody likely, Sonny thought.

"Fine. I'll check. But if she's not home, you'll see me again."

Back in his car, he pulled out his cell phone and speed-dialed Lainie's number. It rang several times, but she didn't answer, and her message didn't kick in. Sonny looked at his own cell, frowning. What the hell? She knew better than to ignore him. He disconnected and tried again but with the same results.

Fuck. What the hell was going on? How could she disappear like that, with no money, no anything? She had no support network. He'd seen to that. So how the hell had this happened, and where for fuck's sake had she

46

vanished to? His gut told him the people at the hospital knew more than they were telling, but making a scene today wasn't going to get him any results. He'd have to formulate a different plan.

He was still fuming, ready to bite nails when he arrived at home. Geoff, who had gone to the house to wait for him, came into the front hall to get a report.

"Well? I don't see her with you. Did they keep her? Ask a bunch of questions?"

Sonny shook his head. "Not only didn't they keep her, it seems they've lost her."

Geoff's jaw dropped. "What the hell? Lost her? How is that possible?"

"I asked that very thing. They said they can't stop people from walking out under their own power." He moved into the library/office where he kept much of the liquor. Pouring an inch of Scotch into a crystal tumbler, he tossed it back in one swallow.

Geoff whistled. "Jesus, Sonny. Take it easy."

"Easy?" Sonny wanted to smash the glass on the floor. "I'll take it easy when that bitch is found. Don't worry. I can handle this."

"Where do you think she went? Who could she go to? I thought you said she wouldn't be moving too well."

"Maybe she's getting used to it." He poured more of the smooth liquor into his glass. "The important thing is, we can't leave her out there flapping her jaw to who the hell knows."

Geoff dropped into the armchair by the desk. "Okay, tell me what I can do to help."

Sonny sat behind his desk with fresh Scotch in his

glass. "Let's make a list of people we can contact—people we trust—who we can call about ways to look for her. This all has to be as far under the table as it can go. I don't need clients to think I can't control my personal business."

"No problem." Geoff took out his phone and pulled up his contacts list. "Let's see who you want to start with and how."

LAINIE SHIFTED IN HER SEAT, trying for a more comfortable position. The seat belt pressed into some of the bruised areas of her abdomen, but she wasn't about to mention it to Zane. She was already damn grateful he was doing this for her, getting her out of the danger zone. The last thing she wanted was for him to think she was a whiner and complainer and call his sister to get him out of this.

She distracted herself by studying him as they rode along. When she'd first seen him, even as much pain as she was in, even with the meds in her system, it was hard not to notice how good-looking he was. Not as tall as Sonny, who was a good six feet plus, but much more masculine. Rugged-looking. A compact muscular figure. His hair, dark-chocolate brown, was thick and a little long, ending barely above the neck of his T-shirt. His square-jawed but lean face was far from handsome, but its rugged masculinity looked even better. A deliberate scruff of a beard covered his chin and part of his cheeks, accentuating his high cheekbones and drawing attention to eyes the color of aged brandy, shielded by the thickest eyelashes she'd ever seen on a man.

Even in her pathetic condition, she was aware of the unconscious sexual magnetism that flowed from him. But she'd also glimpsed a look of agony in his eyes that came from more than physical discomfort. She bet Zane Halstead had some story of his own to tell. Maybe they could swap horror stories over a cold beer. Except she didn't drink beer, and she wanted to bury her own story as deep as possible. Not only because of the pain but to hide her total and utter stupidity at getting caught in her situation to begin with.

She wasn't stupid. At least she didn't like to think so. She had a bachelor's degree in paralegal studies plus the certification. She'd spent ten years building her resume and honing her craft in a small law firm before Sonny Fitzgerald discovered her and hired her for his firm. Danced attention on her. Made her his personal paralegal. Asked her to marry him and moved her into his house.

And then she discovered what the real Sonny was like.

By the time she figured out she needed to get away from him and end it, it was too late. She had no one powerful enough to help her and no one to support her. No one wanted to go up against the almighty litigator Sonny Fitzgerald, a man who had every big name in town in his pocket.

She wondered what Zane's story was. Then she reminded herself not to stick her nose in his business. It was enough that he was taking her someplace where she'd be safe and Sonny would not be able to track her. She hoped, anyway.

"You awake over there, Lainie?"

The sound of his raspy voice was somehow soothing to her.

"Yes. Just…enjoying the quiet."

He barked a short laugh. "I can understand that. Okay. We've been on the road a few hours, and we're close to Chattanooga. I'm gonna stay out of the city, if it's all the same to you. We ought to be able to find a motel on the outskirts and catch a fast-food place before we check in. That work for you?"

"Yes. That sounds fine. Anything is good."

He was silent for a moment.

"Listen, Lainie. It's not a rule that you have to agree with everything I say. You're entitled to your own opinion."

"Uh, okay." But it had been so long since that was the case, she was having trouble adjusting to it. "But I meant what I said. Anything you find works for me. As long as…"

"He's not going to find us." Zane must have been reading her mind. "I've been checking the road regularly and did some lane changing every so often to be sure. But if he'd sent someone after us, I'd have picked it up when we made that stop."

"Did Drea tell you…"

"The other reason Fitzgerald wants you back? She did. And I tell you again, no one's trailing us, and I will keep you safe from the asshole."

She wanted to believe him more than anything, but she knew Sonny, and she knew his connections. She wasn't even sure if Montana would be far enough, but she could hope. The one thing she did know, strange as it was, even shocking, was that from that first moment he touched her, she'd had no fear of Zane Halstead. There was something about him that gave her a sense of security she hadn't felt in a very long time. And she trusted him, also unusual. Maybe Fate had decided she was due for a break.

They rode for another fifteen minutes before Zane spoke again.

"We're coming into the edges of population, Lainie. I'm going to pull off and take the service road until I find what suits us. Okay?"

"Yes. That's good. As long as—"

"I know." He reached over and touched her shoulder, lightly. "We'll be well out of sight."

Zane found a fast-food-chicken drive-through. She told him anything was fine with her and sat quietly while he placed the order. When he found a motel on a cross-street to the service road, he pulled into the parking lot. Instead of getting out of the car, he turned to her.

"Listen, Lainie. I want to tell you this before I register us. I'm not comfortable leaving you in a room by yourself. I'm going to see if they have a room available with two queen beds at the back of the building. That work for you? I promise I'm not making any moves on you. All I'm thinking of is your safety."

She was torn between believing in him because he was Drea's brother and battling her sudden distrust of men. And worrying about what he'd want in exchange. She was hardly in any condition to do anything except try to heal.

But she wasn't looking forward to sleeping in a room alone, either.

"Um, yes. That will be okay." She looked down at her lap. "I don't think at the moment I'd be classified as sexy right now, anyway."

"Look at me, Lainie." His raspy voice, instead of sounding irritated was almost soothing. "Underneath all those bruises and that fear in your eyes, I see a beautiful woman hiding away. If things were different, if I weren't such a fucking mess myself and you weren't hurt and obviously afraid, I'd ask for one bed and we'd make good use of it. But it is what it is, and your safety is my number one concern."

"I—I know. It's okay. Really." She curled her uninjured hand into a fist in her lap. "I'm sorry I'm such a mess. I'll try—"

If he knew what Sonny had done, would he be so reassuring?

"You don't have to try anything," he told her. "We're taking this slow. One step at a time." Then he snapped his fingers. "Shit. I mean, shoot. I—"

She actually allowed herself a tiny laugh. "It's okay, Zane. You can say shit. I'm not a hothouse flower, despite all appearances to the contrary. But what's the problem?"

"Drea told me to be sure and stop at a big box store and get you something to wear besides what you've got on. You need clothes for sleeping, things to change into, personal items…" His voice trailed off.

She almost laughed at the big, bad Navy SEAL buying clothes and cosmetics for her, but then she shook her head. "I can't go into a store. They have security cameras in there. I know it's stupid to think Sonny would even know to look here, but—"

"It's okay," he interrupted. "We talked about that, and she gave me a list. You can look it over and make any changes. How about if we check in here first and eat some dinner while it's hot. Then you can write down your sizes for me, and I'll get someone to help me. I'll tell them it's for my wife."

She was surprised that again she had the urge to laugh. She hadn't laughed in so long, she'd wondered if she'd forgotten how.

"Okay. I hate to ask you to do that though. Shop for my clothes and stuff."

"Hey." He tucked two fingers beneath her chin and turned her to face him. She almost broke down at the kindness in his eyes. "It's okay. I knew what I was signing up for."

"I find that hard to believe." She swallowed. "Listen. I promise as soon as we get to Montana and I can figure things out, I'll find someplace to take myself to and get out of your hair."

"How about if we focus on getting through tonight and go from there. All right?"

She blew out a shaky breath. "Sure. Okay."

Zane drove to the back side of the motel and parked his truck right by the door to their room, which turned out to be nicer than she'd expected. It was roomy even with two queen-sized beds in it. It even had a little table and chairs that they could sit at to eat their dinner. Eating with one hand because the other was basically useless was a little difficult, but Zane had been sensitive enough to get chicken bites and other things she could eat with only a minor struggle. When they were finished, Zane bagged all their trash and stood up.

"I'll take this with me and throw it away. No sense in sleeping with the scent of fried chicken all night." He reached in his pocket and pulled out a folded slip of paper. "How about checking this over, adding anything that's missing, and putting down your sizes?"

She looked at the list and almost smiled at the things Drea had written down for her brother to get. She'd give a penny to watch him go through this but was so grateful he was willing, she had to bite her lip to hold back tears. When she finished, she slid it back across the table to him.

"I don't know how to thank you for this."

He grinned, and she got the feeling he didn't do much of that these days. "It will be a new experience."

"Drea gave you my cash, right?" she verified.

He nodded. "Although I could easily front you the money. No sweat."

"I can't use a credit card, and I want to pay my way. I'm not sure what I'll do when this runs out, but I guess I'll cross that bridge when I come to it."

"Lainie, this is—" What? Exactly what was it? "Why don't I give your money back to you. I'll pay for the stuff tonight, and you can pay me back."

"No." She shook her head. "I feel better knowing you have it. Besides, if I need stuff when we get to Montana, again, I'm not exactly in the ideal shape to go into a store."

"All right. If you insist. But any time you want it back, tell me. For the moment, let me get some fresh ice for your eye. Keep it on there while I'm gone."

In what seemed seconds, he was back with the room ice bucket filled. He grabbed a towel from the bathroom, wrapped some cubes in it, and handed it to her.

She pressed it against her eye. "Speaking of credit cards, did you—"

He shook his head. "No. I got plenty of cash, so I don't need to use one. If Fitzgerald's as powerful as you say, he won't think twice about hacking into every system to find mine and see if it was used. So, no worries on that front."

She visibly relaxed. "Thank you so much."

"Lock the door after me. I'll tap twice and ask for Drea so you'll know it's me."

The moment he left, she turned the lock on the door and put the safety bar in place. Then she sat on the bed farther from the window, ice held to her eye, and tried not to let possible scenarios run through her head. She knew the odds were long that Sonny would have tracked her by this time but, with him, anything was possible. She tried to entertain herself by imagining Zane in the store shopping for panties and a nightshirt for her. However, most of her meds had worn off by this time, so her bruises were throbbing as were her broken fingers. All the pretending in the world didn't make them hurt any worse.

She heaved a sigh of relief when she heard the two taps on the door and that raspy voicing saying, "Drea?"

She managed to get off the bed without too much trouble and opened the door for him. As soon as he was inside, he relocked everything then dropped two bags on the bed she'd been sitting on. Then he took his Glock from the small of his back where he'd stashed it getting out of the truck and placed it on the table. Finally, he unstrapped the knife and put it beside the gun.

Lainie stared at the gun like it had two heads.

"You carry a gun?"

He nodded. "And it's all legal. I don't think the jackass after you will find us, but I like to be prepared." He waved at the bags he'd brought in. "Check all this over and make sure it's okay. As soon as you're ready for bed, I'll give you whatever meds you need. Then we'll put some of the cream Drea gave me on that cut on your arm. After that, we'll try and get some sleep."

CHAPTER 4

"It's not whether you get knocked down, it's whether you get up."

Vince Lombardi

THE NIGHT WAS a mixture of so many things, Zane couldn't sort them all out. Drea phoned while he was shopping for Lainie to tell him Sonny Fitzgerald had shown up at the hospital to get Lainie and pitched ten holy fits when she wasn't there. The entire ED was in an uproar because of it.

"Rick made sure I stayed out of sight. He and Maggie bore the brunt of it, but no matter how Sonny pounded at them, their stories never changed. I hid in the staff lounge while he was here, and they made sure my name never came up. Maggie especially did her tough-broad routine and told him it was not the responsibility of the hospital to restrain patients against their will if they chose to leave."

"Good for her."

"And my name isn't anywhere attached to any orders for her. He doesn't even know I work there," she assured him. "That also means he can't find a connection to you and trace what's going on."

"He'll find out sooner or later," Zane warned her.

"If we get to that point, I can take a couple weeks leave and disappear for a while. The nursing supervisor comes from a bad relationship herself and survived only because a friend helped her, so she's sympathetic."

"You be very careful, sister of mine."

"I will. I promise. Let me know if she settles in okay for the night. Please?"

The first problem came when Lainie took the stuff he'd bought her to sleep in into the bathroom with her. She'd assured him she could get the sling off and change her clothes. But while he was finishing the coffee he'd picked up, the bathroom door opened, and Lainie peeked out.

"Zane?"

"Yeah?" He stood up. "Need help?"

Even with the multicolored bruising on her face, he could see the pink flush that crept up over her skin.

"I, uh, think I need help with the sling."

"No problem." He could do that easily.

It only took him seconds to remove it and place it on the counter for her.

"Thank you."

"Sure. You okay with everything else?"

Again she blushed and looked down at her feet.

"I don't think I can get this shirt off over my head."

He studied the scrubs top she was wearing. "I don't know how you got it on with the shape you're in."

"Drea helped me at the hospital. And I was still pretty drugged."

Anger at how badly she'd been hurt that she couldn't undress herself surged through him, and he had to tamp it down.

"Okay. No sweat. We'll get it off."

Still, she didn't look at him. "I'm not wearing a bra. Drea said I shouldn't put it on. It would hurt my shoulder."

Ookkkaaayyyyy.

"Still not a problem." He hoped.

Working slowly, easing her uninjured arm free first to give him more flexibility with the fabric, he managed to finally get the shirt over her head. He was just glad it was too big for her, giving him room to maneuver. When she was naked from the waist up, what he saw ratcheted his anger up at least ten more notches. He had to bite hard on his tongue not to say anything. From her collarbone to her waist were bruises that he'd bet anything were made by a man's fist. Even her breasts—which were nice and which he had no business looking at—bore the signs of brutal fingerprints.

"As long as we're doing this, I got some stuff at the store to rub on the muscle and help it heal. Okay, if I put it on now?"

She nodded, looking down at her feet.

As he rubbed the cream gently into the muscle then slid the nightshirt on over her head, a strange feeling shot through him. Unfamiliar. A connection with another person, a sense he hadn't had since he left the SEALs except for his sister. Only this was different. Much different. He saw a woman who under other circumstances he could feel things for, and that shocked the shit out of him. He hadn't really wanted to be with a woman in what seemed like forever, but Lainie touched parts of him that had been dead for a long time.

Great, Halstead. Lusting after a badly injured woman.

But it was a lot more than lust. Just that fast, she had become more than someone he'd agreed to help. He wanted to protect her. Make everything better, show her what it was like when someone really cared for you.

In a few short hours? Am I crazy?

Probably, but he was going to do everything he could to help and protect her. If something else was meant to happen, well, at the right time it would. Meanwhile, they had to get past this uncomfortable moment.

He had a million things he wanted to say, but he gritted his teeth and handed her the sleep shirt he'd bought. She still didn't look at him as he eased it over her head and worked to get her arms into the sleeves without doing any damage to her.

"I have easier clothes for you to wear beginning tomorrow."

"Thank you," she whispered, when the top was in place.

Zane tilted her face up so she was forced to look at him.

"It's all good, Lainie. All, that is, except for your bruises. I'll probably have to kill the son of a bitch who did this. But you're fine, and there's nothing to be embarrassed about. You need help; I gave it."

And please, please, don't let his apparently independent cock stand up and salute.

"If you think you can get these flannel pants on yourself, I'll leave you to it. I told the sales girl you'd taken a fall, and she said these would be easy for you to handle. Holler if you need anything else."

"I think I can do it. And, Zane?" She looked directly into his eyes, first time since she'd called him into the bathroom. "Thank you. For helping and for being the good guy you are."

He didn't know what to say to that, so he nodded and walked back into the bedroom.

When she finally came out of the bathroom, she had the scrubs over her good arm. She walked over and dumped them into the wastebasket.

"I can't manage them anyway," she told him. "The stuff you got me is easier. Besides, I didn't want any reminders of the hospital." When he didn't say anything she cleared her throat. "Zane?"

"Yes?"

"He was a lot nicer and smoother when I met him." She just blurted it out, wanting him to know she wasn't too many kinds of an idiot. "And he told me—well, never mind. I really like to think I wasn't taken in that easily."

He studied her for a moment. "There are predators like Sonny Fitzgerald who have made an art out of pulling people in, only to destroy them. Very smart people. You are part of a very distinguished list, so no more excuses, okay?"

"O-okay." She'd try, anyway.

They decided she should leave the sling off while she slept, so he helped her into bed and put a pillow beneath her injured arm and hand. The pills he gave her knocked her out in a hurry, but Zane sat at the little table for a long time, the only light coming from the small lamp on the other side of the bed he was using. He sat there a long time, thinking of everything that had happened today and the damage he'd seen on Lainie's body.

Finally, he texted Drea as he'd promised and brought her up to date on things.

"So far everything okay. Shopping was a success. She's asleep for the night."

"Good. Thanks. Keep checking in."

"Will do. You also."

His mind was still whirling with the details of the situation, and being in the truck for so many hours hadn't done either his leg or his arm much good. He wasn't sure how a full day would affect it.

At last, he'd stripped down to his boxers and climbed into the other bed, but he was a long time falling asleep. Thoughts deep in his brain wanted to come out in the dark. Between fighting to suppress them, he worried he might have a nightmare. What if he did something that scared her? He tried not to tense up as the thought raced through his brain. Then he worried that Lainie might be the one with the bad dreams.

He slept in restless fits and snatches, always aware of the woman in the other bed. Every time she made a noise of any kind, he looked over at her, checking to be sure she was okay. Worried she might be having nightmares of her own.

Morning arrived at last. He hoped Lainie had slept better than he had. He looked over at the other bed and saw her eyes were still closed, although he had no idea if she was asleep or not. Suppressing a sigh, he swallowed some aspirin for his leg and his arm and locked himself in the bathroom. He needed to pull in his frayed edges. They had a full day of travel ahead of them. Good thing all those years with the SEALs had trained him to be alert on very little sleep.

By the time he was out of the shower and dressed again, Lainie was up and out of bed, moving slowly as she gathered her new clothes to wear. She started toward the bathroom then stopped and looked at him, her expression a mixture of helplessness and embarrassment. He could tell by the way she moved her arm it was hurting her and knew she needed to get that sling back on as soon as possible.

"I need to take a shower," she told him. "And I can do that by myself, but I need you to turn the water off and on for me and then…help me with my shirt."

"Sure. No problem. Of course." And his cock better behave at the thought of her naked with water sluicing down her skin. She needed care, not sex.

Right.

"Okay. Let's get you set up."

Maybe he could do it with his eyes closed. If this was a test of his self-discipline, he'd be damned if he'd fail. Whatever else he ended up doing with his life, however this trip to Montana turned out, he would treat Lainie

Taggert with the proper respect and consideration, even if it took every ounce of his self-discipline.

After he got her set up, he told her to yell when she needed help again. Then he stepped outside with his cell and dialed Alex Rossi.

"Yeah, hi. It's Zane. Halstead."

"Good to hear from you." Rossi had a deep voice, one that reminded Zane of his team leader. "I hope you aren't calling to tell me you changed your mind."

"No, far from it." He blew out a breath. "First of all, thanks again for reaching out to me. I don't know how or why, but as things stand right this moment, I'm very grateful."

"Sure. Everything okay?" Rossi asked. "You're still coming, right?"

"Yes, to both questions, but with a little addendum. I sort of picked up a passenger."

"Oh?" Rossi's voice was alert. "What kind of passenger?"

Zane gave him the short version of the story but hit all the main points.

"I couldn't say no," he told the other man. "She's in a desperate situation."

"It's all good. No problem at all. In fact, remind me when you get here to tell you the story of how I met my wife. Meanwhile, give me this asshole's name and I'll see what I can run down on him. And tell me what you'll need when you get here."

Zane would have cried with relief, if he were a crying man. The fact that Alex Rossi was so understanding gave him hope that he could make this situation work to keep

Lainie safe. He gave the man his approximate itinerary and travel schedule and Rossi promised to get things ready for him.

By the time he finished with the call and gone back the room, Lainie was out of the shower and had managed to get herself into her sweatpants and undies and was holding yet another long-sleeved T-shirt.

"Everything fit okay?" he asked.

"Yes. Thanks."

Her face, however, was pinched with pain. The bruising had darkened on her face and exploded in a riot of colors. However, her eye looked slightly better. She held the towel in front of her while he put antibiotic cream on the long cut. Then he helped her on with the shirt, gave her the meds, and helped her put the sling back on.

"How's that feeling?" he asked. "Better? Worse?"

Her try for a smile broke his heart. "I'm doing okay."

"Lainie?" He tipped up her chin with his finger, forcing her to look at him. "We won't get anywhere if you lie to me. I need to know the degree of pain so we can manage it. We've still got a lot of road to cover, but I can help make you more comfortable if I know what hurts and how bad. So, let's make it the first rule of the road that we tell each other the truth. Got it?"

"Does that mean you'll also tell me why you limp when you think I'm not looking, big guy, and why you're rubbing your arm all the time?"

He had to laugh. Despite everything about this situation, despite her physical condition, she'd found a way to make a joke. She had guts, this woman, which was good.

She was going to need them, but his admiration for her grew a little. He'd bet she was a real pistol when she wasn't in this situation.

"You nailed me, but okay. Tit for tat, I guess. A couple of wounds that bounced me out of the SEALs. But it's—"

"Please don't tell me it's nothing, or I'll start lying to you, too."

He grinned. "Okay. Deal. And I'm glad to see you've still got a little spit and fire in you."

Lainie looked down, something he'd come to realize in just this short time was a sign of defeat. Of giving in because the alternative was too awful to bear.

"Lainie, listen to me. It's okay to have that. You're gonna need it to get through this whole thing. Personally, I'm glad to see it. To see it hasn't been totally drummed out of you."

She looked up at him, fear and pain mixing in her eyes.

"I'm still afraid, Zane. A lot. I know what he can do to me."

"But you also know I'm going to help you get through this and protect you. Right?"

She shook her head. "You've known me less than twenty-four hours, and you're already stepping up to my side? You must be bored or nuts."

"Neither. But I believe in treating a woman right and gutting people who don't. So, you be truthful with me about everything and I'm 100 percent on your side. That's the only way we'll make this work."

"Okay. I'll try. I've gotten so used to lying in self-defense, though—"

"I know." He cut her off. "But this is me. Not him. And

you're going to tell me the truth. Meanwhile, let's get some ice in that little cooler and take a couple of towels with us to wrap it in. And please let me help you pack your stuff in the duffel I got for you. I've seen it all, so there's nothing to hide."

She nodded and slid her sunglasses onto her nose with one hand.

"Thank you for these, by the way. They really help."

"I figured you'd need them since we're driving right into the sun. Okay, then, let's head out."

He also took one of the pillows from her bed, leaving a twenty-dollar bill in its place.

"For your arm and shoulder," he told her, setting her up in her seat the way he'd done the night before, with support for her injured body.

"I—" She stopped, swallowed, and tried again. "Thank you. Just—thank you."

Damn. He hoped she wasn't going to start crying.

"Let me make sure you're comfortable." He gave the pillow one more pat then closed the passenger door.

He texted Drea from his truck before they left the motel to let her know everything was okay. Then, when they pulled out of the parking lot, he drove a circuitous route to get back to the service road where he'd seen some of the usual drive-through places. He made a quick stop at one of them for breakfast sandwiches and coffee and then they were back on the road. He figured if they hit Indianapolis by the end of the day, they were good. When he'd planned this trip, he hadn't counted on the wear and tear on his leg, and that was before he'd had Lainie to take care of. While he hated to baby himself, he wouldn't be any good to either of them if by the time they got to Montana he was crippled because he didn't use common sense.

They rode mostly in silence. He knew Lainie had a lot going on in her head, and he really wanted to give her the chance to let it roll out. She needed to get it straight in her mind and try to face it so she could talk to him about it. Alex Rossi might be able to give him data on Sonny Fitzgerald, but Lainie could give him an insight into the guy's mind, and that would be the most help.

When they stopped for lunch, instead of eating in the truck, he found someplace near the restaurant, a tiny parklike area hidden away with no one around. They could eat at a picnic table where she could be outside the truck for a while and he could stretch his leg.

"I used to like going on picnics," Lainie said out of nowhere, watching him stretch and exercise. "I haven't been on one in a long time."

"Maybe we can fix that in Montana," he told her. "We might not even have to leave the house where we'll be staying. I understand it has six acres, so there's bound to be a place we can drop a blanket and have a sandwich or two."

She took a swallow from the bottle of water. "Tell me again why you're going there?"

"To tell you the truth, I'm not real sure myself. All I know is the new sheriff, a guy named Alex Rossi, is cleaning house and reaching out to former SEALs whose names come across his desk." He held up a hand. "And before you ask, I said yes, I'd come out because I couldn't see any other options at the moment and no, I don't know if it will work out, but at least I'll see what's what."

"Oh." She put down her drink. "I guess I thought…"

"What? That I had a job waiting? I probably do, if I want it."

She shrugged. "Drea didn't explain all that much, or maybe she did and I was too scared and zoned out to pay attention. Anyway, however this works out, I'm grateful to you for taking me along. Getting me away from… everything. Thank you."

"It's not a problem. And when we get there, we'll see what's what. But, Lainie, I'm not going to leave you stranded somewhere while I figure out where else to pick up the pieces of my life."

And exactly when had he come to that decision? When he realized what kind of trouble she was in and discovered that his own sense of decency hadn't faded with his injuries.

Christ, Halstead. You can hardly get from one day to the next. How are you going to help someone else?

With the same discipline he'd learned in the SEALs. You just do it.

"I guess," he said, "I'm going to Montana to figure out what to do with the rest of my life."

She sighed. "Maybe I can figure out what to do with mine, too."

"I don't suppose this is the time for you to tell me why Fitzgerald is so scared of what you might tell someone."

She curled her uninjured hand into a fist, took a deep breath, and let it out.

"He killed someone. I overheard him talking about it with his chief bodyguard and ass-kisser."

He stared at her. "Killed someone? Lainie, that's something you have got to tell the cops."

She shook her head. "No. I can't do that. He'll lie his way out of it, plaster money around where it will do him the most good, and I'll be on his radar even more."

"But—"

"See? That's why I didn't want to tell you."

"You have to tell someone eventually," he insisted.

"Check for a story online," she told him. "It's probably all cleaned up, and his name isn't anywhere. Please, Zane. I beg you."

He studied her face for a long time. "Okay. I'll check it out and we'll leave it, at least for the moment."

But he wasn't letting it drop forever. This could be what finally burst Fitzgerald's bubble. Meanwhile, this was the first real discussion they'd had since he put her in his truck. Maybe by the time they reached their destination she'd feel even more comfortable with him. He was going to do everything to make that happen. The thought made him laugh to himself. He, Zane Halstead, who had all but turned into a recluse, was looking forward to a conversation with someone. Maybe Fate had thrown them together, two bruised souls in need of healing.

Maybe.

He started to pack up their debris. "Let me clean up our stuff, and we'll get back on the road. I thought Indy would be a good place to crash for the night."

"All right." She rose to her knees to help him with the

cleanup, clumsily scooping things up with her one working hand.

"Leave that. I'll get it. I really don't think you should be using your bad arm and hand like that."

She looked at him for a long moment. "Uh, Okay. The, um, picnic was nice. Thank you."

He shrugged. "No big deal."

"It was to me. Thank you again."

He tossed the trash in a nearby can then walked back to help her up from the picnic table. When she was on her feet and standing in front of him, he tilted her face up to check out the eye. The bruises were a wild rainbow on her face but the swelling around her eye had gone down. He'd fix her more ice in a towel once they got back in the truck.

Back in the truck.

Another problem.

Like her, he favored the injured parts of his body, but he did his best to show it as little as possible. The less useful he looked, the less useful he became. At least that was what he kept telling himself.

"I think I can climb in by myself," she told him when he opened the passenger side door.

"I'm sure, but let's not try. At least right now. Please."

She caught her bottom lip between her teeth, something he noticed she did when she was upset or embarrassed. Then she sighed.

"I guess you're right. Fine. Let's do it."

Again he managed to boost her up and settle her without jostling the arm in a sling or putting too much strain on her uninjured appendage. He settled her, handed her a towel filled with ice, and double-checked her seat belt before climbing in on the other side.

He had started the engine but was still in park when his cell rang with the distinctive sound he'd programmed in for his sister.

"Yeah, Drea? What's up?"

"Sonny was here again today." Her voice was pitched low. "He met with the hospital administrator. Scott Borges didn't give me any details, but he also didn't give Sonny any information."

"And?"

"Lainie is sitting right next to you," she guessed.

"Uh-huh."

"And you can't talk."

"You're a very smart woman," he told her. "I always said so."

"Mr. Borges thinks we haven't seen the last of him, but he says there is no way he's giving out any information. For all he knows, Lainie decided to put on her clothes and walk out. Everything all right there?"

"Yeah, we're doing okay. Thanks for asking. Lainie's eye actually looks a little better, but I think she'll be happier when her face doesn't look like a rainbow anymore."

"I'm sure. Anyway, if we hear anything else, I'll pass it along."

Zane's fingers tightened on the phone until he was afraid he would crack it. They for sure did not need that asshole Fitzgerald digging around until he found a thread to pull.

"Yes, we're making decent time. I think we'll be stop-

ping in Indianapolis tonight. I'm not pushing it too much."
He forced a chuckle. "Need to take care of my leg. Lainie's
not the only one with physical infirmities."

"Got it."

His sister knew he was deliberately misdirecting
things so Lainie would have no idea what the conversation was about.

"Anyway," she went on, "like I said, I think we have not
seen the last of the asshat, so I'll keep in touch with you.
I'm sure he can't trace you, but…be alert. Okay?"

"Thanks for calling, and yes, I'll keep in touch."

He disconnected and dropped the phone into the cup
holder.

"Drea says hi and she hopes you're feeling better."

"Thanks." Lainie shifted the ice against her eye.
"Everything okay back there?"

"Of course. Why wouldn't it be?"

She took a long moment to answer him.

"Sonny isn't going to stop looking for me. I want you
to know that."

He glanced sideways at her.

"But since I'm not there and neither are you, he's at a
dead end."

"At least for now," she told him. "Sonny doesn't
give up."

"Neither do I. Go ahead and sit back and put that ice
back on your face. We need to hit the road if we want to
make it to Indy tonight. Holler if you need to stop for
anything."

❀

GEOFF DISCONNECTED the last call on his phone and shook his head.

"Sonny, I don't know what else to tell you except she's disappeared. Vanished. Into thin air, it seems."

Sonny curled his hand into a fist and banged it on the desk. He was already on his third drink, and anger was swirling wildly inside him.

"I don't accept that. I won't. She had no money, no car, and I've cut her off from all her friends. There is absolutely no way she could disappear like this."

"Listen. We've talked to everyone we could come up with between us, without making anyone suspicious. No one's heard from her, and you and I are pretty damn good at telling if someone is lying to us."

"Damn it." Sonny smacked the desk again. "I know she didn't walk out of there like everyone says."

Because she was in no shape for it.

He stared at Geoff. "No one can disappear like that without help. Let's hit 'em again. Someone at that hospital knows something."

"Okay, if that's what you want. Maybe we should offer money for any tips that help us locate her."

Sonny shook his head. "Not yet. The medical staff will be insulted and make a stink. The others will make something up in order to scam us. So no, you make one more run at it. Tell them I'm distraught, and you're trying to help me out. If that doesn't work, I'll call the administrator and play the outraged, indignant fiancé again. Maybe I'll even call the chairman of the board of directors. Threaten to sue them for every nickel if they don't tell me what happened to the bitch."

Geoff chuckled. "I'd call her something besides bitch when you talk to them though."

"Yeah, yeah, yeah." Sonny picked up a gold pen and began rocking it back and forth. "I'll be on my best outraged behavior. Meanwhile, I'm going to do more checking on my own." He swore again. "Damn it. A woman with no friends and no resources can't simply evaporate into thin air like that. She had to have help."

"You sure she hasn't been in contact with anyone?"

Sonny nodded. "Trust me. I watched her like a hawk. Monitored her calls. And after she started having her little 'accidents,' I cut her off from everything. She didn't need to be discussing shit with someone."

"Just out of curiosity," Geoff asked, "what was the purpose in isolating her?"

"Focusing," Sonny explained. "I wanted her to use her brains and her body for my benefit. Talk to my clients at social events, show them I had someone with a brain who could work in their best interest. Actively solicit other clients for me, but as I directed her to."

"Like you don't have enough?"

Sonny shook his head. "There's never such a thing as enough. I liked her spirit. It was one of the first things that attracted me to her. I planned to take that spirit and mold it to what I wanted. To her serving all my needs."

"All your needs?" Geoff grinned. "I take it she had objections to some of them."

Sonny swallowed the sudden rise of bile in his throat.

"You could say that. Meanwhile, take that run at the hospital before I step back into it."

After Geoff left, Sonny leaned back in his chair and

picked up the gold pen again. Somehow he had miscalculated the situation with Lainie Taggart. She had been so bright and eager in the office. Clients loved her, and even the staff got along with her. She ate up the legal guidance he gave her, told him how much she admired him, so he was sure moving to the next steps would be a breeze. How was he to know they had two different definitions of the word molding.

She should have respected the fact he had a temper, which he kept in check for the most part. But damn! She sure pushed his buttons. And she wouldn't learn not to do it.

Okay. Geoff was off to the hospital, which he fully expected would yield nothing. Geoff was good at what he did, but he was well-known as Sonny Fitzgerald's right-hand man, so there were boundaries he could not push. But Sonny had other people who did what he called scut work for him. They could get into dark corners and leave nothing that would trace back to him. He pulled a special cell phone from his desk and speed-dialed a number.

"Antonio? Yeah, it's me. I have a little assignment for you guys."

CHAPTER 5

"BELIEVE YOU CAN, and you're halfway there."
   Theodore Roosevelt

LAINIE WAS fidgety as their lunch wound down, casting glances as if she expected Sonny Fitzgerald or one of his goons to suddenly walk up to them.

"He's not following us," he assured her again. "Believe me, I know how to check, and we're clear. I promise."

"Okay." But she didn't sound as reassured as he wished.

After lunch, Zane finally got her to admit that riding in the truck jostled her bruises and her sprained shoulder, so she had taken her meds again. He knew her fingers were bothering her, too, but she kept telling him she was fine. Yeah, right. Fine. He was beginning to think this woman had more guts than she knew, certainly more than some other people he'd met.

He knew she was taking a big chance running away,

knowing what would happen if, god forbid, Sonny Fitzgerald managed to track her down. He still wondered how she'd gotten herself into this situation to begin with. What her real story was and if he'd ever find out. Maybe when they got to Montana…

Shit, Halstead. You have no idea what's going to happen then. One day at a time.

But unexpectedly, he felt himself drawn to her, and what the hell was that all about anyway?

Half an hour after they hit the interstate, she was asleep. He hoped she stayed that way for a while. Riding wasn't comfortable for her, and they were still five hours away from Indy. He'd replotted the trip, breaking it up into more digestible pieces, which meant he'd be an extra couple of days getting to Montana. Tonight he ought to check in with Alex Rossi and bring him up to speed.

He also needed to do some intense research on Sonny Fitzgerald. He didn't read the newspapers, either in print or online, and he found the news too depressing to watch. Tampa had never been his home, anyway, so it wasn't as if he was plugged into whatever was going on. He wished he knew someone with connections he could plug into, but he'd isolated himself so much after his discharge that he hadn't the vaguest idea who to call.

He tried to recall some names people had given him when he was floundering for a direction, and he'd had a dozen security agencies mentioned to him. Maybe he could contact one of them and have them do some digging. He really needed to know what he was up against. He hoped Alex Rossi wasn't going to kick him out on his ass for bringing some kind of mess with him. He had to prepare Lainie to tell the sheriff everything when they got there. Whatever that everything was.

Okay. Alternative. Tonight after Lainie fell asleep, he would plug in his laptop and search for as much as he could find on Fitzgerald. He knew he wouldn't be able to dig up the nitty-gritty stuff, but he was pretty sure whatever he did find would give him a rough picture of the man. His gut churned again as he thought of Lainie's injuries. He didn't have to wonder what kind of man did that to a woman. He'd seen it before, and the answer was always ugly. Anger boiled in him every time he looked at Lainie.

The cut on her right arm ran from wrist to elbow. It wasn't deep enough to require stitches, and Drea told him he needed to keep the medicine on it to avoid infection. Her face still looked like it had been used for a punching bag and, every time he looked at it, he cringed at the pain he knew she must be feeling. The swelling around her eye was slowly receding, but the area around it was still puffy, and the entire left side of her face looked as if someone had thrown a painter's palette at it. And then there were the bruises on her body, as if someone had repeatedly punched her.

He also worried about the two broken fingers that were taped together. Whenever he helped her with her sling, he managed to eyeball them. So far, they looked okay, not showing any of the bad signs his sister had told him to be on the lookout for.

By eight that night, they were checked into a nice, quiet motel on the outskirts of Indianapolis. Once again, Zane had picked up food for dinner—pizza and salad this time—and they ate quietly, both of them tired from the drive. For Lainie, he knew it was the effort of dealing with her pain in the discomfort of the ride. For himself, his leg again was sending loud protests at being forced into a pretty much stationary position for a length of time.

He popped two aspirins while waiting for their dinner order. He'd take two more when he got into bed. And he'd have to carve out fifteen minutes to do the stretching exercises the physical therapist told him were mandatory every day. Mandatory, right. And ditto for his arm. He also stopped at a drugstore and bought a box of disposable plastic gloves.

"So you can shower more easily," he told Lainie. "We'll fit it over the hand with the broken fingers and tape it shut at your wrist. That should work."

She blinked away the tears in her eyes when he showed her the box, and yet again he wanted to destroy Sonny Fitzgerald piece by piece.

"I'm not quite sure how to thank you for all of this. You don't even know me, Zane, yet you opened up your life to me to help me when I needed it. And the respect you treat me with is...unbelievable."

He smiled, an unfamiliar twist of his lips that he'd found himself doing more in the past two days than the past six months.

"Maybe it gives me a chance to focus on something other than myself," he told her. "Besides, haven't you ever heard that all SEALs are heroes? This gives me a chance to prove everyone right. Besides, I respect all women unless they show me a reason not to."

She shook her head and looked down at her feet,

something he thought she'd done way too often in the past couple of days. If Fitzgerald had done this to her, he'd like to treat him to a few hours of painful torture.

Still, she was a tad less withdrawn than she'd been when he picked her up. Not as tense with him and showing faint signs of trusting him. He figured the farther away from Tampa they got the safer she felt, although it hadn't even been forty-eight hours since he'd picked her up. Then he remembered something his team leader had told them on their first mission.

"You all are still getting to know each other, so keep this in mind. Facing danger and fighting an enemy together gives birth to trust between people."

They ate dinner in silence. Although Lainie had been a tiny bit more talkative today, he could tell she was still drawn into herself. He could tell by her posture and the pinched look on her face that she was still wrapped up in fear and pain.

Well, of course, you asshole. Did you think two days was going to fix that?

And he'd been in self-imposed social isolation for so long he'd lost all his conversational skills. He'd have to figure out a way to make her more comfortable so she'd talk to him. By the time they got to Montana, he needed to know enough about her to be able to handle their situation.

"I'll clean up," he told her when they finished with their meal. "You get the first shower."

"Thank you." One corner of her mouth ticked up in the hint of a smile. "I'm going to take advantage of those gloves."

"Let me take a look at that eye first." He cupped her chin and studied her face. The swelling on the eye had reduced significantly, enough that she was now able to see out of it. The discoloration was in full bloom, but only time would fade it.

"It feels better," she told him.

"It looks better, too. I think one more day with the ice on and off should do it."

She sighed. "Too bad my face will take longer. Thanks for not making me go into anyplace again where people would stare at me."

"No problem. We got lucky at that truck stop today. The restrooms were accessed from outside the building."

She caught her bottom lip between her teeth, the little gesture that drove him wild.

"I hope you know how much I appreciate this. I don't know how I'll ever repay you, but—"

"I'm not doing it for repayment, Lainie, so let's drop that, okay? Go take your shower. Got that little bag of stuff you need?"

She nodded. "And thanks for that, too."

When he'd shopped for her, the salesperson also recommended a cosmetic bag with the minimal things his "friend" would need. He could almost hear the quotation marks. He couldn't believe how grateful she'd been for them. He helped her gather her things and carry them into the bathroom then fixed the disposable glove on her hand.

She stopped and stood there for a moment, looking down at her feet. He'd fix that no matter what. She had nothing to be ashamed of.

"Need help again?"

She nodded, wordlessly.

"No problem. I think I can get the hang of it."

They repeated the process from the previous night. Removing the sling and then her T-shirt. He gathered all the items she'd need and put them on the ledge of the tub, rather than the soap dish in the wall where she'd have to reach for them. He placed her sleep shirt and pants on the counter for her.

He'd done his best to be calm about the bruises on her body, now the same horrific multicolors as those on her face. One of these days he'd find Sonny Fitzgerald and show him what it felt like to be pounded by a SEAL.

"Okay?" He looked down at her.

"Yes. Thank you. Oh, and if you can turn on the water, that would be great."

He managed to keep himself under control until he walked out of the bathroom. He couldn't break anything or pound the walls, so all he said was, "Fuck." Then sat down to wait for her.

And rearrange his brain. He thought about last night when he'd watched her walk toward the bathroom, his eyes fixed on the sexy curve of her hips and the sway of her hair. His cock, that hadn't had a relationship for months with anything but his fist, had perked up with interest.

Damn! Not what he needed!

Nice going, Halstead, he told himself, and gave himself a mental smack. Leching after a woman in her condition, for god's sake. But he hadn't been with a woman in so long he'd about forgotten what it was like, and there was something about Lainie Taggert, even in her condition, that had lit a tiny fire under his hormones. He'd damn well better call on that SEAL training to keep that fire under control. But then the image of her half-naked and looking as bruised as if an elephant had stepped on her appeared in his mind, and rage wiped away every other feeling.

Tamping down his anger, he pulled a pair of sweatpants from his duffel, shucked his jeans, and yanked on the sweats. For the next fifteen minutes he went through his exercise routine, gritting his teeth against the pain of stretching the tortured muscles. By the time he'd finished the program for his arm, the bathroom door opened, and Lainie motioned to him. She had managed to get the lounge pants on, but she held the T-shirt in her hand. Her skin—at least the part not covered in bruises—looked soft and silky. And she had a towel wrapped sloppily around her head. When she pulled it off with her good hand, he saw her hair was wet and streaming down her back.

"I need help again. Please." She let out a small breath. "I'm sorry to be such a pest."

"You washed your hair." What a stupid comment, he thought. Any fool can see it.

"I did." Her mouth curved in a tentative smile. "It's amazing what you can do with one arm and one hand. I had to wash out the hospital smell. But I can't get the shirt on again, and I can't dry my hair by myself."

Okay. Right. How the hell was she supposed to dry it with one hand?

"They have a dryer here, but…"

Suck it up, Halstead, and help the woman. You don't have to be a stylist, just a little handy with the tools.

"No problem. I'm happy to help you."

She actually laughed. "It's okay, Zane. I don't expect you to be my stylist. It'll air dry."

He shook his head. "You can't go to sleep with wet hair. Come on. We'll figure this out together."

"I—" She hesitated then nodded. "All right. Thank you."

He gave her a crooked grin. "Be forewarned, this isn't one of my skills."

"It's okay. We'll figure it out."

But after he helped her get the shirt on, he swallowed a groan as he eyed her wet head and tried to figure out what to do. He'd never dried a woman's hair before or paid much attention when they did it. He was surprised when he heard her laugh.

"It's not that bad. I'll talk you through it."

Which was exactly what she did. They stood in front of the bathroom mirror so they could both see what he was doing. He tried not to think how silky her hair felt in his hands, or how the faint flowery scent drifting from her skin teased at his nostrils. For fuck's sake! He was protecting her, not dating her. He breathed a sigh of relief when he was finished, her hair now dry and straight, exactly what she'd told him she wanted.

"All set," he told her, setting down the brush.

She managed a smile. "Thank you, Zane. I appreciate it, and you didn't do a bad job at all. Tomorrow, if I can pull it into a ponytail, that will help."

"We'll work on it. If you're getting into bed for the

night, we leave the sling off again. But you need to take your pills."

"I think I'm ready for them," she told him. "I won't lie to you. Everything hurts."

"I can believe it. Travel is wearing."

Not to mention the fact her body had been used as a punching bag.

She insisted she could get into bed by herself, and that was fine with Zane. He did, however, insist on helping her brace her injured arm with a pillow under it, as he'd had her do the night before.

"Thank you," she said again.

"Lainie, you really don't have to keep thanking me for every little thing."

A look of hurt flashed in her eyes, and he wanted to bite his tongue.

"I just—"

"It's me," he interrupted. "Not you. But it's important to me that you know I'm happy to do this. All of it."

And the strange thing was, he meant it. Strange, because he'd become such an isolationist.

As soon as Lainie was tucked in, he showered, pulled on sweatpants again, and settled himself on the other bed with his laptop. Glancing over to make sure Lainie's eyes were closed, he opened Google and typed Sonny Fitzgerald Tampa in the search bar. He was stunned at the list of articles and documents that came up.

While he searched and read, he kept glancing over at the next bed. He was relieved Lainie hadn't objected to them sharing a room because no way was he leaving her alone for even a minute, especially after reading all the crap about Fitzgerald. How the fuck had she gotten herself mixed up with him? He'd have to ask Drea. He also had to keep reminding himself she was a victim who had been entrusted to his care and protection. He was shocked, puzzled, and bothered by the fact that she was also giving his libido a big kick in the ass.

His one connection with a woman in the past year had been hot and brief, but when it was over, he was embarrassed to say he could hardly remember her name. Before his injuries kicked him out of the SEALs, he was focused on his team and nothing else. Since then, the last thing he wanted was a woman who would give him a pity fuck or, worse yet, be disgusted by his injuries. So why, after being thankfully dormant for months, had his dick decided it was time to wake up and send him messages?

He sure didn't want Lainie Taggert, the woman in his protective care, to think he was going to put the moves on her. After what she had experienced, he wondered if she'd ever want a man to touch her again. But even with her bruises and injuries, there was something so femininely appealing about her. Even though you could still smell the fear coming from her, she was trying her best to pull herself together.

He already knew, despite his original misgivings, that when they got to Montana he was going to keep her with him as long as she needed protection. No handing her over to someone else, whoever that might be. He'd use every bit of his SEAL training to protect her and get Alex Rossi and maybe some others to help him with that. But he also knew to make it work, they had to eliminate the source of the threat. They'd take Sonny Fitzgerald down, and then... Well, who knew, right?

Sending a stern message to his misbehaving cock, he went back to his Internet search. Every so often, he'd glance at the other bed, reassuring himself Lainie was okay. That her arm was still propped on the pillow and she wasn't doing anything to aggravate her physical condition.

An hour later, he'd definitely decided Sonny Fitzgerald was the scum of the earth and, given the chance, he'd happily obliterate him. His law firm was considered one of the most powerful in the state, although many of his clients might not pass the smell taste. At the top of the list was Steelman Consolidated, a conglomerate whose owners were named something other than Steelman. It appeared that they had a habit of finding smaller companies they wanted, looking for something they could sue them for then having their attorney, none other than Sonny Fitzgerald, litigate them into selling their company for pennies on the dollar. And if the subtle hints were right, those he couldn't litigate into obscurity found their business faltering and their health endangered.

Steelman's officers also appeared to walk the edge of legitimacy. Several of the media reported they had so much in personal wealth in addition to their corporate shares that they could probably buy and sell small countries. It appeared that people who pissed him off disappeared, and either no one bothered to look for them, or their bodies were found in places where they could serve as a warning.

This guy had a network that could take down anyone

anywhere, if they weren't smart. Well, he was fucking smart. He was a SEAL, even if he was no longer active. The training never went away, and physical challenges could be accommodated if you had a brain. A lot would depend on seeing exactly what the situation with Alex Rossi turned out to be.

Zane stared at the screen where the latest article stared back at him. Everything he read only emphasized even more the danger that Lainie was in. Lainie was smart to be afraid of him.

Shit!

The question that kept circling his brain, though, was how she got involved with him in the first place. In the morning, he'd find a way to call Alex Rossi, share information with him, and see if Rossi had picked up anything else on Fitzgerald. He'd have to plan this whole thing like a mission, but he wondered if he'd lost those skills.

Shutting down the computer, he placed it on the nightstand, checked the alarm on his watch, and closed his eyes, willing himself to sleep.

And then the scream woke him.

"You little slut. You ungrateful bitch."

The fist slammed into her face, catching her eye and cheekbone.

Lainie gritted her teeth to keep from crying out, but it was hard. The pain was almost unbearable.

"I—I'm sorry."

God, she hated apologizing. It made her feel weak, but it seemed to be the only thing that took the edge off his anger. The past couple of months, his anger seemed to be bubbling closer to the surface than it ever had.

"Sorry? Sorry doesn't cut it."

He slapped her so hard she fell to the floor. While she was trying to scuttle away, he kicked her. Oh god. Tonight he really might kill her. This was the worst rage she'd seen yet.

"Sonny, please." She tried to draw air, but it hurt to breathe.

"Please? I'll show you please."

He drew back his fist, and she opened her mouth to scream—

"Lainie?"

Hands were touching her, and she fought desperately to push them away.

"No, no, no. Get away from me." She struggled hard to get away. She was sure she'd be dead if she didn't. But these hands were gentle, not vicious. And the voice was different. What—

"Come on, Lainie. Wake up. It's okay. You're safe. Open your eyes."

She tried to scuttle away from the touch, but something stopped her. A pillow. More than one. How on earth did a pillow get on the floor with her?

"Can you open your eyes?" the voice asked again. "Come on. It's me. Zane."

Zane? Not Sonny?

She forced her eyes open and blinked at the sudden light. The face looking at her was not Sonny's but Zane Halstead's. His slightly ragged hair was sticking up in all directions, and a frown creased his forehead, but his eyes were filled with worry, not hate. His hands rested lightly on her waist, enough to steady her.

"Breathe. That's it. Come on, Lainie. Slow breaths. You were having a bad dream."

No kidding. She was so confused. Where was she? Had she been dreaming about that night again? She drew in one ragged breath and let it out then another.

"That's it. Good girl. Okay, okay. Lainie, I'm putting your hands in your lap. Please don't move them. I'll be right back. And keep taking slow breaths."

She thought it strange that the sound of the voice had her fear dissipating. She left her hands in her lap where he'd placed them, but then when she tried to move them, pain shot through her left one. Oh yeah. Sprained shoulder and broken fingers.

It came back to her now. The dream. Sonny, in a drunken rage, kicking and hitting her. A chill skittered over her as it came back in every vivid detail.

"Here, Lainie. Drink this." Zane held out a glass of water. "It'll help settle you. I'm going to sit on the edge of the bed again. Is that okay?"

She took the glass with her uninjured hand and sipped the liquid slowly. Zane sat on the edge of the bed again, close to her but not touching her. He waited while she drank more water then took the glass from her and set it on the nightstand.

"Better?"

"Yes. Thank you." She looked down at her lap. "I'm sorry. I feel like an idiot, waking you up and all."

"Don't worry about that, but you did scare the shit out of me." Then he asked again, "Bad dream?"

"Yes." She was so ashamed she could hardly look at him. Ashamed of the position she'd gotten herself into.

Ashamed that she hadn't found a way to leave before. Ashamed that this man who might be rough around the edges was being so good to her and probably thought she was some kind of nutcase.

"Let's sit here for a minute, then, until you calm down. Is it all right if I look at your arm and fingers and make sure you didn't do any damage to them?"

"Sure." She looked away while he gently probed her injuries, testing to see if there was additional swelling or discoloration.

"Seems okay. Let me look at your eye."

His touch when he tilted her face up so he could see it was so tender she again felt tears threatening. She sniffled and blotted her face with the sleeve of her T-shirt.

"You probably wish you'd never set eyes on me. Or told your sister no way were you hauling this nutcase to Montana with you."

"That's really not true at all." He turned her face so she was forced to look at him. "The minute I laid eyes on you, I knew we had to get you away from your situation. And I know my sister. For one thing, she'd have wanted you out of the city and as far away from that asshole as you could get. For another, she knows my first instincts would be to protect you, no matter what."

"I'll bet you didn't count on me being a basket case," she protested.

He glanced away from her, and a strange, faraway look came into his eyes.

"We're all basket cases in one form or another, Lainie."

She wondered what exactly his story was. Would he tell her if she asked? Not tonight, that was for sure. But they'd be together for some time. She'd figure out how to get him to open up.

"Would you like one of those pills to help you get back to sleep?" he asked.

"No." She shook her head. "They'll make me be all out of it tomorrow. But I could use another couple of Tylenol."

"Coming right up."

He fetched two of them and dropped the caplets into her palm, and she swallowed them with the last of the water.

"Thanks." She set the glass on the nightstand then lay back with one pillow under her injured arm. "Zane?"

"Yeah?"

He'll probably leave me on the highway if I keep asking for things.

"Could I ask one more favor? Not that you haven't gone above and beyond already."

"Ask away."

"Would it bother you if I leave the light on my nightstand lit? I...don't think I want to be in the dark, but I don't want to keep you up."

"Honey, I could sleep in a bright sun at high noon. No problem at all." He studied her with an intense look in his eyes. "You sure you're okay for the rest of the night?"

"Yes. It will be better with the light on. Thank you."

He nodded. "Good, then. And, Lainie?"

"Yes?"

"Sometimes it helps to get things out in the open. If you ever want to talk, I'm a good listener."

"Thanks, but I'm not sure I want you to know how

stupid I was to get myself into this situation. I'm a college graduate, Zane, with paralegal certification. I should have known better."

"Don't beat yourself up, kiddo. Smarter people than you have gotten tangled up in worse situations. Anyway, I'm a good listener, and I don't judge. But keep this in mind. Once we get to Montana and settle into our situation there, I'll need to know at least the nuts and bolts. Otherwise, I won't be able to properly protect you."

She stared up at him. "I thought for sure when we got there you'd figure out how to send me off on my own."

He shook his head. "Not happening, so get that out of your mind. Listen. I want you to know, I've been doing some research on Fitzgerald, and also had Sheriff Rossi looking into him for me. We want to make sure to keep you safe. And, Lainie? Whatever you think, as long as you're with me, Sonny Fitzgerald will never get to you and never lay a hand on you again."

Now she really did want to cry. She had felt so isolated, so adrift and helpless. Then Drea Halstead, whose friendship she had ignored, had created this situation with her brother to provide safety and protection, and no one seemed to want anything for it. If it worked, how would she ever thank them?

"Whatever's in your head, shut it off for the night," Zane told her. "Time to get some sleep."

Sleep. Yes. She could only hope. Yet, when she closed her eyes all she could see was Zane Halstead, a man dealing with his own demons, reaching out to her to take care of her and make her feel safe. How was it possible with her wounds all still so fresh, visions of another man danced in her brain?

God!

She'd been positive she'd be sitting up in bed wide awake for whatever was left of the night, so it shocked her when she popped her eyes open again and realized it was morning.

And she was still alive.

Thank you, Zane Halstead.

CHAPTER 6

"THE MOST DIFFICULT thing is the decision to act, the rest is merely tenacity. The fears are paper tigers. You can do anything you decide to. You can act to change and control your life; and the procedure, the process, is its own reward."

Amelia Earhart

DESPITE HIS BROKEN sleep of the previous night, Zane still had his act together in the morning. He showered and dressed while Lainie slept. He thought about trimming his scruff beard but decided he liked it a little longer. A new look for a new life.

Yeah. Ha ha. He could only hope.

Still, for the first time in months he thought maybe there was a chance for one. Was something good going to come out of all this mess?

He packed all his gear and then woke Lainie.

"I don't need to shower," she told him. "I took care of

everything last night. Give me a few minutes, and I'll be ready."

"Take your time."

"I want to get going. That's all."

He stopped what he was doing and took her uninjured hand in both of his.

"I know my saying it might not be enough for you, but I promise, I am watching carefully. I learned the tricks of the trade as a SEAL, and if anyone was on our tail, I'd know it. And take care of it."

"Okay. I believe you. Thanks."

But he knew she wasn't completely reassured. Damn! He wanted to punch the bastard's lights out. Instead, he repacked everything in his duffle and stashed it in the truck then climbed into the front seat and called Drea.

"Can you talk?"

"For a few," she told him. "I started my shift an hour ago, but it's a little slow right at the moment."

"Slow in an ED? That's a joke, right?"

"Yeah. Ha ha. What's up?"

He told her about Lainie's nightmare.

"It was a bad one, I think. I didn't ask her any of the details, and she didn't seem as if she wanted to tell me. But she certainly looked scared shitless when she finally woke out of it."

"Sonny Fitzgerald would scare anyone shitless." Drea's voice was laced with more venom than Zane had ever heard her use. "Having treated her injuries and read her file, I can only imagine what she was dreaming."

"I did some searching on the guy last night. Shit, Drea. The guy is a scumbag of the first order. His clients are scumbags, too, I don't care how much money they all have. And she thinks he's worried about whatever she knows about his clients."

"He'll kill her for sure," Drea told him, "if he thinks she's got information that can damage him. Take care of her, Zane. Please. She... She..."

"It's okay, kiddo. Consider it a done deal. I already planned to set her up with me in Montana. Maybe she's what I need to quit feeling sorry for myself."

"You could do that on your own, if you wanted to," she told him, "but thank you. From the bottom of my heart. She and I were close once, and I'm hoping we can be again."

"Has anyone been around again looking for her? Maybe the same guy as yesterday?"

"No, but that doesn't mean the danger is past. I expect Sonny himself to come back looking for her and threatening the hospital."

Zane hated that any of it might spill over to Drea.

"You stay out of sight if he does. You hear me?"

"Loud and clear." She sighed. "Okay. Gotta go. I'll text you later today with an update."

His next call was to Alex Rossi.

"How's it going?" the man asked. "How far on the road are you?"

"Indianapolis. I plan to make Des Moines by tonight and then Montana the following day. I'm taking it easy because she's in such shit condition."

"If I told you what I'd like to do to men like Fitzgerald," Rossi said, "I'd have to arrest myself."

"I hear you. Listen, I did some digging on him last night."

"I did, too. None of it good. When you get here, we need to compare notes."

"She's also worried about information she's gathered here and there that might damage Fitzgerald. That's a death sentence for sure."

"Got it. You can believe she'll be safe with us. If Fitzgerald somehow finds her, we'll take care of him."

Zane took a moment to gather his thoughts. He had never expected such a connection with this man.

"Listen, I'm not sure how to thank you—"

"Forget it. Wait until you hear the stories I have to tell. I'm just glad you're coming out here. Text me along the way."

"Will do."

"One more question." Pause. "How involved are you with this woman?"

Zane thought for a moment. "Good question. When I picked her up two days ago, I would have said not at all. And I've been such a loner for so long that I didn't even see myself as someone getting involved. With anyone. But…"

"Okay. I get it. I'm taking the temperature of the situation to see how things stand. Whatever it is, we'll all make it work."

Zane blew out a sigh of relief. "Thanks. For everything."

"No problem. Keep in touch."

He had no idea what was going to happen, but by the time they got to Montana he owed it to Alex to tell him things might be changing. In a little over two days, Lainie Taggert had become more than a victim who needed his protection. He was shocked to find himself even thinking in that direction. He'd only known the woman for two days, for fuck's sake. She was a victim of abuse who probably didn't want anything to do with a man at the moment. He'd never been great with relationships in the best of circumstances, and this was hardly that.

For the first time in his memory, he felt something for a woman besides the desire for hot-and-heavy sex and a quick goodbye. Not that he didn't want the sex when she was ready, if ever, but his body had a mind of its own. Now? he asked himself. Now my dick wants to come out and play? Last night, when she'd been wrestling with demons in her nightmare and looking so vulnerable when he woke her, he was afraid it could turn into more than that. Well, hell. He'd need all of his SEAL training to keep himself together because Lainie Taggart was in no condition for anyone to put the moves on her.

When he unlocked the door and walked back into the motel room, she had managed to dress herself and somehow pull her hair into a ponytail. The pinched look around her eyes and mouth told him it had been a struggle, however, but she apparently wasn't going to ask for help unless she desperately needed it. And the way she held her arm told him she needed that sling.

Yeah, she definitely wasn't a weakling. Which made him ask himself yet again how the fuck she'd gotten into her situation with Fitzgerald.

Lainie stopped in the middle of one-handedly stuffing

things into the tote Zane had bought for her and studied his face.

"Everything okay?"

"Yeah, sure. Why do you ask?"

"You, um, look mad at the world," she told him.

Zane hauled in a deep breath and blew it out slowly. He had to learn to control his feelings better. He didn't want to do or say anything to frighten her. "Nothing a little time and energy won't fix. But everything's fine. *You're* fine, and I'm going to keep it that way."

She caught her bottom lip between her teeth again, that little habit that for whatever reason always sent a message to his suddenly rebellious cock.

"I don't want you to think—" She shook her head. "Never mind."

In two strides, he was in front of her, his hand gentle as he touched her face.

"Whatever you're thinking, get it out of your mind. Shit happens to people." He paused. "I've got my own nightmares about situations I'd give my left nut to go back and change. What's important is that inside I see a strong woman pushing to get out again. A woman willing to drive across the country with a man she's never met and trust her safety to him."

"Maybe I didn't have a choice," she pointed out. "Or maybe it was taken away from me."

He shook his head. "No, I think you finally decided to make a choice that could help you." He studied her face, especially her eye. "I think we can do without the ice. Most of the swelling's gone down. Let's get that sling on and get moving. I want to hit the drive-through for some breakfast, and I definitely need coffee."

"I'm ready." Her lips turned up in one of those almost-smiles. "And thank you."

"My pleasure."

The funny thing was, he discovered he actually meant it.

SONNY FITZGERALD SAT BACK in the leather chair and looked at the man on the other side of the large desk. He would have thought the man would have been more accommodating, more respectful, considering the circumstances. At the very least offered him a cup of coffee. Sunshine flooded the room from the two large glass windows that overlooked Tampa Bay, but it did nothing to help his state of mind. He did his best to conceal the anger that vibrated through his body.

This meeting with director of the hospital, Stan Borges, was not going well. He was a man definitely in charge of his universe, and he wasn't about to be pressured by anything Sonny said or threatened.

"I'd love to help you, Mr. Fitzgerald, but my hands are tied. If a patient chooses to leave the hospital under his or her own power, there's really nothing I can do about it."

"But she's injured," Sonny pointed out. "From a bad fall."

Had the expression on the man's face hardened, a knowing look swum fleetingly in his eyes?

"I don't personally know the extent of the injuries,"

Borges told him, "but I did ask for her chart to be sent up. I also spoke with the doctor who treated her. Dr. Cavallo said yes, she had injuries but she was able to move on her own power. For whatever reason, she decided to leave the x-ray department waiting area and the hospital."

"I want to know how she did that," Sonny demanded. "I'm telling you, I don't think that's possible."

Borges' expression didn't vary. Did he know something? What had he been told and by whom?

"I offered to call the police," he reminded Sonny. "The day she walked out of here. But you chose not to do that."

"The police would only remind us that a person isn't missing until twenty-four hours have passed." He didn't want the damn police sticking their noses in his business. Besides, they'd only tell him they couldn't do a thing for twenty-four hours.

Of course, he had no intention of calling the cops, but he'd thought it would be an effective threat to get some answers. Apparently not.

"Of course, that would be unfortunate for the hospital," Borges said in a flat voice. "But if that's your course of action, of course I can't stop you."

Okay, time to try something else. He made his tone as conciliatory as possible.

"What if I said I'm in a position to make a substantial gift to the hospital?" Maybe that would change the bastard's mind. What the hell was his problem anyway? He'd have thought for sure they'd do anything so the hospital didn't get blamed for losing a patient.

Borges leaned forward and picked up an electronic tablet on his desk.

"Let me ask you some questions, Mr. Fitzgerald. I have a copy of Miss Taggert's chart here. In fact, her entire hospital file. I see this is her fourth visit to our emergency department in less than a year, all with similar injuries." He placed the tablet back on his desk. "I'm thinking the police might be interested in that, also." He lifted an eyebrow. "Don't you?"

Sonny had to bite down hard to keep his temper under control.

"Are you accusing me of something, Borges? Because if you are, I'll sue your ass."

The other man fixed him with a cold look but said nothing.

"I'm not accusing you of anything, merely pointing out the facts. I have questioned everyone in the ED, and all questions have been answered to my satisfaction. Miss Taggart was treated and taken for X-Rays. When the technician came to get her, she was nowhere."

"And no one went looking for her?" Sonny wanted to pound something. "Do you make a habit of letting patients disappear like that?"

"Of course we searched for her." Something flashed in Borges' eyes. "We're a responsible medical facility. I understand the staff went through all of this when you came to pick the patient up and she was gone."

Sonny ground his teeth. "So, you're saying it's okay that she just walked out of here and no one knows where she went."

"Mr. Fitzgerald." Borges shook his head. "I'm sorry we can't help you. When we discovered Miss Taggert was missing, of course we instituted a full search. We'd have been irresponsible not to. But we've had patients walk out of here like that before. We cannot keep someone against their will."

He realized if he pushed harder, Borges might bring up Lainie's medical history again, and he'd be the one answering questions from the cops.

Fuck.

He stood up, glaring at Borges.

"You haven't heard the last of this. I promise you."

"I'm here any time you want to talk. All you have to do is call my secretary, and she'll let you know if I have time available."

He had to tamp down the urge to punch the asshole in the nose. Instead, he stormed out of the office and out of the hospital.

Geoff was waiting for him in the turnaround by his car.

"Did you get anything?"

Sonny shook his head. "No, and that jerkwad had Lainie's medical records on his desk. I didn't want him asking questions."

Geoff shook his head. "I kept telling you to go easier on her. That it would come back to bite you in the ass."

"She shouldn't piss me off. You know that." He climbed into the back seat.

Geoff got into the driver's seat, and in a moment they were rolling out toward the street.

"So what now?"

Sonny took out his cell. "I called Antonio and told him what I want. He'll check every one of her friends for the past ten years and make sure none of them have seen her.

Then he'll get all the dirt on everyone at the hospital and see who we can leverage to tell us what really happened."

"I don't know how he always gets the info you want, stuff I sometimes think even the government can't get its hands on."

"That's his special talent," Sonny told him. "He can even find out where people buy their underwear and if they prefer a shower or the tub."

"Be careful where you step. You've got another big deal coming up. You don't want it to fall apart."

"You've known me a long time, Geoff, so you know these two things. I never fuck up a deal, and I never lose a situation like this. Okay. Let's get to the office. I have a meeting to prepare for."

DREA LOOKED across the desk at hospital administrator Stan Borges and hoped she wasn't going to lose her job.

"You know he'll be back again," she told hm. "He's not the type to give up."

"I'm well aware of that, but I can handle Sonny Fitzgerald."

She looked down at her lap. "I'm truly sorry if I put the hospital in a bad situation—"

Borges held up his hand. "We'll weather it. It wasn't the first time someone just walked out of the ED and disappeared, and it won't be the last. You know that. I'm sure it was like that at Harper General where you were before you accepted the position here."

"You're right, and I know that. I also know there isn't

anything the nurses and doctors can do about it. If you catch them before they walk out, you can point out they have to sign an AMA. But if they slip out when you aren't looking, there's nothing we can do. But I don't want us to get sued or anything."

Borges gave a short laugh. "I think the last thing Sonny Fitzgerald wants is the police. If I show them her hospital records that document the abuse, he'll be in bigger trouble than he can ever cause for us. Drea, you're one of my best ED nurses. That's why we made you the job offer. You're not in any trouble."

"I could not let him get his hands on her again," she told Borges, relieved she wasn't in trouble. "She was terrified when she came in, and that's an anomaly. The Lainie Taggert I knew wasn't afraid of anything."

The administrator looked at her for a long time before he spoke again.

"I knew someone who was in an abusive relationship," he said at last. "It isn't always by choice. Sometimes the person is very clever and fools you, until you're caught in the trap."

Drea wondered if it was a family member or a good friend or what, but she knew better than to ask questions. If he wanted to tell her he would.

"I'm sure that's what happened to her. She's not a dummy."

"People like Fitzgerald know exactly how to turn on the charm and how to exert control little by little. I'm glad you did this, Drea. You probably saved her life."

She blew out a breath. "Thank you."

"You watch out for yourself," he told her. "He'll see

your name sooner or later. If you and Lainie Taggert were friends, and he knew about it—"

She held up her hand. "I get the message, and I'll be very careful and alert." She stood up. "And thanks for not firing me."

"Are you kidding? We probably should give you a medal. Let me know if you need anything from me."

"Thank you, sir. Thank you very, very much."

Back at the ED, she stepped outside for a moment and speed-dialed Zane.

"How is everything going?" she asked when he answered.

"So far, so good. Here. I'll let her tell you herself."

In a moment, Lainie's soft voice came over the connection.

"Drea? Thank you so much for doing this. Your brother is a godsend."

Drea laughed. "I'm not sure anyone's ever called him that before, but I'm glad he's taking care of you. I'm sure he's happy to do it."

"I'm not so sure about that, but he's being great about everything. Here. I'll let you speak to him again."

"She sounds a little better, Zane. Whatever you're doing, thanks."

"No sweat. Everything okay there?"

She knew he was asking if Sonny had been around and causing trouble.

"Everything's under control, at least for the moment. He showed up and tried some heavy-handed plays but everyone in the ED played dumb, and the hospital director practically told him to get lost. Asked if he wanted the hospital to hand over the information about her other visits."

"I'm guessing not."

"Zane? He's far from finished. You know that. If for no other reason than it wouldn't do his public image any good for people to find out he's an abuser of the first order."

"You got that right. Okay. Keep me up to date on everything, and, Drea, I mean everything. I'll text later."

"Sounds good. And, Zane?" She paused. "Thanks again for doing this."

"It's all good."

Drea stood there for a moment after the call ended, running things through her mind. Lainie sounded better than when she'd left here. Of course, considering her condition at the time, that didn't take much. She needed to give some thought to her own situation. And soon.

CHAPTER 7

"Keep your face always toward the sunshine, and shadows will fall behind you."
  Walt Whitman

It was late afternoon two days later when they entered the foothills of the Crazy Mountains in Montana. After four days—no, almost five—on the road with Zane, Lainie had adjusted to his presence, even to the point where she felt comfortable with him. Each day she'd felt more secure with him, even a little relaxed.

Well, you should. You shared a motel room with him four nights running. And he's seen you all but naked.

She wasn't sure if she should be embarrassed that Zane had seen her body mostly naked or humiliated that he'd seen the awful signs of Sonny's abuse. That first night when he'd had to help her change clothes, she'd wished a hole would open up in the floor and swallow her. Any other man she'd known would have either made suggestive comments or asked a million questions about her bruises. But he simply went about taking care of her and made no comments at all. The only indication she had that he'd noticed was the momentary clenching of his fists, but then he was all about taking care of her.

In only a few days, she'd come to realize Zane Halstead wasn't like any other man she'd ever met. Maybe it was the fact he was dealing with his own life-changing injuries. It was hard not to be aware of how the long days of driving made his limp more noticeable when they stopped for the night. Or the fact that he never complained about either them or the burden of bringing her with him.

She should not have been surprised. Despite the shape she was in, she had seen beneath his gruff exterior that first day and been reassured by his underlying kindness, like the sunglasses to shield her eyes and the pillow to support her shoulder. Learned all his little quirks and habits. It was so nice to be with someone who was not always demanding and criticizing. It drove her crazy that it had taken her so long to see beneath Sonny Fitzgerald's pleasant surface. She'd never be that stupid again. The difference between Sonny and Zane was that with Zane there was no pretense. What you saw was what you got. It hadn't taken her long to figure that out.

She was healing physically, if not yet emotionally. Her sprained shoulder was not quite so achy and, with the applications of ice, the swelling on her eye was almost gone. The bruising on her face and body would take longer to disappear, but she couldn't do anything about that.

And in less than forty-eight hours, she'd realized the impossible seemed to be happening; Zane Halstead was growing on her, and in ways she never expected. She was shocked one morning when he finished helping her pull on her shirt to look up into his eyes and see a spark of heat there. More surprising, an answering flare in her own body. Her bruised body. She hadn't thought about sex as a pleasure for longer than she could remember. Now her independent nipples hardened when he touched her skin, and the pulse points in her body were sending her strange signals.

T Gruff, tough Zane Halstead had a raw kind of sex appeal that, shockingly, appealed to her. Not that she could do anything about it. Or that *he'd* want to act on it. But it was nice to have even a hint of that feeling again after a long drought. What would happen between those two bruised souls, alone in a house on the plains of Montana?

Don't think about it. At least, not yet.

She still had the specter of Sonny Fitzgerald hanging over her. And Zane was right. She had to tell Alex Rossi whatever she knew. It wasn't fair to anyone if she didn't. They had to be prepared in case Sonny did find out where she was. Thinking about it made her sick to her stomach.

Surprisingly, despite everything, she managed to be curious about her surroundings. When Zane hit a truck stop to fill the gas tank, he'd picked up a magazine about the Crazies, as he called them, for her that he found inside.

He had told her the area around the Crazy Mountains was completely rural, although it wasn't that far to Bozeman. That the town they'd be near was very small, and that Sheriff Alex Rossi's office sat on land donated to the county. That was because, she read, they were completely surrounded by private land. People either owned the property or rented from landowners.

She could see the mountains rising white-capped and majestic in the distance, stark peaks against an incredibly blue sky. The magazine description said they rose more than six thousand vertical feet above the prairie, which at the moment was filled with a riot of wildflowers and clusters of tall evergreens.

Lainie stared out the window, awed by the rolling landscape and the majestic mountains that rose from it.

"What do you think?" Zane asked as he navigated a turn in the road.

"I think it's possibly the most beautiful place I've ever seen." She couldn't help being awestruck by the wonder of it.

"Like I said, there's not a lot to do around here. Most people are into ranching or businesses that support it. But I promise to get you to Bozeman every chance I get."

"Um, Zane? This probably sounds stupid to you, but the less time I spend in cities right now, the happier I'll be." She turned her head and stared out the window. "It's so beautiful here, and peaceful. And…" her voice trailed off for a moment. "Safe."

"I can't say anything about the cities, but I can tell you in this area in the Crazy foothills, I think Sheriff Alex Rossi has a lot to do with it. I haven't told you his story because I want you to meet him first. He'll fill you in."

Lainie tensed. Was her being here going to be a problem? Would he tell Zane to cut her loose? She had developed an unhealthy but protective wariness about men. Of course, that made her connection with Zane all the more unusual.

She swallowed and forced herself to ask the question. "Why? Is there something wrong with him?"

Zane shook his head. "Not a thing. We need more people like him."

"Then, is he upset about me? About you being stuck and having to drag me along with you?"

Zane did something totally unexpected. He reached over and squeezed her thigh lightly. She supposed it was in case she had bruises there he hadn't seen.

"First of all, I am not stuck, and I am not dragging you anywhere. It was my choice to bring you, so let's get past that. Second, if he's upset with anyone, it's with Sonny Fitzgerald. When I told him about you, his reaction was to think of ways to keep you safe. I think it's part of SEAL DNA."

Lainie had to squeeze her eyes shut tight to keep the tears from running down her cheeks. It had been too long since anyone had treated her like this. Sonny had fancied her his own possession to do his bidding and to knock around when she pissed him off. These two men—one she'd known less than a week and the other she hadn't even met—were more concerned for her well-being than Sonny had ever been.

Zane cleared his throat, a rough, gravelly sound.

"You okay, Lainie?"

She had to swallow twice before answering him.

"Yes. I guess I'm startled that a man who's only known

me for a few days could be so concerned for my welfare. I'm not used to it."

He gave her leg another soft squeeze before moving his hand.

"I can't presume to ask you how you got to this place in your life. What I can do, however, is let you know your value as a person and help you stay safe and off Sonny Fitzgerald's radar."

"It amazes me that you even want to do that." And wasn't that an understatement.

"Yeah, well, it's one of the few good qualities I have left. Anyway, how about changing the subject? How does everything out here look to you?"

"Wonderful," she breathed. "Beautiful."

Who could not fall in love with the acres of gorgeous scenery, with small valleys and upland prairies and the majestic Crazy Mountains rising in dramatic peaks from the land.

"Like I said earlier," Zane told her, "There are only a few very small towns until you make the drive to Bozeman or farther to Billings. Not a lot to do."

"I keep telling you," she insisted, "that works fine for me. The fewer people I see the better. Besides." Her voice dropped. "I really don't want too many people looking at me in this condition."

"Okay, then. We're all good. But, Lainie?"

"Yes?" Uh-oh, she thought. Here it comes, whatever it is.

"You have nothing to be ashamed of. I told you that. End of story."

No, that wasn't what she expected. She only hoped she

could get her head into that mode. Maybe when her injuries healed a little more.

They rounded a curve in the two-lane highway, and Zane turned down a short gravel road, coming to a stop in the parking lot next to a one-story block building painted a light tan. A porch ran across the front, and double doors opened to the interior. There was limited parking in the front but more to the side, the area surrounded by tall conifers. A plaque beside the doors identified this as the sheriff's office.

Zane climbed out of the truck, and Lainie noticed him trying to hide a grimace as he stretched his leg and his arms.

"You shouldn't have driven so much these past few days," she admonished. She started to add that he'd have done better if he hadn't had to cater to her situation, but he'd made it plain he didn't want to hear any more of that, so she kept quiet. Instead, she opened the passenger door and tried to extricate herself from the truck. Easier said than done.

"I've got you." He was beside her in seconds, amazing her with how quickly he moved. "Let's do this the smart way."

More gently than she'd have thought possible, he slid the pillow from beneath her arm, lifted her from the seat, and set her on the ground.

"You okay to walk inside?"

"Yes." She even managed a smile. "Thanks to you, I'm doing better."

Nevertheless, he kept his hand beneath her elbow to steady her as they climbed the three steps and entered the building. A woman sitting at a desk in the reception area looked up and smiled.

"Well, hello. You must be Zane Halstead. And I'm guessing this young lady is the friend the sheriff said was traveling with you."

Lainie picked up on the fact the woman had not been given her name and swallowed a sigh of relief. The possibility that Sonny could track her here was remote but not impossible.

"I am. Is Sheriff Rossi here?"

"He is." A tall man wearing knife-creased pants that covered the longest legs she'd ever seen, with a holstered gun riding one lean hip, came through a door that led to the rest of the office. He held out his hand to Zane. "Alex Rossi."

Lainie watched Zane shake the man's hand. "Zane Halstead."

Alex smiled at both of them. "Come on back to my office, and we'll get things squared away."

His office was in one corner of a large room that held a dispatch station, desks, and a common area for electronic equipment. Alex ushered them in and closed the door.

"Glad to see you made it okay and aren't too much the worse for wear." He got them settled in chairs before he sat down behind his desk.

Lainie said her piece right away, getting it out in the open.

"I hope it doesn't screw things up for Zane, me showing up with him and all."

"Not a bit. What he's doing is a good indication of the

kind of person he is. Would either of you like coffee? Something cold to drink?"

They both shook their heads. Lainie had a fierce urge to spit out what she had to say. Then, if the sheriff didn't throw her out, find out exactly what had brought Zane to Montana and where they'd be staying. She took a good look at the man across from them who, for whatever reason, was offering them a lifeline. She'd already seen how tall he was. She looked up at the very masculine square-jawed face with its high cheekbones framed by thick, dark-brown hair the color of chocolate, eyes some women night call a fierce blue. But she wasn't interested in his physical attributes, only in the power of the sheriff's badge he wore on his shirt.

And the fact that he had a look in his eyes that told the world they'd better not try any shit around him. She felt herself relax marginally.

Zane chuffed a little laugh. "Yeah. Turned out to be more adventurous than I expected."

Lainie wasn't going to allow herself to be discussed in oblique references.

"I believe he means he hadn't expected to leave Tampa with a woman in a dangerous situation, sporting injuries, whose fiancé might try to hunt them down and kill them."

She couldn't believe she'd laid it out there like that, but each day with Zane she'd begun to feel a tiny bit stronger. The person she'd been before Sonny, the one hungry for life, fighting for her place in the world, was inching its way back in a very short time. She could thank Zane for that. If only she were strong enough to embrace it fully.

The sheriff laughed, a low chuckle. "I'm glad to see you're not trying to gloss this over."

She shook her head. "I think I did that for too long. And now Zane's got me on his hands when he really came out here to see about starting a new phase in his life."

"The way I see it," Zane told her in his rough voice, "at least for the moment you're part of that new start."

"And by the way," she added, looking at the sheriff, "thanks for not pulling the offer because of me."

Zane watched Rossi look carefully at each of them, studying them.

"I don't know what you were looking for when you reached out to me," Zane told him, "but I'd like to hear what's on the table."

"And you, Lainie?"

She looked from one man to the other. "I'd like nothing more than to be someplace safe where I can heal and figure out what to do with the rest of my life."

"We'll make sure of that." Alex looked directly at Zane. "I admire a man who puts others beyond his own wants. That's why I'm looking at former SEALs." He shifted in his chair. "Not that every Special Forces group isn't spectacular in its own way, but I'm going with what I know."

"Well, thank you just the same."

"Good. On to Sonny Fitzgerald. I did some research on him," Rossi told them.

"As did I," Zane said.

"The nicest thing I can say about him is he's a nasty individual. He'd never get away with half the junk he does if it weren't for all the people in high places who owe him favors."

Lainie nodded at his words. "He makes a point of getting people in his debt so he can do whatever he wants. And the people who head large businesses and corporations know they can grow with little expense if Sonny leads the charge." She swallowed. "I guess Zane also told you that Sonny's worried about any information I might have. It has to do with something that happened the night before I—the night before I left. I don't have real proof, so he'll want to eliminate me before I can do any damage."

"Not on my watch," the sheriff said.

"Or on mine," Zane added. "But maybe this is the time to say what it is."

Nausea roiled up inside her again. She drew a breath then laid out the story about Sonny and the woman he'd killed.

"The thing is," she told both of them, "I know he's got that mess all cleaned up by this time, at least as far as anyone knows. It's been nearly a week, and no one is pointing a finger at him for it. If I come along and open my mouth, he'll convince the police I'm crazy and have me done away with."

"Not if you're with us," Alex assured her. "No one messes with the sheriff."

Lainie shook her head. "I'm telling you, you don't know this man. He makes sure there are no bubbles on the surface then gets rid of anyone who might cause them."

"Yes, I do. He leaned forward in his chair. "My wife, Micki, is a prosecuting attorney. Until she moved back here, she worked in Hillsborough County in Florida. The city of Tampa. She's very familiar with Sonny Fitzgerald."

Zane sensed Lainie tense beside him, heard her indrawn breath.

"Why didn't you say something before this?" she asked.

"I wanted to wait until you got here," he explained. "I knew you'd have questions, and there wasn't much sense in letting you drive yourself crazy on the road."

"She's told you about him?"

"You bet. As soon as I explained this situation. She said she supports anything we can do to wipe this scum off the face of the earth."

Lainie blew out a breath. "Okay, then. So you really know what we're up against."

He nodded. "I've done a lot of research on him." He looked at Lainie. "Between your story, what Micki told me, and what I read, I'd say this man hardly deserves to keep living."

She felt the heat creep up her cheeks as embarrassment flooded her.

"I'm so ashamed I got involved with him. I'm not a stupid person."

"No, you're not," Zane was quick to say.

Alex nodded in agreement. "From what I've read, a lot of very smart people have fallen victim to him. He has the ability to charm people into his orbit and then decide how they'll benefit him. I got the impression if he wasn't such a bastard litigator—excuse my language—he wouldn't have the support of so many powerful people."

"Same impression I got," Zane agreed. "And my number one priority right at this moment is to keep Lainie safe from him."

Thank you, Zane.

From the moment he'd first lifted her into his truck, he'd demanded nothing and treated her with respect. She hadn't had that in a long time.

"My first concern is for Lainie's safety," he added. "Maybe we should discuss that first."

Alex nodded. "I agree. I took the liberty of doing something that I hope is okay with you."

Zane frowned. "I'm sure it is, but like what?"

"I called a good friend at the Montana Bureau of Justice. They have equipment and resources much more sophisticated than mine. I'm going to guess Sonny Fitzgerald is going to use every dirty trick to try and find Lainie. And if he somehow learns she's with you, he'll try to trace you."

"Shit." Zane's face lost a little color. "My sister. If he's able to find out Drea helped set this up, he'll be after her, too. Can you extend that to her?"

Alex nodded. "I'll get her flagged. If he tries to do a search for credit card purchases or cell phone records on either of you, it will pop up and give us a heads-up on it. Also, give me your email password."

Zane lifted an eyebrow. "Email password?"

Alex nodded. "Justice has a great tech superstar who can hack into anything and get information." He grinned. "Strictly for legal purposes, of course." Then the grin disappeared. "He'll keep checking to make sure your account isn't hacked. From what you said and what my wife told me, this guy will stop at nothing."

"He's right," Lainie chimed in. "I heard him mention stuff like this before when he didn't know I was listening."

"Even if I have two-factor authentication?"

"Even if." Alex pushed paper and pencil at Zane. "Here. Write her name down for me and yours and the passwords."

He picked up his phone and punched in a number.

"You should call Drea," Lainie told him while Alex made his phone call. "Let her know what's happening. She needs to be careful, although she's met Sonny and knows what he's like. I can tell you, she's not crazy about him. She had his number from Day One. Why didn't I listen to her? If somehow he finds out..."

"I'll do it as soon as we're in the truck. And that's water under the bridge, Lainie. There are things all of us should have done. We just move forward from here, right?"

Alex nodded. "Lainie, there are a lot of ways to do this. I promise we'll figure out the one that's the safest for you."

"Thank you."

"Next." Zane looked over at Alex. Then he took his gun from the small of his back and placed it on his desk. "I checked, and Montana does not require a permit."

Alex nodded. "Good. I'm glad you're armed, although it's no less than I'd expect. If you decide to take my offer, however, we'll issue you the same weapon the rest of us carry. Of course, you're free to also carry your own weapon in an ankle holster."

Zane nodded. "Good enough."

"That's what this place is known for," Rossi told her. "Figuring out the rest of your life. We had to clean out a bunch of very bad people to get to that point though."

"What you mentioned on the phone?" Zane asked.

Rossi nodded. "After you get settled, I'll tell you about it. The sad thing was the former sheriff was in it up to his neck, and I haven't been sure which of the deputies he left me I could trust."

"Where is he now?" Lainie asked.

"In prison. That's part of the story." He cleared his throat. "Like you, Zane, I was a SEAL. Three tours of duty. The need to serve never seems to go away, but I had reached burnout stage. Time to get out. I ended up here because another SEAL, Scot Nolan, became part of an organization headquartered here in the Crazies called Brotherhood Protectors. Long story short, Scot reached out to me and put me together with Hank Patterson who runs the agency, but my head wasn't into private security." He leaned back in his chair. "The county was, however, in desperate need of a new sheriff. So here I am."

"And?" Zane prompted.

"And, I have two things on my plate that dovetail with each other. I'm cleaning house here and looking for former SEALs to add to my staff. I was a SEAL, and I know that's who I can depend on. The deputies who were Bartell's friends are gone. The dispatcher is a heads-up lady, and the two younger deputies are okay. Miranda Golden, my senior deputy, has been here awhile and is top of the line. She said she did a little dance the day they carted former Sheriff Bartell off to jail. She knows the area and the people and her law and is a real asset."

"So you've got three deputies," Zane commented.

"Actually, four. Miranda fetched a kid out of college who's still pretty much wet behind the ears but hell-bent on law enforcement. When he graduated Montana State, he went to Missoula where his college girlfriend lived with the idea the two of them were a thing. By the time he'd gone through the academy in Missoula, he discovered he was the only one who felt that way. Miranda snatched him up so here he is, nursing a slightly broken heart and eager to enforce the law."

Zane grinned, a full-out smile, which amazed Lainie. She hadn't thought he had it in him.

"Sounds like the raw recruits we get in SEALs." Then he sobered. "But that doesn't give you much of a staff, right?"

Alex nodded. "The four I've got are okay for the moment and the state police will step in if there's some kind of emergency. But yeah, we're a little short on hands. But I wanted to build my own staff." He paused. "And I wanted former SEALs, guys like me who were looking for a comfortable place to use their skills."

"But not in private security," Zane said.

"Right. Listen. Hank Patterson's Brotherhood Protectors is a first-rate operation. He and I are very good friends. I'd recommend them to anyone anytime. In fact, Hank's the one who got me into this job. My head was not into going private."

Zane nodded. "Got it. So, how did you get my name?"

Rossi paused for a moment.

"When I was processing out, I spent some time with Andy Ryan. I understand you know him—"

"Wait a sec." Zane sat forward. "This isn't some kind of emotional therapy or something, is it?"

"Hell, no. But he and I are good friends, and he knows my goal is to build a first-rate staff with former SEALs looking for the next place to serve. To regain their footing. He's kind of my recruiter out there."

Lainie wasn't sure for a moment if Zane was going to punch Rossi in the jaw. Get up and walk out of there or what. She and the sheriff were both shocked when he burst out laughing.

"Rebuilding the heroes, is it?"

Rossi smiled but shook his head. "Only if they're up for it. Andy said he thought you'd be a good candidate."

Lainie held her breath, waiting to see what Zane would say. If he turned this down, where did they go from here? Where did *she* go?

"Sounds good to me," he said at last.

"One more thing." Alex slid a slip of paper across the desk. "Phone number for Mark Sandoval. He's the local general practitioner." He looked at Lainie. "Zane didn't tell me a lot about your condition, nothing more than the basics, but I figured you'd need some kind of medical attention."

She didn't know whether to laugh or cry or curl up in embarrassment.

"Thank you," she whispered, as Zane pocketed the slip.

The sheriff rose from his chair. "Let's go look at the house I've got set up for you. It goes with the job, by the way. It's easy to set up security, and you can stay as long as you want, check out the area while you make up your mind."

"Sounds good," Zane told him.

He smiled. "My wife did a little grocery shopping. Hope she got what you need until you're ready to make a trip to the store. Then we'll see where we go from here. That work for you?"

Zane looked at Lainie then nodded. "As long as Lainie's good with it."

Lainie hadn't realized she'd be part of the decision-making process, but she was glad she wasn't being left to twist in the wind. Not that she had a right to expect any more, but in a few days, she'd become comfortable with gruff yet sensitive Zane Halstead. Strange considering the hell she'd lived in the past months. She certainly wasn't ready to try out anything else yet, but she was shocked at how comfortable she'd become with this man in a few days. Maybe because he was so different from Sonny and some of the other men she'd known.

The first thing Zane did when they were in the truck was call Drea, as Lainie had said, and warn her. She listened carefully to his side of the conversation.

"Yeah, that's right. Know you've met him. That should give you caution. Do you have someone you can stay with for a while?" Pause. "Well, please give it some thought. And we'll check in with you regularly. Okay, Later."

"She says she'll be careful," he told Lainie, "but she doesn't think he can find out about her. She spoke to the hospital administrator, and he's on her side. She can get help there if she needs it."

"Zane, that man can find out anything. He's got hackers who I'm sure could even breach Homeland Security. She needs to be careful."

He nodded. "She understands. She's got Sonny's number, so she'll be extra cautious. She's no dummy."

"Fine, but let's keep checking on her."

"I plan to. And thanks for being so concerned about her."

"I have to. She's my only friend. I mean, besides you." She glanced over at him. "We are friends, right?"

He grinned. "We're definitely something."

They followed the sheriff from his office, not wanting to leave the truck there and be without wheels. He took them down a narrow gravel road that led away from the highway, through a stand of ponderosa pines, and brought them into a small clearing. Lainie caught her breath.

A small house—actually a one-story log cabin—sat in the clearing surrounded by gravel with more trees at the back. To the right was a small barn and a corral. Prairie dotted with little clusters of trees stretched beyond that. They parked next to Alex, and Zane helped her out of the truck and up onto the porch.

"It's not the fanciest place in the world," Alex Rossi was saying as he unlocked the front door, "but it's clean."

"I think it's beautiful," Lainie told him.

The sheriff chuckled. "You've hardly seen it yet."

She stood there, hand tucked into Zane's arm for stability, and looked at the trees and prairie.

"It's beautiful and secluded. The secluded part is especially appealing."

"Let's see the rest of it." The sheriff opened the door and ushered them in.

Lainie caught her breath. It was so different from what she was used to in Florida, but that was part of its beauty. The living room was wide with big picture windows, plank floors, and a fireplace. As Alex led them through it, she saw two nice-sized bedrooms and a bathroom bigger than she would have expected. The kitchen was big enough to hold a table and chairs plus barstools at a counter.

"Like I said, Mick was more than happy to lay in supplies for you." He showed them the pantry cupboard and the refrigerator and freezer. "So you didn't have to run to the store right away. However, I left a list of the stores you'll be needing the names of right away. The rest you can absorb as you go along."

"Thank her for us," Lainie told him.

Alex turned back to Zane. "I guess part of this also depends on how long you expect Lainie to be with you."

"I don't—" she started to say when Zane interrupted her.

"A long time. I promised to protect her, and I intend to do that."

"I imagine you want some time to think about the sheriff's deputy position. See if you like the area. I will tell you that Lainie from this moment onward becomes someone for my staff, such as it is, to protect, so we're here for whatever you need." He handed Zane a folder he'd carried with him from the office. "These are the details. Look it over for a few days. Get a feel for the place."

"Don't you have someone else who might be wanting this place? I can't be the only candidate for this job."

Alex's mouth hitched in a half grin. "The only one I'm interested in at the moment. I know the kind of people I want to hire and I'm being very choosy. Oh, and by the way. You said you grew up on a horse farm? There are two mares who belong in that barn. They came with the original owner. With no one living here we moved them over to the ranch, but I think they're homesick. Since you'll be living here, though, I think I'll move them back. Get you back into the horseflesh business."

"Might be easier said than done."

"We'll see."

"Who did live in this house before?"

"A friend of Micki's brother. He worked on the ranch for some time but left to go work on a ranch in Australia, of all places. There are a few apartments for rent here, but you're my first SEAL recruit, so my wife and I thought you should have this. Also, having someone with you tipped the scales."

"What happens when you hire the next one?"

Alex grinned. "We'll figure it out. Anyway, when you're ready, my wife and I would like you both to have dinner with us. I'd invite you to the ranch, but Micki refuses to set foot in that house. Hasn't since the whole mess." The smile left his face. "The trials of the four other men dragged for months until finally their attorneys convinced them to take a plea. Told them the longer it went on the worse the sentencing would be. I think we were all glad when it was over."

"Pardon my being nosy, but who lives at the ranch, and where do you and Micki live?"

"She took a small parcel at one end of the ranch property, which as close as she'd come, and we built a house there. Her brother Jason, who is living temporarily out there until it sells, convinced her to do it. Said the ground wasn't tainted by what happened."

Zane whistled. "What a nightmare to live through."

"Tell me about it. Anyway, we'd love to have you over when you're ready."

"Thanks. I think I want to give Lainie a chance to settle down first."

Alex nodded. "One step at a time. Meanwhile, you've got both my office and cell numbers. Call me anytime."

He shook hands with both of them and headed out the door.

"Oh, Zane," Lainie breathed. "It's almost too good to be true."

He took her uninjured hand in his and gave it a gentle squeeze.

"Here's the deal, Lainie. Tell me if this works for you. The protection is a given, for as long as it's needed. And as long as you want to stay."

She studied him. "Are you sure?"

"Yes. I'm going to ask Alex about installing a security system, which I think will make both of us feel better. But —" He stopped a moment. "But you're the first person I've felt comfortable with in a very long time. Except the members of my team, and that's different. We've only known each other a few days. You're banged up because some bastard wanted to take his anger out on you, and I have no idea how you even feel about being with me for a while. But I'm in no hurry for you to leave. Maybe not ever."

He turned away, giving her time to absorb his words, which shocked her. She knew about instant connections. She'd made a series of bad choices that way. But Zane was different. Sure, he had his problems, still dealing with the leftovers from his last mission and adjusting to a new life.

But she wasn't the least bit afraid of this man. The gentle way he'd helped her the past few days, in what could have been embarrassing situations, told her he was a different breed from her usual bad choices.

Was it really possible—

Get past this, Lainie. And see what it's like after more than a week before you rush into something again.

"Lainie?"

Zane's voice disrupted her thoughts. She couldn't believe she'd zoned out like that.

She gave herself a mental shake, absently noticing he still held her hand.

"Sorry. Didn't mean to zone out like that."

He did that thing again where he cupped her chin, forcing her to look into his eyes.

"Think about this. You're doing me as much good as I am you. I was in a bad place the day I picked you up. You've made me look outside myself." He looked away for a moment. "Not that I don't have a long way to go."

"We both do." She wet her lips. "Maybe we can get there together."

He smiled, and it transformed his face. "Maybe we can."

CHAPTER 8

"But man is not made for defeat. A man can be destroyed but not defeated."

Ernest Hemingway

"Sonny, you're driving yourself crazy."

Geoff Miller swiped his phone shut and looked at his boss. "You hardly concentrate on the clients because you're so obsessed with finding that bitch who screwed you over."

"Focused," Sonny corrected him.

"What?" Geoff frowned.

"I said I'm focused, not obsessed." He rose from behind his desk and walked to the large window in his office. "Focused is what gets the job done."

"Yeah?" Geoff quirked an eyebrow. "How's that working out for you?"

Sonny tossed his pen down on the desk. He didn't need Geoff's smart mouth today, unless it was to tell him where he could find Lainie. The bitch. The absolutely ungrateful bitch. He'd given her anything she could possibly want, and this was how she repaid him?

"If you've got nothing to say, keep your mouth shut."

Geoff held up his hands. "Okay, okay, make yourself miserable all you want."

"I take it no one you spoke to has laid eyes on her?"

Geoff shrugged and shook his head.

"What the fuck?" Sonny wanted to throw something. "Nobody disappears like that. Not unless they've got a ton of money behind them. Which she does not."

"Well, someone helped her," Geoff pointed out. "They had to."

"If you don't quit repeating the obvious, you'll be the next one to disappear. I'll—" The cell phone on his desk rang, and he snatched it up. Looked at the readout. "Yeah, Antonio? Have you finally got something for me? What? I gave you the job almost seventy-two hours ago. What the fuck takes so long? All right, all right. Send over what you've got."

He slammed the cell phone down on the desk.

"Careful," Geoff commented, "or you'll break it. Anything?"

"Frank says they plucked the entire roster of hospital employees off their system, and he has his crew running them through every database he's got. But since we didn't know what names to flag, he's sending us the raw list while he has his guys run profiles on all of them."

"Holy shit, Sonny. That could take forever."

Sonny shook his head. "Not with Frank. He's got the

most sophisticated setup you'd ever want to see. Anyway, he's sending over what he's got as we speak."

He turned to his computer and opened his email, waiting for the one from Frank to pop up. Of course, the moment it showed up, the intercom on his desk buzzed. Fuck. Now what?

He pushed the button. "What is it?"

"I'm sorry, Mr. Fitzgerald, but you told me to let you know when the Calabreses arrived."

Double fuck. Angelo Calabrese and his brother, Paolo, were the principle owners of Steelman Consolidated, a multimillion-dollar conglomerate that bought and sold other companies. Usually, they targeted a company, Sonny created an adversarial situation, the company sued, Sonny litigated them out of existence, and the Calabreses got something practically for free. And Sonny got a big fat fee.

It was a sign of his unusual distraction that he'd forgotten all about the appointment. They were right smack in the middle of one of these deals, and he needed to get his head out of his ass and into it or he'd lose his biggest cash cow and his seat of power.

"Okay. Put them in the conference room. You sent someone out for those pastries they like, right?"

"Yes, sir. They'll be all set."

"Good. Thanks. Tell them I'll be right with them."

Why did he have the feeling his life was falling apart, when he had devoted so much attention to carefully constructing it.

"Better get your shit together for them," Geoff warned.

"No kidding. Will you—"

Geoff held up a hand and rose from the chair. "I'll pull up the list he sent you and see if anything pops up at me. You go be the tiger-eating shark."

Which was exactly the reputation he'd worked so hard to build. He was not about to let that bitch ruin it for him.

∼

"Lainie?"

Zane had finished a walk-through of the house, making mental notes of spots that need security equipment. He knew Lainie must be exhausted and wanted her to lie down for a while before they decided what to do about dinner.

"In here."

He walked into the kitchen and saw her standing by the counter, looking out the wide window at the barn and corral and the prairie beyond. He could tell by the posture of her body and the way she braced herself with her good hand against the counter that she had about reached the end of her rope. And why not? They'd been on the road for most of five days. And her body had to be protesting.

"Come with me." He touched her free elbow. "You need to lie down, and I need to check your injuries. Come on."

"But dinner, and all our things," she began. "We have to—"

"We don't have to do a thing, and we'll eat when we get hungry. The nice thing is we're not on anyone's schedule but our own. Come on."

With his hand still gently but firmly on her arm, he led

her to the larger of the two bedrooms. He knew he was limping and hoped Lainie wouldn't bring it up. His leg ached like a son of a bitch from all the days of steady driving. Even doing his exercises at night had offered minimum relief. He wouldn't mind stretching his leg out for a while and easing the ache. Damn! He was beginning to feel his age. At thirty-eight, that wasn't so good.

He folded back the spread on the bed, urged Lainie to sit down, and crouched by her feet to remove her shoes. He'd already memorized the routine for removing the sling, and he checked her broken fingers where they were taped.

"We need to get this checked out," he told her. "Tomorrow I'm calling the doc whose name Alex gave us."

He saw her start to object then change her mind. "Okay. I won't argue."

Zane swallowed a smile. "That'll be a nice change. Okay, sling's off. Lie down so I can brace your arm with a pillow."

She offered no resistance as he arranged her body for comfort. He had to grind his teeth to keep from running a hand over the lush curves and stroking the skin that despite the bruises looked so soft and silky.

Shit, Halstead. You're turning into a real lech. Behave yourself. The woman's barely five days out of the hospital.

Maybe it was the fact he'd mostly been without a woman for so long. His choice but still. No, that wasn't it. There was something very very special about this woman. He was torn between wanting to worship her body and beat the shit out of Sonny Fitzgerald. But he needed to go very slow here. They'd be alone in this house for who knew how long. He could take it slow. See if it was meant to be.

"Zane?"

Her soft voice was like a song to him.

"You need something?" He snapped his fingers. "Pills. Of course. I think there are only two left. I'll get your duffel from the truck." He stood up, trying to conceal the wince as pain shot through his thigh. "For sure we'll go see that doctor tomorrow."

"Tylenol, please," she called. "It's late in the afternoon, and I don't want to be up all night."

He found a glass in the kitchen, filled it with water, and brought it to her with the Tylenol. His leg was beginning to throb, and he was having a hard time not showing how much it hurt. He wanted to get Lainie settled, though, before he gave in to his own situation.

"Thanks," she told him, handing him back the glass of water.

"You rest, okay?" He started to leave the room.

"Zane?" He stopped, gritting his teeth against the stab of pain in his thigh.

"Yeah?"

"Will you, um, come lie down with me?"

The rest of his muscles tightened, and his cock stirred hopefully. No. Uh-uh. Not going there.

"I'm not so sure that's a good idea." Because she was touching places in him that he'd thought dead, and she was in no shape for anything besides conversation.

"I think it's a great idea." She paused. "Please? I really don't want to be alone right this moment. Besides, I can see how your leg is bothering you, and I know you're going to lie down somewhere. So why not here?"

Because, because, because.

He sighed. "Okay, but just until you fall asleep."

He was pretty sure he'd regret this. He went to the other side of the bed and kicked off his shoes. Then, moving slowly, he lay down about six inches away from Lainie. He was so acutely aware of her lying there next to him he was sure she could hear his nerves vibrating.

"Do you need to do anything special for your leg?" she asked.

"It'll be okay if I'm off it for a while. I'm going to take a hot shower pretty soon. That always helps."

What he could really use was a long soak in a hot tub. However, he wasn't about to sit naked in the bathtub. The bathroom door probably had a lock, but somehow the tub made him feel more vulnerable.

"You could go take your shower," she told him. "I'll be okay until you're done."

"It's all good," he told her, hopefully.

He lay there, willing himself to relax, trying to think over the pain in his leg. When he felt Lainie's small fingers creep into his hand, heat shot up his arm and through his body.

"This is nice," she murmured.

"To tell the truth, I'm not sure how you can even stand a man to touch you after what that bastard put you through."

There was little humor in the sound of her short laugh.

"Maybe I need something to let me know there are

other kinds of men in the world." She paused. "Maybe I see how different you are from Sonny, and I want to know what your touch is like. Maybe I have to have something to tell me there are other options, although I do seem to keep choosing the wrong ones."

"Much as I hate to say it," he told her, "I've seen too many men who make a habit of coming on to a woman as one person when they really are another."

"But not SEALs," she guessed.

"No, not SEALs."

She threaded her fingers through his, and his cock tried to stand up and say hello.

Good going, Halstead. Show her you're one of the assholes.

At least the throbbing in his leg had begun to ease.

"Zane? How come you're not with a woman?"

He bit back all the things he wanted to say and decided being truthful might explain why them together was such a bad idea.

"When I was with the Teams, I was so focused on that and the mission that I didn't want to fracture my concentration. I didn't think it would be fair to a woman always coming in second."

"But lots of SEALs are married, or in a committed relationship," she persisted. "Right?"

"Everyone is different," he finally said. "Maybe I wasn't ready. Anyway, you need to close your eyes and get some rest."

"I talk too much sometimes." She sighed. "Okay, okay. But keep this in mind. I'm not done with the subject yet."

Wonderful, was all he could think.

Maybe, if he took things slowly with her, after they

destroyed Sonny Fitzgerald, he could find a way to move forward with Lainie. She was sweet but with an emerging core of steel.

But then, in what seemed like minutes, he felt Lainie's hand relax in his and heard the soft purr of her breath. He knew he should pull away from her but somehow he couldn't make himself. He hadn't felt a touch like that in what seemed forever. And inappropriate as it might be at the moment, he was going to let himself enjoy it a little longer.

Lying there, thinking about what she'd look like without all those bruises and other damage, he realized he was in trouble. He'd need every bit of self-discipline not to fuck this up.

Finally, when he could tell by the rhythm of her breathing that she was sound asleep, he slipped her hand from his and eased himself off the bed. He managed to get their things out of the truck without making too much noise, and, after taking out clean clothes for himself, he headed for the bathroom. He waited until the water was as hot as he could stand it before he stepped in and pulled the shower curtain closed.

He adjusted his stance so his left leg got the force of the stream, beating into the injured muscle and tendons. He realized the scar from the surgery had not improved much in six months, and why the hell did he expect it to anyway. The surgeon had done a great job—he was happy he could still walk—but ugly was still ugly. No one else had seen it except the therapist since then. Not Drea and certainly not the one woman he'd been with. They'd spent the entire time in the dark.

But then he thought of Lainie's nasty bruises and injuries and realized he needed to get a grip. She'd managed to stand there without falling apart while he helped her with her clothing and tended to her. The damn woman had more courage than he did. And thinking of Lainie and her body, still so tempting and appealing even bruised as it was, his cock swelled and ached.

Okay, he needed to do something about that before she woke up. And before it got out of control and he embarrassed himself. Alex's wife had been thoughtful enough to stock some necessities in the bathroom, so he poured liquid soap into his hand and lathered up. As soon as he'd covered his body, he braced himself with one hand against the tiled wall and gripped his cock with the other hand.

Closing his eyes, he stroked himself over and over, conjuring up an image of Lainie as he did so. But in his mind, she was unbruised, uninjured, and standing naked in the prairie outside this house. The wind blew her hair and made her nipples harden and peak. She was smiling and reaching out to him. The image made his dick throb, and he stroked harder and faster, gritting his teeth so he wouldn't make a sound.

With his eyes closed, he held onto her image, imagining it was her hand on him, her other hand lightly squeezing his balls. He imagined what it would be like to have her naked body under him, her legs wrapped around him as he slid into her tight wet heat. Feeling her slick muscles squeezing him. Sucking those tempting nipples into swollen buds.

His own hand moved at a greater speed, the soap

making it slick on his hard shaft. And then, like a strike of lightning, he exploded, his semen spilling over his fingers as he squeezed himself and stroked and tugged. Finally, finally, the orgasm subsided, and he leaned weakly against the tiled wall.

It took him a while to catch his breath, but when he did, he rinsed off and turned off the water. The hot water had helped his leg a lot, and the orgasm diminished the raging need in his body. But then what? He couldn't jump in the shower every time looking at her made him hard.

At last, dressed in clean clothes, he went to check on Lainie.

One thing at a time, buddy. Let's get her healed first.

SONNY SAT at his desk staring at the report from Frank. As usual, the man had been thorough and ferreted out every single employee at the hospital. Geoff had already printed out the list while he was meeting with the Calabreses and was going over it again, but Sonny wanted his own eyes on it. He would spot names that Geoff might not be familiar with. Every so often he would stop and check someone out on the computer, but it always turned out to be a false lead. As a major urban hospital, its roster listed more than ten thousand on staff in both medical and nonmedical positions.

He was still at it when it grew dark outside and everyone else had left the office. He was at his desk, and Geoff was sprawled on the couch with his half of the list. His eyes were burning, and the excessive amount of coffee he'd consumed was like acid in his stomach when he finally hit something.

"Shit." He stared at the list. "God damn fuck and double shit."

Geoff sat up. "Find something?"

"Something? Yeah, I found something. The worst possible something."

"Well?" Geoff leaned forward. "Is it a big secret?"

Sonny made a rude noise. "When Lainie and I met, she had a friend named Drea Halstead. She was a nurse in the emergency department at a hospital across town. Nosy bitch. She was one of the first ones I locked out of Lainie's life."

"She can't have been too happy about that. Neither of them would have been. If anyone knows how women are, Sonny, it's you."

"Yeah, well, some are easier to handle than others. I thought this bitch was a bad influence on Lainie, always sticking her nose in our business. Her name never came up again, so I figured she was out of our life for good."

"Yeah? So?"

"So she started working at this hospital a month ago. In the emergency department."

"And you think she was there the day Lainie was," Geoff guessed.

"It could explain how she managed to disappear as slick as she did," Sonny pointed out. He took a sip of cold coffee, made a face, and put the cup down. "But then where the hell was she when I was there?"

The familiar rage was building inside him.

"You didn't see her anywhere?" Geoff asked.

"No, damn it." He wanted to punch someone or something. "And, of course, not knowing at the time she worked there, I didn't ask."

"And if she'd helped Lainie at all, you can be sure she'd hide when she saw you coming." Geoff frowned. "So what now?"

"We take her life apart. If she was able to get Lainie out of that hospital slick as grease, she had to have help. I want to know her friends and relatives, where she shops, where she eats. Everything about her. But first, I want to know her address. We'll put a tail on her."

"You think she's hiding Lainie somewhere in the city?"

Sonny shook his head. "Not necessarily. But we have to start someplace. Find out her relatives and contacts. And maybe scare the shit out of her while we're doing it." He looked at Geoff. "No one walks away from me. You hear me. Absolutely no one."

"How well I know."

Sonny picked up his cell. His calls to Antonio did not go through a business phone or any other landline.

"Did you get the list I sent?" Antonio asked, without even a hello.

"Got it, and I found a name. Drea Halstead. I want you to tear her life apart. Friends, relatives, coworkers, everything. I want her charge card info so I can see her purchases. The works."

"Already doing that for everyone," Antonio told him.

"Yeah, but that could take a while, and we don't have any time to spare. I have another deal with the Calabreses next week, and I can't afford to let anyone fuck it up. Put one of your guys on her specifically and fast-track it. But, in the meantime, get me her address. Text it to me. Also the hours of her shift at the hospital."

"On it."

"Anything on Lainie yet?" He'd set Antonio on Lainie's trail the moment he'd left the hospital.

"Nada. It's like the earth swallowed her up."

"She's out there somewhere. How many times do I have to say this? She can't disappear like this on her own. Look deeper."

"Okay. Here comes the list."

In seconds, Sonny's cell phone beeped at him, and he saw the text from Antonio. He smiled.

"Got it."

"Not to rain on your parade," Geoff told him, "but how can you be sure she's the one? You might be wasting your time with her while the person you really want disappears along with Lainie."

"That's your department. Work with Charlie on eliminating everyone but the real possibilities. Then have him pull up everything he can find on them." His phone dinged, and he looked at the screen then tapped it. "Okay, Antonio's got her address for me and her work schedule."

"That was fast."

"That's how good he is." He checked his watch and stood up. "I'm telling you, I have a gut feeling this is who we want. I never liked her, and she never liked me. It would be Lainie's style to pull a stunt like this."

"Where are you going now? And do you want me to hang out here or at the house?"

"The house. You know whatever you need electronically I have there, already set up. I don't want anyone in this office overhearing anything."

"Got it." He gathered up the papers he'd been working with as well as his phone and his jacket. "Check in with me so I'll know you haven't gotten arrested as a Peeping Tom."

"No chance of that. I'm too slick for them to catch me."

"Famous last words. You be very careful, Sonny. You've got a good thing going. I don't want to see you destroy it because of some stupid bitch."

"Neither do I, but people have to be taught a lesson, so no one will do it again."

"Don't take the SUV or Mercedes. Too noticeable. Take that ugly sedan you keep around for stuff like this."

"Planning on it. And don't worry. I've got it under control."

He hoped.

CHAPTER 9

"THERE IS no charm equal to tenderness of heart."
   Jane Austen

LAINIE OPENED HER EYES SLOWLY, blinking, unsure for the moment where she was and how she got into this strange bedroom. It didn't look like any motel room she'd ever seen, with its four-poster bed, ruffled curtains at the windows, and a big antique-looking dresser. Beautiful still-life prints hung on the walls, and candlestick lamps graced each nightstand.

She shifted position and swallowed a groan as pain stabbed her in various places. But one thing she noticed. It wasn't nearly as bad as the day she'd left the hospital. The hot showers each night had worked magic on her body. Today they were more twinges than anything else. When she shifted her weight, her shoulder still protested, but again, not like it had been the day she ended up in the emergency department. Sleeping with her arm on a pillow relieved a lot of the strain, and the pain meds and Tylenol dulled the worst of it.

Her fingers were still a problem, but there wasn't much she could do beyond what she was already doing. She guessed that tomorrow when Zane took her to the doctor whose name Alex had given him, she'd get a better read on the situation. She hoped she didn't have to show him the bruises on her body that were barely starting to fade. She couldn't do much about her face, but that was already fading a little, and the ice had made the swelling nearly disappear. He'd probably think she was as much of an idiot as she called herself for getting in this situation.

And Zane! What must he think? He probably looked at her as a pitiful loser who made bad choices in life. Well, he wouldn't be far from wrong. She had certainly made a series of bad choices. She seemed to have picked up the habit from her mother, which was one of the reasons she'd left home a long time ago. Apparently, however, for a supposedly smart woman she hadn't learned a thing. It seemed her choices kept getting worse.

And here she was, with a man totally unlike any she'd ever been with before. Not outgoing. Not gregarious. Withdrawn into himself because of his own situation. Yet putting himself out there for her and treating her like something special. She wasn't sure she even knew how to act. But one thing she did know, and it shocked her more than anything else. They had a connection unlike anything she'd ever had with a man before. Even with his injuries and depression he projected strength and honor. His body might be damaged in some way, but it didn't matter to her. And it wasn't just sex. She wanted to curl up in his arms and stay there for the rest of her life.

"Lainie?"

She opened her eyes to see Zane standing next to her. His hair was wet, a sign he'd showered, and combed back, which made his lean, very masculine face more stark. And more appealing, if she let herself think like that. He was dressed in a clean T-shirt that emphasized his abs and sweatpants that hung from narrow hips. If she hadn't been in such discomfort, she might have actually drooled.

He sat down on the bed next to her, being careful not to jar her bad arm, and studied her face.

"Looking a lot better," he told her. "The swelling around the eye is gone, and the bruising is already starting to fade."

"Please," she said. "You don't have to sugarcoat it. I know what I look like."

He frowned. "I don't know how you got such a negative opinion of yourself. If it was the guy who did this to you, I have a few things I'd like to do to him. Lainie, you're a beautiful woman, even with the bruises, and easy to be with. Probably more than any other woman I've ever spent time with." He snorted. "Although for the past six months there hasn't been anyone to really compare to."

She didn't know what to say to that, so she decided to change the subject.

"How's your leg?"

He shook his head. "It's as good as it's going to get, I guess. You know. It is what it is. I have to make sure to do my exercises every day, is all."

She laughed, a tentative sound. "We're quite a pair, aren't we?"

"I'd say so." His smile transformed his face but disappeared as quickly as it appeared. "Listen. I know I'm no bargain for a lot of reasons, but somehow we're okay together. Like I keep trying to convince you, my plan is to take care of you and, if needed, protect you. I'm doing it because I want to, so let's drop the subject. We're done discussing it. At the moment, I want to check you over."

The bed dipped with his weight as he sat next to her and checked the bruises on her face with a gentle touch.

"They hardly even hurt anymore," she told him.

"They've been healing pretty quickly," he acknowledged. "Tomorrow I'll ask the doc what we can get to put on them to help the process along. Uh, is it okay if I look underneath your shirt?"

He looked so uncomfortable asking that Lainie actually giggled.

"Nothing there you haven't already seen. Sure. Go ahead."

"Let's shift you a little so I don't hurt your shoulder."

He helped her move to lie flat on her back then lifted the hem of her shirt. She thought it cute that a man as totally male as Zane Halstead was embarrassed to look at parts of her body normally covered up. She thought again of how he'd helped her dress and undress on the road, doing his best not to embarrass her. She wondered how many other men would have been as sensitive to her feelings and her situation.

Certainly none of the ones I've known.

And that led her to catalogue in her head the string of

bad choices she'd made where men were concerned. She asked herself for what was probably the millionth time, how was it possible that someone who'd graduated with a high GPA from high school and with honors from a university could be so damn stupid about men?

She saw his reaction to her condition by the tightening of the muscles in his face.

"Still bad?"

He shook his head and let go of the shirt. "Getting better every day. Bruises take about two weeks to heal, but like I said, we'll find out if we can help that along."

She managed a smile. "My shoulder feels better, so that's something. That stuff you got has really helped it, plus bracing it on a pillow. Did you learn all this in the SEALs?"

"Basic stuff. Everyone gets TCCC, tactical combat casualty care, which is very good training. It means we can temporarily patch each other up until we can get to a medic or a doctor."

She managed another smile. "I should thank the SEALs, then."

His mouth curved again in another rare grin. "Yeah, I guess I should, too."

Lainie studied his face. "You miss it, don't you?"

It was a long moment before he answered her.

"It was my life for fifteen years. My teammates were my best friends. My brothers in arms. The Teams were my life."

"And with your discharge you're out of it and can't figure out how to fill that void in your life. Right?"

"Yeah. You could say."

"I do say." She lifted her good hand and touched his jaw. "Zane, you have a chance to start a new life here, a really good one. This place is beautiful, Alex Rossi seems like a good guy, and he's going to let you adjust at your own pace. You can make a fresh start here."

When he looked at her, she saw some unnamed emotion swirling in his eyes.

"Maybe I can make it with you."

She stared at him. "Zane. We haven't known each other a week. I'm a physical wreck, you're still healing, you have no idea what you want to do, and I have a madman after me."

He actually grinned. "At least we're not boring." Then he sobered. "You don't have to know how someone likes their steak or if they prefer chocolate or vanilla to get a sense you might fit together. Let's see how it goes. At least for the moment, I feel more comfortable with you than I've felt with anyone for months. Okay?"

She nodded, stunned to realize she felt the same way. How crazy was this anyway? Would she wake up tomorrow and discover none of this was real?

Oh, please, no.

"Feel okay to get up?" Zane asked. "I thought we'd see what Alex's wife left that we could put together for dinner."

"Sure, but…" She stopped and bit her bottom lip.

"What is it? Something wrong?"

"This is probably selfish and stupid, but I'd love to take a bath. The showers were great, but that big tub looks too inviting. Plus, I think it would do my shoulder and my bruises a lot of good."

"I'm not sure that's such a good idea."

She frowned. "Why not? Wet heat is supposed to be good for all of this."

Zane cleared his throat. "Uh, Lainie, you can't do this by yourself. You can't reach and stretch, and I don't want you banging your body up even more."

"Then you'll just have to help me. God, Zane. It's not as if I have any secrets from you, and I'm pretty sure you're not going to attack me or anything." She stifled a laugh at his obvious discomfort. "Are you?"

A muscle twitched in his cheek. "Of course not."

"We'll make it work." She said it with more confidence than she felt. What the hell anyway. He'd seen almost everything, and her embarrassment was outweighed by her overwhelming desire to lie in a tub of hot water.

"We will if that's what you want."

"Then let's get busy."

He'd brought in her things from the truck, and she managed to open the duffle and take out what she needed. Even though it was only dinnertime, she planned to put on the sleep shirt. Not much sense getting dressed again for such a short time.

She was delighted and surprised to see that Alex's wife had left a bottle of bubble bath on the vanity counter.

"We have to get a really nice present for this woman," she told Zane.

He nodded his agreement. "She's got the bathroom fully stocked, that's for sure."

As the tub began to fill, Zane took the bottle from her and shook some of it into the water. In seconds, the room was filled with the faint scent of lavender, and a froth of bubbles appeared on the surface.

"Okay." He turned to her. "Let's get you ready for this."

Unlike the first time he'd had to help her undress, this time Lainie felt self-conscious for a different reason. The sling was no problem, but as he eased the T-shirt over her head, her nipples swelled and hardened. She felt the heat creep up her cheeks as his gaze lowered to her breasts.

Then he dropped her T-shirt on the counter and stood waiting, unsure of what to do next.

Lainie sighed and swallowed her embarrassment.

Lordy, how do I handle this?

"Okay, here's the deal. I can probably finish undressing by myself, but I think I need help to get into the tub. How about if I keep my panties on. Will that help?"

Zane shook his head and then grinned. "Let's act like the two adults we're supposed to be, okay? I'm not putting any moves on you of any kind while you're in this condition, so don't worry about it. And you can't take a bath in your underwear so let's do it. It's okay."

"What if I want you to?" The words popped out of her mouth before she could stop them.

Zane froze and stared at her. "Excuse me? What did you just say?"

She shook her head, feeling her cheeks flush with heat. "I'm an idiot, that's all. I said what if I wanted you to make a move on me? Could I sound any dumber?"

He paused in the process of placing towels in easy reach of her.

"How about if we get this out in the open and then move forward. That work for you?"

Oh god. He was going to tell her he wasn't interested. And why would he be?

"It's okay," she began. "Forget I opened my big mouth and consider me not in my right mind. I—"

"I know it's only been a few days." His words rode right over hers. "I think we're both some kind of emotional mess. I know I have a lot of shit to sort out. And my first priority, as I keep saying, is your protection."

"And you're taking care of that," she told him. "I trust you to keep doing it."

"That's one part of my SEAL training that I haven't lost. But damn, Lainie, I don't ever remember being this attracted to a woman before, at least since I was young, and my hormones were running all over the place. Especially one in your condition. I'm doing my best to show my respect for you and make sure I take care of you."

She turned to him, took one of his large hands, and placed it over her breast. When he tried to draw it back, she pressed on it more tightly.

"I want to tell you something." She looked down at her feet then back up. "You're the first man I've really trusted in a very long time. I've done poorly with instant connections, but somehow this is different. You're different. I thought Sonny was someone I could trust, but I think that says more about my susceptibility to the wrong kind of man than anything else. And my poor choices. But in less than five days, Zane, I feel safe with you. And that's saying something."

He quirked an eyebrow. "After just a few days?"

"Sometimes you can spend months with someone and still not know them. Other times you can connect instantly and know it's good. Trust me. I know what I'm talking about."

He stared at her, heat and hunger and uncertainty swirling in his eyes.

"There's not much we can do right this minute, but, Zane? I know this sounds stupid, but I feel as if I've been waiting for you my entire life."

"Lainie." His voice was tight, but he didn't move his hand. "You feel that way because I offer you a safe escape from your situation."

"Don't diminish yourself like that. I've made enough bad choices in my life to know when I'm making a good one. I don't know if I can put it into the right words, but we made a connection that first day, even when I was doped up and in ten kinds of pain. We have to take it slowly, and we have challenges to face, but let's not lose it because you're being noble. Or because you think I'm an idiot for getting in my situation in the first place."

His fingers tightened the slightest bit on her breast, and his eyes bored into hers.

"I don't think you're stupid, so please stop saying that. I don't want to hear it again. I don't know your history, Lainie, and I hope you'll feel comfortable enough to tell me what it is, but hear this. I haven't met Sonny Fitzgerald, but from what you and my sister tell me, he's like a lot of other assholes I've met. A real piece of shit but with golden charm when he wants to use it. So let's not hear any more about this being your fault. Okay? Are you hearing me?"

He sounded so fierce, Lainie had to stop herself from smiling.

"Okay. I hear you. Uh, thank you."

They both suddenly realized his hand was still on her breast. With an unexpected movement, he dipped his head and kissed the flesh around the nipple. Then he stood back.

"Let's get you in the tub. I think a good soak will do you a world of good."

She pushed her pants and panties down with one hand and stepped out of them. It was impossible to miss the sudden hunger in his eyes as his gaze raked her from head to toe. Doing her best not to be self-conscious, she gripped his arm for stability as she moved to get into the tub.

"Okay. Let's do this."

"Hold on a minute," he told her. "We forgot something."

He helped her to sit down on the little bench that slid under the counter.

"What's the matter?"

"Your hand. Hold on."

He draped a towel around her before he rushed out of the room. When he returned, he had one of the plastic gloves in his hand on a roll of tape.

"I had it shoved into my duffel and forgot to take it out. Let's get you fixed up."

When he had her injured hand securely protected, he lifted her in his arms and got into the tub.

"I could get in myself if you help me," she protested.

"But it's safer this way." He stopped, his gaze skimming over the bruises on her body. "You let me know if I hurt you in any way."

She couldn't help being embarrassed by her nakedness, especially in her dreadful condition.

"Don't look at me," she whispered.

His mouth curved in that smile she'd come to look for, the one that gave the impression he didn't use it much.

"I like looking at you, no matter what. It's a beautiful body."

"Even though it looks like someone used it for a punching bag?"

He locked his gaze with hers. "One of these days I'm going to kiss every one of those spots."

She was shocked by his words, and it seemed he was, too, because he shifted his gaze to the tub itself. As if embarrassed by his show of emotion and desire, he lowered her into the water, easing her down, making sure he didn't bump her hand or her shoulder. He positioned her so she lay back against the tub, and she closed her eyes.

"This is nice," she murmured.

"Stay exactly like that, with your eyes closed. If I do something you don't like, all you have to do is tell me."

Her eyes widened, and a flush spread over her body. "You're going to bathe me?"

"It's a lot better for you than trying to do it yourself."

"But your leg. How will you kneel here?"

"I'll put a towel under it. That'll work."

She had no idea how she was going to make it through this or how she was going to keep herself under control. She couldn't believe that in her condition she was aroused by this man, or how badly she suddenly wanted him. And what was with that?

"I can smell your brain burning." His pleasantly gruff voice interrupted her thoughts. "Turn it off and relax."

She closed her eyes and tried to let the scent of the bubble bath and the pleasant movement of the water against her body soothe her. The bruises were fading but they still were sore, her shoulder ached, and she was too aware of the pain in her broken fingers. Unfortunately, none of that was enough to counteract the feel of Zane's calloused yet gentle hands on her body as he smoothed the soapy lather on her skin and then washed it away with a washcloth.

How had this happened? She was naked in a tub with a man she'd known for less than a week, scared to death that the last man she trusted would find her and kill her, yet her body was reacting as if this was some erotic interlude. She could feel the tingling in her nipples and a pulse throbbing in her sex so intensely she was embarrassed. She wanted his hands on her breasts again and his fingers exploring her hungry sex. One minute she'd been terrified for her life, and the next she was lusting after a man she'd known for less than a week. How was that even possible? She deliberately kept her eyes closed, not only to enjoy the sensations racing through her but also because she was afraid of what she would see on Zane's face if she opened them.

"You okay?" Zane's deep, hoarse voice broke into her thoughts.

"What?" Her eyes flew open.

"You had a funny look on your face. Everything all right?"

No. I'm losing my mind.

"Yes. Fine." She wet her lips. "Thank you for taking care of me like this."

Heat flared in his eyes. "Would you smack me if I told you I'd like to take even better care of you, but in a different way?"

Lainie looked directly into his eyes. "Would you think I'm terrible if I said I wanted that, too?"

He broke out his smile again. Lainie wished he'd do it more often. It completely transformed his stern face.

"No, I'd say we have something to look forward to." He cupped a breast with a soap-slicked hand. "And when we get to it, make a note I plan to take my time."

She studied his face. "I never thought I'd want to be with a man again."

"And I had no desire to be with a woman again, ever." He shrugged. "Funny how things change."

She stared directly into his eyes, trying to read what was in there. "Yes, funny. Zane, are we rushing into something here? I feel as if a whole year has been crammed into what feels like a few short days."

"That happens in situations like that. I learned that with the SEALs. A crisis intensifies situations and relationships." He skated a palm over first one breast and then the other. "Until the other day, I had lost all desire to be with a woman. Any woman. My life was a mess, and I thought I had nothing to give."

"And now?" She hoped she didn't sound as anxious as she felt.

"Now? Now I think, as messed up as we are, we might have something to look forward to."

"I hope so," she whispered.

"Me, too." He squeezed out the washcloth. "And I think it's time to get you out of this tub before I forget I'm supposed to be acting like a gentleman." He rose to his feet. "Don't do anything. Let me get you out of here. I want to put some more of that ointment on your shoulder and the antiseptic cream on the cut on your arm."

Lainie looked at it. "It looks like it's healing well. And my fingers aren't swollen so much, either."

"Good. I like progress."

She had no idea how he managed to be so gentle lifting her from the tub, setting her on her feet, and drying her off. She was stunned when he placed a gentle kiss on each breast before finishing his tasks. And more shocked when he did the same to her lips, barely brushing his mouth over hers. By the time she could say anything, he had her in the nightshirt, her arm back in the sling, and was cleaning up the bathroom.

"I don't know about you," he said when he was done, "but I'm ready to see what they left us for dinner."

"Me, too."

"I think you could use some Tylenol, too. You don't say much, but I can tell by the way you move your shoulder's hurting you. Plus, those bruises are still healing."

She sighed. "Yes, to everything."

"Okay, then. Let's check out the kitchen."

As they headed out of the bathroom, all Lainie could think of was how lucky she was. And hope nothing changed it.

CHAPTER 10

"THAT WHICH DOES NOT KILL us makes us stronger."
  Friedrich Nietzsche

I SHOULD HAVE HAD Antonio send someone to sit on their ass out here. Or Geoff. He'd do it.

Sonny had managed to find a spot close to the emergency department entrance, off to the side where he could see both the entrance and where Drea Halstead's car was parked. Antonio had texted him the make and license number so he knew which one was hers, plus the hours of her shift. But that had come and gone, and she had yet to emerge from the hospital. What the fuck was keeping her?

The longer he sat there, the greater the chance that someone would spot him and come over to question him. Or worse, send a hospital security officer to ask what he was doing there. If he said he was waiting for his friend/wife/girlfriend, they'd be sure to ask for a name, which he had no intention of giving them.

He figured he was good for a little longer. Unless someone looked hard, they wouldn't notice the nondescript dark-blue car sitting there. He slouched down in the seat, cursing the discomfort but needing to make himself as invisible as possible. He was about to text Antonio and tell him to get into the hospital computers again and double-check the shifts Drea Halstead worked. But then the emergency department doors slid open and a small group of people hurried out.

And there she was, right in the middle, but waving goodbye as she headed for her car. As she hurried along, tote hooked on one shoulder, keys in her hand, he could tell she still had that arrogant air about her, the one that royally pissed him off. The last time he'd seen her, she and Lainie had been having lunch downtown in one of the new trendy cafes. He had a prescribed list of people Lainie could socialize with, people who traveled in the top social circles in Tampa and who also respected Sonny's position in Lainie's life. Drea Halstead wasn't one of them.

He still remembered that day. He'd had Geoff follow Lainie when she left the house and take a booth near the women. Sometime before that, he'd had Geoff place tiny listening devices in all of Lainie's handbags. When the man had heard Drea tell Lainie how much she despised him and that she needed to move out of the house and get away from him, he knew it was time to cut the cord.

He still remembered the scene when he'd walked into the restaurant, marched up to the booth, and told Lainie it was time to leave. It hadn't been pleasant and, when they got home, he'd had to teach her a lesson about who she could spend her time with. But it had been worth it. That was the last of Drea Halstead.

Or so he thought.

She had to be the one who'd handled this. Someone had to get Lainie out of the hospital, and who more likely than a nurse? The last Sonny knew, the woman had been working at Harper General across town, but now it seemed she'd changed jobs recently. If so, she definitely was the one who maneuvered Lainie's disappearing act. No doubt about it.

He was so tempted to reach for his gun and blast her to hell, but then he'd never find out where Lainie was. Patience, he told himself. Have patience. It would be worth it. He had too much invested in Lainie Taggert to let her walk away.

He'd worked his ass off to build his position in this town and his reputation as the litigator who cut the throats of the opposition. He had carefully cultivated all the right people, heavily supported the key politicians, created a place for himself that others envied. Then he'd needed to find the right woman. Not one of the overblown society groupies who would do anything for his money but didn't have half a brain. Someone who had smarts and would be a great addition to his image.

When he'd hired Lainie Taggert as a paralegal in his office, he'd done it because she was sharp. Smart. Beautiful. Comfortable in any situation and with a keen legal mind. He'd brought her onto his personal staff and cultivated the relationship, sure she'd be the final star in his crown. When he asked her to marry him and moved her into his house, he'd relaxed, sure he'd reach the top of every ladder.

He should have realized that women like Lainie were too smart to put up with his shit. The more she saw of the real Sonny, the scrappy street fighter with the peculiar sexual tastes, the more the relationship fractured. That's when his temper began to get the best of him and things really began to go to hell.

Well, he'd be damned if she'd get away from him. It wasn't the idea of losing her that bothered him the most. He wasn't even worried she'd report the physical situation because he was sure she wouldn't do that. No, it was her brain he was worried about. He had no idea what she might have overheard that could destroy him, or at the very least do him some damage. Like what happened the night this all blew up. Had she heard his conversation with Geoff? Figured out what happened?

Drea Halstead was going to tell him where Lainie had disappeared to, or he'd wring her neck. Maybe he would anyway.

The hospital was in downtown Tampa, and the late-afternoon traffic was thick. He had to maneuver carefully not to lose her. But at least he had her home address if he did. He knew she lived in an apartment at the edge of downtown in a midrise that had security codes for all the doors. If he couldn't catch her in her car before she walked inside, he'd have to figure something else out. At least he didn't have to negotiate the usual logjam on the interstate.

While he was navigating the traffic and doing his best

to stay at least two car lengths behind Drea, he called Antonio.

"Did you get those security codes for Drea Halstead's building yet? I can't exactly park and walk in with her. If I follow someone else in, they might remember me later."

"Working on it," Antonio told him. "They must have had some computer genius program it though. It's a tough one to crack."

"I thought you could hack anything," Sonny growled.

"I can, but some things take longer than others."

"I'll be there in the next fifteen minutes or so, depending on how thick the traffic stays, so gas it up."

"Doing my best," Antonio assured him.

"Yeah? Well, make it better than your best."

Sonny punched the button on the steering wheel to disconnect the call. Lately, it seemed things were not going as well as he was used to. He couldn't afford a string of bad luck. He had too many major situations percolating that he needed to stay on top of. Finding Lainie was critical on his list of things to do, and he'd have someone beat the shit out of Drea Halstead to cough up the location if that what was needed.

He had a momentary scare when Drea switched rapidly to the inside lane, leaving him no choice but to squeeze in after her or lose her. He had no idea why she did that since they had several blocks still to go before nearing her destination. He needed to find a way to get vehicles between them again. Maybe after the next traffic light.

But when they reached that intersection, the light was

yellow, and Drea gassed it and shot through. Sonny had to slam on his brakes or risk being part of a multicar collision, and that he didn't need. He cursed loudly and banged his fist on the steering wheel as Drea's car moved farther and farther away from him. He really needed those security codes because he had to get into her building.

Shit.

This was why he always sent others to do this kind of dirty work. On top of it all, he didn't need to get caught doing this. With the codes, he could get into her building and take it from there, but he needed to do it damn fast. When he reached her building, he drove into the attached multilevel parking garage. Antonio had also given him the number of Drea's assigned parking spot, so he took a quick pass through the garage and damn! Her spot was empty.

Where the fuck was she anyway?

He drove around the block once, cursing the slow traffic in the crowded downtown area. Finally, a spot opened up across the street from her building, and he pulled in, keeping an eye out for any action. Then he punched Antonio's number.

"I can't get any work done if you keep calling me," Antonio complained.

"For what I pay you," Sonny growled, "you should be able to do both."

"What's the problem?"

"I lost the bitch."

God! He hated to admit it. He'd killed men for less.

To his credit, Antonio didn't make any sarcastic remarks.

"The best I can tell you, Sonny, is I'll hack the CCTV and see if we can find her car anywhere, but you know it's like looking for a needle in a haystack."

"Any luck on Lainie's whereabouts from your end."

"No, but two seconds ago I got some more info on the Halstead broad." *Click, click, click.* "Her family owns a horse farm in Ocala. I pulled up their website, and I'm forwarding the link to you. I sent two guys who can blend in with the area to check it out. Maybe she took your girl up to her folks and is hiding her there."

Sonny perked up.

"Yeah? Maye I should take a ride out there myself."

"No, I've got one for you to check out first that's closer." Antoni paused. "Drea Halstead has a brother, Zane, a former SEAL. My information shows he was wounded and medically discharged six months ago. And get this."

"Get what?" Sonny didn't have time to play games.

"He's renting an apartment right there in Tampa. Maybe she thinks a SEAL is the best protection for your girl. I hear they're damn good with guns."

A tiny sliver of excitement wriggled through him. "Text me the address. I'll find it on GPS. Does he work or anything?"

"Uh-uh. Word is he's depressed about his situation and keeps pretty much to himself. She could be locked up there with him and his armory. Or maybe that's where Drea Halstead went instead of to her place. Anyway, you're closer than my guys, and I thought you might want to check this one out yourself."

"Thanks, Antonio. But don't let up on all the other stuff."

"Got it."

One way or another, he'd find out where Lainie was and teach her a good lesson. His upbeat mood lasted until he reached the apartment complex where Antonio had told him Zane Halstead was living, only to find an empty apartment.

"He's gone."

Sonny turned to a man who had climbed the stairs behind him. "Gone?"

The man nodded. "Left a few days ago. I'd come home to get something, and I saw him throw a duffel in his truck and take off."

"Hmmm. Did he say where he was headed? I might have some work for him."

The man shrugged. "Not to me. He's pretty much a loner."

Sonny frowned. "Did he have anyone with him?"

The man shook his head. "Nope. All by himself. You could call the leasing office to see if he left a forwarding number or address."

Sonny held onto his temper with great effort. If Zane Halstead had Lainie with him, he wouldn't be leaving any information around for people to follow.

"Thanks for your information," he told the man.

"Yeah. Sorry I wasn't more help."

Sonny climbed back into his car and speed-dialed Antonio.

"The place is emptier than a baseball stadium in a snowstorm. He's in the wind. I want you to get the make and license plate of his car and reach out to all your dark web friends. See if anyone has a way to track him. Find out where he is. Dig into his life. I want every single fact there is about Zane Halstead. And—"

"I know, I know. You want it yesterday."

"And also check on the Halstead woman's friends. Social media, wherever. If she's gone to ground, I want to know where."

"On it."

Sonny disconnected the call and sat in his car for a moment. Five days had passed since Lainie had walked out of the hospital or been helped out. Five days of increasing rage and frustration. Five days of disciplining himself to conduct his business as usual. He knew Antonio was checking things as fast as he could, but not every database could be easily breached. And Drea Halstead, who he was sure could provide him a clue, had disappeared. He was getting nowhere fast. He wanted to slit someone's throat.

He was too frustrated to go home, and getting drunk wouldn't solve the problem. What he needed was a woman who knew when to shut up and was into his brand of sex. Something to take the edge off. Pulling up his Call list, he punched a number.

"Me. I'll be there in thirty minutes. If anyone's there, throw them out."

He sure hoped this day didn't get any worse.

MICKI ROSSI, Alex's wife, had outdone herself stocking the house. The refrigerator, freezer, and pantry were stocked with things that would appeal to almost anyone.

Not knowing their particular tastes, she'd guessed pretty well at a lot of the things. And instead of buying it at the deli, she'd roasted a chicken with potatoes and carrots, and left it with instructions taped to the pan for heating. There also was a freshly made salad with two kinds of dressing.

"I don't know how we'll repay these people for their kindness." Lainie wiped away tears. "Why are they even doing this?"

"I don't know Alex's entire backstory," Zane told her. "Only that he was a SEAL, came out here to work for Hank Patterson's Brotherhood Protectors, and ended up being the sheriff. I do know he relates to those of us looking to find a niche for ourselves again and wants to make this as comfortable as possible. His wife's story, though, is pretty gut-wrenching. I'll tell you about it after we check in with Alex."

"We'll have to do something nice for them," she told him.

"I agree. Maybe after we get to meet his wife, you can —" He was interrupted by his phone playing Drea's signal. "Hey. What's up?"

"I need to pass something along to you," she told him, "and please don't freak. You were right about Sonny finding out about me though."

Zane's breath froze for a moment. He did his best not to show anything, but the way Lainie looked at him, he knew she saw the tension grab him.

"What's going on?" He made his voice as even as he possibly could. "Are you okay?"

"Lainie's with you, right?"

"Uh-huh. But you didn't answer me. Are you alright?"

"What is it?" Lainie was staring at him.

He held up a hand, indicating to hold on.

"Go on," he told Drea.

"When I left work today, a dark-blue sedan pulled out after me. I thought maybe it was a patient or whatever leaving at the same time, except no one came out of the door when I did."

He squeezed the phone even tighter. "And?"

"I did my usual route going home, and he kept two or three car lengths behind me all the way. Again, it could have been nothing more than my imagination, but—"

"But you're not an alarmist." Lainie was looking at him with eyebrows raised. "So, what happened?"

"About six blocks from my apartment building, I decided to give it a test and yanked my car over into the right-hand lane. The blue car nearly caused an accident pulling over behind me."

"What happened then?"

"I slowed down as we approached a traffic light then floored it to go through on the yellow right before it turned red. The blue car was left behind."

"So you ditched him. Please tell me you did not go home."

"Of course not. But I did pull into the restaurant lot across from my building and parked behind a big van. The sedan drove into our parking garage and, after about five minutes, came out."

"So he definitely was looking for you."

"Uh-huh. I'm super alert about stuff like that ever since I saw that television special." She gave a tiny little laugh. "I guess that's why they say television is educational. Plus, I've been on the alert for Sonny ever since the scene he caused here."

"Smart girl. Listen, don't go home."

"Are you kidding? Give me credit for brains. I'm across the bridge at Clearwater Beach with my friend, Nan Sipe. She says I can hang as long as I need to. And I called Borges at the hospital, and he told me not to come to work."

"Good advice. Well, we know who it was, but damn! He got onto us quicker than I expected."

"From what I learned online," Zane told her, "I'm not surprised."

"Are you going to tell Lainie?"

"Not that I want to, but she needs to know the truth. I'm not hiding anything from her."

"Good for you. I think that woman has guts. She won't shrivel up and hide."

"I want you to check in with me twice a day," he ordered. "No excuses."

"No problem. Later."

"Well?" Lainie was staring at him.

He gave her the short version of the conversation. She turned pale but didn't flinch.

"That's his style. I'm surprised, though, that he didn't have one of his private goons doing it. I hate for her to be put in danger because of me."

"He can't get to her where she is. There's no record of her even knowing this woman. I'm guessing he's pissed off because he wanted the confrontation himself. Figured he could push Drea around a little and get information from her." His lips curved in a ghost of a grin. "He doesn't know my sister."

"You've got that right. She's one of the strongest women I've ever met." She set her fork down on her plate. "But, Zane? If he found out about Drea, then he knows about you. He's got people who can hack into almost anything. He'll know what kind of truck you drive, what the license plate is. He'll—"

He touched a fingertip to her lips.

"He thinks he's dealing with a greenhorn here. He's not. He's facing off with a SEAL. A former one, but the skills never die. I'm going to take care of this situation. We'll be prepared for whatever happens. Let's get some rest, and tomorrow we'll attack each problem one at a time."

When she sat there, immobile, staring down at her plate, he cupped her chin and tilted her face up.

"We're in this together. Right? And we'll deal with that asshole together. Trust me. It will all work out."

Her skin was so pale, it made Zane wonder if she was going to pass out, but she looked him in the eye and nodded.

"I'm tired of being scared. Frightened of my own shadow. And I'm tired of men who turn out to be vengeful losers. Whatever you've got up your sleeve, I'm on board with it."

Zane couldn't help smiling at her. "That's my girl. Okay, then. Let's finish dinner."

They had both lost their appetites, but they managed to swallow a few more bites before Zane put everything away in the fridge. Then, while Lainie drank the cup of tea he brewed for her, he called Alex and filled him in.

"If this guy has top-notch hackers working for him, and he sounds like the kind of guy who does, they're already into the make and model of your truck, the license plate, maybe even your cell phone. You know how these guys operate."

He did indeed. In his SEAL missions, he'd run across terrorists like that, who had contacts who could do anything electronic.

"Come into the office tomorrow," the sheriff went on. "We'll work something out."

"I'm taking Lainie to see the doctor in the morning. Is right after that good for you?"

"It is, but, if I were you, I'd take the sim card out of my phone and not use it again."

Zane's eyebrows shot up. "You think he has equipment that can tap into it from this far away?"

Alex snorted. "You want to take the chance he doesn't?"

"You're right. Where's the best place to get a burner phone in town?"

"Pendell's Variety, right on Main Street. I'd get a couple of them."

"Okay. Tomorrow at your office. And, Alex? Uh, thanks."

"You know what they say in the SEALs." He grinned. "The only easy day was yesterday."

"Hooyah."

He called Drea and told her to ditch her phone and get a burner. To have her friend call the hospital with that number and only give it to Dr. Cavallo and to Stan Borges, the hospital administrator. And to destroy her current phone and sim card.

Lainie sat there, the expression on her face a combination of miserable and mad.

"I seem to be messing up everyone's life."

He cupped her chin in a now familiar gesture.

"Not you, Lainie. Sonny Fitzgerald. But this time he messed with the wrong people."

Zane slept better than he expected, although he'd woken off and on and quietly gone to check on Lainie. He knew all the hours of riding in the truck and moving around hadn't helped her situation any, so he insisted she take the last two pills Drea had given him.

His own trouble came from the images of a naked Lainie in the tub, trying to tell his dick to go to sleep when he wanted to slide it into the warmth of her body. He couldn't remember the last time he'd been this attracted to a woman or the last time it had been in a situation as bad as this. His self-control was certainly being put to the test. If he had his druthers, he'd take both of them up into the Crazy Mountains and shut out the rest of the world. Maybe when this was all over, they'd have the chance to do that.

Because it would be over one of these days. He was smart enough to know they couldn't hope to hide from Sonny forever. He only hoped to buy enough time to give them both a better footing here, and for him, himself, to be sure he had backup with the sheriff and anyone else. The deputy's job looked attractive, but he wasn't obligating himself to anything that would take him away from Lainie until this mess with Fitzgerald was put to bed.

He made breakfast for both of them, doing his best to keep his distance from Lainie so she wouldn't get the idea she owed him anything. There was also that little fact that he'd enjoyed bathing her way too much. Keeping his hands to himself was going to be a true test of his discipline. No other woman had ever gotten to him the way she did, and it wasn't that he'd been without for so long or that he felt sorry for her. He wasn't into pity sex. No, it was the way her body, bruises and all, turned him on so that he struggled to deal with a perpetual hard-on.

But it was Lainie who grabbed the front of his shirt when he bent to set her plate on the table. And Lainie who placed her mouth on his, running her tongue over his lips and humming to herself with satisfaction. God, she tasted good. He had to tamp down the urge to thrust his tongue into her mouth and coax her own to dance with it.

"You keep doing that," he told her in a breathless voice, "I'm going to forget all my good intentions."

"Maybe I want you to," she whispered.

"Let's get you healed first," he told her.

"Is it my bruises that turn you off?" Pain flickered in her eyes.

He sighed. "Lainie, nothing about you turns me off, not bruises, not anything else. That's my problem."

"Promise? Because right this minute I don't think very much of myself."

He brushed a stray hair back from her forehead. "Listen to me. This shocks me as much as it does you. I don't even know how to deal with these feelings. But in a few days you've become someone very special to me. When you're better? I promise, you'll have to fight me off."

THEN THEY HEADED for the little town and the doctor's office. Dr. Mark Sandoval, the general practitioner Alex had sent them to, examined Lainie completely. Zane offered to step outside of the room when he went to remove her sling and T-shirt, but she grabbed his hand.

"No. Stay. You've seen it before." She looked at Sandoval. "Before we start, I want to make sure you know that Zane wasn't the one who did this to me."

The doctor nodded and looked at Zane. "I know. Alex Rossi would have you in jail instead of sitting in this office if it were. Okay. Let's take a look at what we've got here."

He was positive he was more embarrassed than Lainie was, but he stoically sat through the examination then helped her put her T-shirt back on. The part that made him want to kill someone was when she lowered her yoga pants to her hips and he got yet another view of the vicious treatment she'd received. He could cheerfully wring Sonny Fitzgerald's neck and not lose a wink of sleep.

"I know you said you got some over-the-counter stuff for the bruises," he told them, "but I'm going to give you a prescription for something that will work a little faster and also ease the pain from them. I wrote out some instructions for the shoulder, too. The X-ray of the fingers shows a clean break in both of them and it looks to be healing nicely. Don't get the splint wet." He grinned at them. "And don't try swinging an axe or anything like that."

"Thank you." She flashed him a brief smile.

Zane shook hands with Sandoval and thanked him, also. Back in the truck, he started the engine then reached for her hand. "We need to get your prescriptions filled and pick up a few groceries. Alex's wife did an incredible job stocking the house, but there are a couple of things I'd like to pick up. I'll bet you feel the same."

She nodded but then caught her bottom lip between her teeth. He was finding that habit so sexy, it was teasing at his self-control.

"I'm not sure I'm ready to go into any stores yet," she told him. "My face still looks like someone used it for a battering ram, and then there's the sling and stuff." She paused. "And I know it's silly, but I don't know what Sonny's found out about where we are, and I don't think I want to be in public where people could see me and remember me. Like I said, it's not as if I can blend in."

He took her uninjured hand in his, lifted it to his mouth, and kissed her palm. It occurred to him that while he'd had plenty of women and more than his share of sex, he had a connection with Lainie that he'd never experienced before. The shrink he'd seen right after his discharge had told him he'd experience life changes when he least expected them. Well, the guy got that one right.

"Okay, how about this. I have to go see the sheriff about this stuff with Sonny that's come up. Let's take care of that and then I'm sure you can hang out there while I get your prescription filled. We don't have to hit any stores today unless there's something we really want. We can leave that for a couple of days and figure out how best to do it."

"I'm a real drag." She sighed. "Never mind. I can brave the public if you don't mind being seen with me."

"First of all, I never mind being seen with you, but you may be right. Calling attention to yourself right now isn't the smartest move. Let's not create public notice until we find out if Sonny's onto us."

"Okay." She managed a half smile.

Before he realized what he was doing, he leaned over the console and pressed his mouth to hers. She tasted so sweet that for a moment he felt dizzy. Without thinking, he caressed her lips with his tongue before easing it into her mouth. When she opened for him, his entire body responded. He'd never had a kiss affect him like this before, and he'd probably kissed far more women than he should. Not only did his cock swell, but an ache settled into his balls, and his pulse ratcheted up a notch or two. When they finally were able to have sex—when, not if— he knew it was going to blow his mind.

When he suddenly realized they were still in the parking lot and someone could drive in at any moment, he pulled back but only a fraction. Lainie stared at him as if she'd been struck by a thunderbolt, and he knew how she felt. This wasn't their first kiss, although the other had been so brief it might not have happened. They weren't kids, either, and well past the stage of being thunderstruck by a kiss. Nevertheless, there it was.

He smiled, and, for a change, it felt very good. Lainie was staring at him as if she, too, had been hit by a roaring train.

"Zane? What are we doing?"

"I think it's called kissing, but if you have to ask, I must not be doing it right."

"B-But...I mean...I still look like a freight train ran over me, and I'm less than a week out of the emergency department. You're still trying to figure out what to do with the rest of your life. You sure got more than you bargained for having to drag me off to Montana. On top of it, I've got a maniac after your sister as well as us. I mean...what's going on with us?"

He sighed and brushed a few strands of hair back from her forehead. "Something is, that's for sure. But, every-thing else aside, for the first time in months I feel some-thing for someone. I think you do, too. Let's take care of the trouble following us, get you healed up, and see where this goes. Okay?"

"Okay, but right at this moment I think we should get out of this parking lot before we embarrass ourselves."

He nodded. "No kidding."

He was still grinning all the way to the pharmacy and then to the sheriff's office. But the grin disappeared fast when they sat down with Alex.

The sheriff looked at Lainie. "You were right about Fitzgerald."

"W-what do you mean?"

"Sonny Fitzgerald doesn't let any grass grow under his feet, does he? First, the woman he killed was found dead by her eldest son, a victim of a fall in her home. A weird accident, the report says. I had a friend of mine with the Hillsborough County Sheriff's Office check it out. If you walked in there today and told your story, they'd think you were crazy. We'll have to figure something out. I refuse to let a man get away with murder."

"I don't know what you can do though."

"We'll see. But, unfortunately, that's not the only problem."

Lainie turned ten shades paler. "What do you mean? What's happened?"

"Remember yesterday I said I'd get your names flagged in case Sonny set his minions doing any searches for you?"

She nodded, her uninjured hand balling into a fist.

"I heard from my friend at the Montana Bureau of Justice a little while ago. Lainie, Sonny's got someone tracking your credit cards, your driver's license, any other database you might be in. He's probably frustrated that he isn't getting anything. I told my friend to email me any updates."

Lainie looked at Zane then back at Alex, and Zane saw the blood drain from her face.

"He can't track us here, can he?"

Alex shook his head. "Not unless he puts out a description of your truck and the license plate. Plus, he'd have to know you were headed here to begin with."

"There's no one to give him that information," Zane told him. "I've been pretty much a loner since I got back to Florida. My sister is one of the few people I told, and she's hiding out in a friend's cottage on the beach."

Lainie shook her head. "Don't count on him not finding out. He's got people everywhere who can find out anything."

"What worries me," Alex told them, "is if someone

manages to hack into your email account, Zane. Again, he's got the resources to do about anything he wants to."

Lainie nodded her agreement. "I know that for a fact. That's how he was able to win so many cases. He'd have someone dig around to find out everything about the other person or business then use it as a club."

"He'll have a pretty hard time. In the SEALs," Alex said, "they taught us to be damn suspicious, so I have two-factor authentication. He might get past the first firewall, but it will take him a long time to get past the pin. I had a friend who works for a security firm set it up for me."

"Good. Then it won't be easy for him to find the email from me."

"No, but as I told you before, if he's got a good tech on spyware, he can also get your cell phone number and track you that way."

"Yeah, I pulled the card but held onto it for emergencies. I can't be without a phone. It's our only contact to the world. What do you suggest?"

"Are you going right home?"

"Yes." Zane nodded. "We have to stop and pick up some meds for Lainie first but that's all."

"And your burner phones," Alex reminded him.

"I told my sister to do the same thing, but we won't have each other's numbers, not if we're both using new phones."

"Buy your phones in a fake name then call me and give me the numbers. And take the sim card out of yours. If you need anything, we'll arrange to get it for you, at least for the time being. Staying out of sight is more important."

Zane nodded in agreement. "I also want to get a security system installed, if that's okay. I don't know who owns the property, but—"

"My wife does," Alex told him. "It's one of the rental sites her father owned. In fact, let me call the company that did the ranch and get them out there today."

Zane relaxed a fraction. He knew he'd be wound up tight as a drum until Sonny Fitzgerald was put away for good.

"Thanks."

"I assume you've got plenty of ammo? Not that you want to use it but just to be ready."

Again, Zane nodded. "I'm set." He glanced over at Lainie, who looked paler than snow. "Okay. Time to go."

"I agree." He pushed himself back from the desk. "And so you know, I added the house to the regular patrol assignments, so we'll be keeping an eye on things. I also got a picture of Sonny and gave it to each of the deputies. Just in case. I'll be by later to check on things. Lainie, we're going to take good care of you. I promise you that. I know men like Fitzgerald, and I take great pleasure in crushing them. And you couldn't have a better man than Zane to watch out for you."

"I know." She swallowed. "Thank you."

"And remember, Micki, my wife, is anxious to meet you. You've got an open invite for dinner whenever you're ready."

"From what I've read, she's quite a woman."

Alex snorted. "No kidding."

"Working as a prosecutor in Hillsborough County, she must have heard plenty about Fitzgerald."

Alex nodded. "She filled me in on a lot of details. That's why, Zane, the fact that you scooped Lainie up and brought her out here to get her out of his target sights made my opinion of you rise even more. I know you're aware of what we needed to do to keep her safe."

Lainie stared at him, her mouth open. "I'm stunned."

"Yup. I printed out his picture and handed it to my deputies and also the state police. If he dares show his face around here, we'll be ready for him." He looked at Lainie. "Is it okay if Micki gives you a call later, nothing more than to say hello? You might find it a good thing to talk to her."

Lainie swallowed. "I'd love that, especially considering the situation. But does she know what a wreck I am?"

"All she'll know is what a nice person you are," Alex assured her. "Really. And Zane can tell you her story on the way home. I'll pass the message to her. Okay, you guys head out."

When they were back in the truck, Zane took a moment after he'd cranked the engine. He cupped her head and leaned over the console to place a gentle kiss on her lips.

"It's my plan to take care of Sonny and get him out of your life once and for all. That's a promise. And Alex is going to help me."

He was rewarded with a tiny smile.

"Okay. Time to tell me Micki's story."

Still, despite the smile, he heard the underlying fear in her tone of voice. He meant what he said. He'd get rid of that bastard once and for all.

CHAPTER 11

When we are no longer able to change a situation – we are challenged to change ourselves.
Viktor E. Frankl

SITTING in a meeting all afternoon had stretched and tested every bit of Sonny's self-discipline. Antonio had given him scant information about either of the Halsteads. Drea seemed to have disappeared off the face of the earth, and wherever Zane was, he wasn't using credit cards. He'd tried hacking into Zane's email account, but it had two-factor protection, so he had a program running to discover it. He'd managed to get the guy's cell phone number, but it had suddenly gone suspiciously dead, and they had no location on it.

He was beyond pissed, and having a new case to litigate that required all his skills didn't help his state of mind.

Meanwhile, a funeral had been held for the woman

he'd killed. He attended because people knew they'd been in business discussions and it would look bad if he was a no-show. He'd put on a good performance, and her friends thanked him for coming. If they only knew, he thought.

Geoff was waiting outside in the car with the motor running.

"I hate funerals," he told Sonny.

"Yeah me, too. But if I didn't show up, too many people would ask too many questions." He pulled his cell from his pocket and took it off Mute. When he looked at the screen, several messages rolled through, all of them from Antonio.

Still working on cracking email password but close.

Still can't find Drea Halstead but have team there looking. Team scouring area, checking hospital.

Lainie's cell phone dead after she reached hospital. Doesn't show up anywhere.

Found location of brother's cell but nothing for two days.

He punched the button for Antonio's number. "Where did you locate him?"

"Des Moines, Iowa, if you can believe it. But that was two days ago and nothing since then."

"Fuck, Antonio." Sonny wanted to hit something. "For all the money I pay you, I expect more than this."

"Not even Homeland Security could do better than this," Antonio snapped. "You can take that to the bank."

Sonny gritted his teeth. "Goddammit. I have to find her. I could be—" he stopped.

"Be what?"

"Never mind. If you need more money, I'll deposit it in

your account. Hire more men, if necessary, but each day that passes, I'm in danger from what she knows, and that is simply unacceptable. Do I need to come see you in person?"

There was a long moment of silence.

"Sonny." Antonio's tone of voice was a cross between irritation and cold steel. "We've been doing business for a long time. I think you've learned by this time that threats don't work well with me. You want to find someone else to do your dirty work, be my guest."

Sonny gripped the cell so hard he was afraid he'd crack the case.

"You know I don't want to do that. I'm walking a very fine line here."

"Nothing out of the ordinary. I'm getting back to work. You will hear from me when I have something."

The call was disconnected.

"Shit! Fucking damn shit!"

"You should know threats don't work with that man. Besides, he's the last person I'd want pissed off at me. You could find your life plastered all over social media and the news sites, with all your dirty little secrets."

"Yeah, yeah, yeah." He stared out the windshield. "We're running out of time. At any moment she could decide to call the cops with what she knows."

"So what?" Geoff shrugged. "She has no proof. We cleaned things up good. There was no trace of you when we got done."

"Nothing is absolute. Meanwhile, you've got a new takeover you're studying. Get back to work. Bury yourself at the office. Antonio will find her."

"I wish I could be as sure as you are. What if she ran off with Drea Halstead's brother?"

"She doesn't even know the man," Geoff pointed out. "You monitored her cell phone. She didn't call either the woman or her brother, so how would they hook up?"

"Who knows? But I'm telling you, it's more than coincidence that right after that Halstead woman starts working at the hospital, Lainie checks into emergency and then disappears."

"Maybe, or maybe not. Let me drop you at your office and then see what I can find out. I don't have Antonio's resources, but I'm smart enough to know how to construct a timeline. Okay?"

"Yeah, okay. Find me something. Anything. I need to find that bitch and wipe her off the face of the earth."

"And leave no trace," Geoff reminded him.

"And leave no trace," Sonny echoed. "Thanks."

"For what?"

"Being exactly what I need."

Geoff laughed. "We do it all together, right?"

"Right."

"You should lie down for a little while," Zane told Lainie as soon as they were in the house. "Maybe take one of those pills Dr. Sandoval prescribed."

"Not yet. I don't want to be zonked out. But I will sit in the rocker in the living room." She smiled. "And I'd love some tea if you don't mind making it."

"Sure. Coming right up."

She was sitting there, staring out at the beautiful view out the big back picture window when Zane came in with her tea in one hand and the sack from Pendell's in the other.

"I got four cell phones," he told her, "just in case."

"In case Sonny finds a way to track one of them?"

He nodded. "I paid cash for all of them, so there's no records. If the number appears anywhere, it will show as anonymous."

"You must have brought a big wad of cash along with you."

He grinned. "Maybe I wanted to impress you with how rich I am."

Lainie looked at him over the rim of her cup. "Zane, I've known you less than a week, but I've already figured out you're not interested in impressing anyone."

"Except maybe you." He winked.

She snorted. "Yeah, right."

But he'd already impressed her in so many ways. Why couldn't she have met a man like this before everything else in her life happened? Why couldn't she have met *him*? Each day they were together, she found herself more and more attracted to him, unbelievable considering her situation and condition. What would he want with her anyway? She was damaged goods.

"I can smell your brain burning." He was programming one of the phones and didn't look up.

Lainie was glad of that because she could feel the heat climbing her cheeks and knew her face was red.

"Thinking how fortunate I am that you were heading out here to Montana exactly when I needed help, and that you were willing to take me with you. How did I get so lucky?"

He looked over at her.

"I think I'm the lucky one, Lainie. I was drowning in my own self-pity until this. You've given my life purpose, and that's a major thing."

He texted Alex Rossi to give him the number of the new phone, at least this one.

"That's good," he said after the information exchange. "Thanks a lot. For everything."

"What are you thanking him for besides telling us to get the phones?"

"He's already called the security people. They're on their way, and so is he. He wants to make sure they install what we need."

"I can't believe he's being so nice to us."

"You need to start getting used to the fact there are a lot of really nice people in the world. You've been hanging around with the wrong kind."

Boy, wasn't that the truth?

Zane was such a complete opposite. Where Sonny thought showing kindness except when he wanted something was a weakness, Zane seemed to have it built into his system. But on top of that, shocking her, was her growing attraction for him. Was it possible that someone in her condition could even feel attraction? The brief kiss, the quick caress had told her two things. He was as attracted to her as she was to him, and fighting it equally as hard. She wished she felt well enough to find out if she was only imagining this.

"Penny for them."

She looked up, jerking her hand and almost spilling her tea. "What?"

"You look like those are some deep thoughts running through your head. Care to share them?"

"Just thinking about…things."

He placed the second phone on the coffee table and moved over to crouch beside her.

"One of the many, many things I learned in the SEALs was to enjoy life as you find it because tomorrow it could all be gone. I forgot that after I was told I'd be medically discharged and spent way too long feeling sorry for myself. Convinced I no longer had a place in life. Then two things happened. Alex Rossi emailed me, and my sister called about you. Looking at the big picture, I realized that, yes, things can come at you when you least expect, but don't be a fool and ignore it."

"But—"

He touched her lips with the tip of a finger.

"No buts. Maybe Fate decided we both needed something good in our lives. I feel it, Lainie, and I know you do, too. Let's let it play out. I can promise you that the minute you're in better shape, I'm going to spend an entire night making love to you, in every way possible." He chuckled. "That is, if I haven't forgotten how."

Heat roared through her, the pulse in her sex throbbed with an almost forgotten intensity, and her nipples hardened painfully. Considering her physical condition, she thought that was quite a tribute to Zane Halstead and his ability to arouse her with just words.

"Zane, I—"

In the middle of her sentence, she was interrupted by

the doorbell. Zane went to answer it and when he returned, he had not one but two people with him. Next to the sheriff was a woman about Lainie's height, maybe five foot six, with rich, thick brown hair pulled back in a ponytail and green eyes that looked out from beneath thick lashes. She wore a soft knit shirt with jeans and boots and had a big smile on her face. She walked directly to Lainie.

"Micki Rossi. I'm sorry to barge in this way, but I wanted to meet you and tell you in person that I'm here to help with anything you need."

"You'll have to forgive her," Alex said. "We've told her she needs to be more outgoing, but she's stubborn and won't listen."

Lainie smiled and accepted the other woman's outstretched hand. She couldn't help herself. There was something about the woman's enthusiasm that was catching.

"It's okay. I'm fine. And, Micki, thank you for coming over. I'm sorry, though, that you have to see me in this condition. I'm not at my best, as you can tell."

"Actually," the woman said, "after Alex's description of your injuries, you look a lot better than I expected." She glanced from Lainie to Zane and back. "Looks like our SEAL here has been taking good care of you."

Lainie relaxed a fraction.

"He's doing his best. I have to admit, I feel a thousand percent better than I did when Zane picked me up to leave town."

"She's got grit and determination," Zane told them. "I

don't think riding nearly five days in a truck helped but she's a trouper, and she's been following instructions."

The doorbell rang again.

"That'll be the security people," Alex told them. "I wanted to meet them out here and the three of us do a walk-through while their tech sketches a diagram. You ladies good for the moment?"

"We're fine." Micki made a shooing motion. "Go on. Take care of business." She turned back to Lainie. "Can I get you anything? More tea?"

Lainie held up a hand. "I'm good, thanks. And thank you for coming over to visit."

"Feel free to kick me out if you have to lie down or anything." Her face sobered, and she took Lainie's free hand in hers. "I'm having a vacation week and enjoying every minute."

"Zane said you used to work for the prosecutor's office in Hillsborough County, but he didn't say what you currently do."

Micki laughed. "After the whole…incident that my father's death touched off, I didn't feel like doing much of anything. I was depressed about it all, revolted that he'd had anything to do with the rapes. My mother was a basket case and had gone off to stay with my aunt."

"I imagine it had to be terrible for you."

A look of unbearable sadness washed across Micki's face, only for an instant. Then it was gone.

"Alex finally told me if I didn't find something to do, he was going to get me a job washing dishes. We were married by then, and I think it was hard for him to see me unable to get past everything, no matter how hard I tried." Her smile was back. "The county prosecutor's office staff is fairly small because the population of the county is only thirty-five thousand. One lead prosecutor and two assistants in addition to the clerical staff. It so happened, one of the positions of assistant district attorney had come open right about then. Alex pushed me to apply, and, well, here I am. And enjoying it, believe it or not. We get a fair number of cases, believe it or not, but it's not nearly as busy as it was in Florida."

"I understand when you lived in Tampa you knew about Sonny Fitzgerald."

Micki's forehead creased in a scowl. "That asshole. Everyone knows him. We've been after him for years for some of his legal shenanigans, but it's not as easy to take down someone so rich and powerful."

Micki's opinion made Lainie feel a lot better.

"No kidding." She shook her head. "I can't believe I ever got mixed up with him."

"Lainie, you are far from the only one. I told Alex all about him. If he dares to show up here, he won't like the reception he'll get. Trust me, we're all ready to protect you and take him down."

Lainie felt herself relax. She hadn't been sure how this woman would react to her situation, but it helped that she knew all about Sonny.

"Another thing, although feel free to tell me it's none of my business. Alex thought I might be able to help you talk through the trauma and figure out how to deal with it. I suppose you know all about mine." When Lainie didn't answer she smiled, nothing more than a soft upturn of her lips. "It's okay. I lived closed off with it for years, but Alex has really helped me work my way through it. Alex says Zane seems to him ready to do that with you."

"I feel so helpless," Lainie said, "which is not really me. At least it didn't used to be, before I made a really bad choice. I don't want him to look at me as a burden."

Micki laughed, a soft, musical sound. "From what little I saw and from what Alex told me, I'd say there's no worries there. Not from what I see." She pulled over a hassock and sat next to Lainie's chair. "Let me tell you a little about my own hangups and how I got past them. The guys will be out there playing with their toys for a while yet."

Lainie had no idea how long they sat there, talking and chatting, Micki's presence was so soothing, and listening to her talk about her challenges of recovering from what happened to her and moving forward with Alex made her look at her own situation from a different point of view. She could accept responsibility for getting herself into the situation, but it was up to her to move past it. She wanted to do that. She wasn't used to being weak.

She found herself telling Micki everything, things she hadn't told Zane, or even Drea in the short time they'd been together. It all came rolling out like a tidal wave until, exhausted, she sat back in her chair.

"Well." Micki studied her for a moment. "That's quite a story. You have nothing to blame yourself for. Abusers are very, very clever about how they do things, either by cajoling or threatening. They seduce you with their words and actions until they think they have control and then wham!"

"But Zane said you and the others didn't even know who the men were."

Micki nodded. "They used fear, and very well. The rapes were brutal and the threats delivered in such a way that they scared most of the girls silent for years. Please don't beat yourself up over this."

Lainie sighed. "No kidding. I think I'm already bruised enough."

"See there? You already made a turn. You're no weak sister. I can tell."

And god, how she wanted Zane to look at her as a strong and healing woman. Not some pathetic wreck. She said as much to Micki.

"I'd say pathetic is hardly what he thinks, at least according to my husband. Who, by the way, is very good at reading people. Not many women as injured as you are would embark on a cross-country journey with a man she didn't know and never complain or bitch. Give yourself a break." She grinned. "Anyway. I'm pretty good at reading people. I only had a couple of minutes to observe, but I'd say from the way Zane looks at you, he's got a pretty high opinion of you." She looked at Lainie's empty mug. "Can I fix you another cup of tea?"

"Let me do it," Lainie protested. "I can. Really. And I can fix tea or coffee for you. I'd feel so much better if I got to wait on someone else for a change."

"Okay, but I'm your backup if you need it."

They were sitting at the kitchen table with their cups when Alex and Zane came back into the house.

"The technicians will be coming into the house shortly," Zane announced to Lainie. "They'll be setting sensors on all the windows and doors and setting up the feed for the cameras. Is that okay? You want to lie down, and I'll save the bedroom for last?"

She shook her head. "No. I'm fine." When he raised his eyebrows, she said, "Really. Fine."

"She is," Micki agreed. "I'd say your girl's got a lot of grit, Zane Halstead."

He cocked one eyebrow at her but, to her surprise, he nodded.

"I noticed that on this trip, which was far from a pleasure jaunt. She's a keeper."

Lainie stared at him, unsure what he meant but still clinging to his words.

Alex left shortly after to go back to his office, and Lainie finally decided to lie down for a little while. Her shoulder was bothering her a little, and she wanted to ice it. Zane was still busy with the security people, so Micki ran home to fix lunch and bring it back.

"I don't know how to thank you for all this," Lainie told her.

"No big deal. I enjoy it."

When the security system was all set, the crew chief walked Lainie through the whole setup, showing her where all the sensors were as well as the positioning of the cameras.

"Everything's covered," he told her, "including the barn. Someone will have a nearly impossible time sneaking up on you. We'll set up the monitor in the kitchen since you've got the counter space for it." He handed her a cell phone. "If there's any breach, press the number eight. It rings right into our control center, and we'll get our handy dandy sheriff on his way ASAP."

"And, of course, I will always be here," Zane told her.

"But the more firepower we have with him," Lainie said, "the better I'll feel. He and his goons wouldn't hesitate to shoot us in a hot minute."

"You know," Micki said, "there's always been gossip around the courthouse that Fitzgerald had what he called his dark crew that did his dirty work for him, both physical and electronic. A lot of people would love to get their hands on them."

"Especially me," Zane growled, and put his arm around Lainie's good shoulder.

For the first time since she'd awakened in the emergency department, Lainie felt there was hope.

CHAPTER 12

"If you don't like the road you're walking, start paving another one."

Dolly Parton

TODAY IS THE DAY.

Zane had fixed coffee for them both, as he did each morning, and while he headed to the bathroom to shower, Lainie enjoyed a few more minutes in bed, savoring the last of the coffee.

She had been planning and plotting in her mind. After that first visit with Micki Rossi, she had decided she'd spent enough time bemoaning her situation. And the more time they spent together, the more she realized she needed to quit being a victim. People could tell her all they wanted to that Sonny Fitzgerald was a master at controlling people, at setting them up to get what he wanted. But she knew the underlying truth. If she hadn't wanted what he was offering so badly to begin with, none of this would have happened.

Of course, without this situation, she never would have met Zane, who was turning out to be the brightest spot in her entire life. He was sending her very gentle signals that she was doing her best not to misread, signals that when she was healed and ready, he wanted to take their relationship to a new level. She had to pinch herself to realize that a man like him actually wanted her. And *liked* her, on top of that.

They had shared more kisses, each one a little deeper and more lasting than the previous one. But he still treated her as if she was made of glass. Okay, so she still looked like she'd gone ten rounds in the ring but not nearly so much as she had in the beginning. But in a few days she pulled herself together mentally and emotionally, thanks to Micki Rossi, realizing that if she didn't, in Zane's eyes she would always be a victim, and she couldn't abide that.

Zane had again taken her to see Dr. Sandoval, who said she was healing nicely.

She iced her shoulder twice a day, took her anti-inflammatory meds, and had Zane rub the ointment into it morning and night. Today she was going to try going all day without the sling. She'd have to be careful though. No makeup yet, not until the bruises healed a little more, but Zane didn't look at her like she was part of a freak show—not that he had, even in the beginning. But sympathy could be equally as bad.

Get going, she told herself, before she lost her courage. What she had in mind was the boldest step she'd taken in a long time. Gathering her clothes, she headed toward the bathroom. Figuring he was close to being finished, she knocked on the door before opening and called out, "Incoming."

When she opened the door, he hadn't yet wrapped a towel around his waist, and this was her first good look at him naked from head to toe. She had already seen the scars from surgery on his upper arm and thigh, but the sight of his thick cock standing at attention took her breath away. God, the man was truly well-endowed. It was more than she could resist. She dropped her things on the vanity counter and knelt before him.

"Lainie." He tried to nudge her to her feet without touching any of her bruises.

She refused to budge. She hadn't been this bold in a very long time, but this would be part of the new-old Lainie. She studied his cock for a very long moment, admiring its length and thickness and the way it stood so rigidly at attention. The head was a soft purple, and a vein that wrapped itself around his length was pulsing. Then, taking a deep breath and letting it out, hoping her hand didn't shake, she wound her fingers around his cock and swept her tongue against the velvety head. She did it once then again and again. He groaned his pleasure, so she slipped her hand between his thighs and cupped his balls, squeezing them.

"Lainie." The word was a groan.

She looked up to see Zane staring down at her. Heat flaring in his eyes, a muscle jumping in his cheek.

"Not good?" She asked the question in an innocent tone of voice, even though she knew the answer.

"Too good. You have to stop before you hurt yourself."

"I won't be the one who's hurting if I do. Close your eyes, Zane. Let me do this. Please."

She took his silence for an answer and went back to what she was doing. She set up a rhythm with her hand and her mouth, up and down, up and down, sometimes letting her tongue drag the length, too. And she kept up a rhythmic squeezing of his balls, timing it with each stroke. He filled her mouth and then some, so she had to tilt her head back to take in the entire length of him.

"Lainie, this is too much for you. You have to… I need you to… Aw shit."

Better than that, she thought, as his cock exploded in her mouth, pumping his juices into her. She sucked and licked and swallowed and squeezed until she'd drawn every drop from his body. Only then did she release him from her mouth, but she still kept her fingers around his thick shaft and her hand between his legs, stroking the soft skin there. She couldn't remember the last time she'd enjoyed giving a man pleasure. Sonny Fitzgerald had taken all that away.

"I need to sit down," he told her in a shaky voice.

"Okay."

She backed away enough to allow him to move and sit on the rim of the tub.

"Jesus, Lainie. I thought you were going to suck my brains out. That's the best…the best…"

"So, it was good?" She held her breath.

"Good? Damn. It was way more than that. That word is too mild for what you did." He was still trying to even out his breathing. "That was incredible. Holy shit. I might not be any good for the rest of the day." Then his face sobered. "Did you hurt yourself? Because if you did—"

Relief surged through her. She reached up with her good arm and touched her fingers to his lips. "I'm not stupid enough to do that. Trust me. Besides, I'm doing so much better." She looked down at her body where even though they had faded, a lot her bruises were still apparent. "Really."

"Really?" He let his gaze roam over her body and was about to say something when his cell phone on the counter rang with Alex's programmed sound. "Hey. Yeah? Okay, thanks. I'll be ready."

"What's going on?" she asked when he disconnected the call.

"Alex and Micki are bringing the horses over today, along with a load of hay. And the feed store is on its way to deliver an order. He said everyone will be here in about thirty."

"I need to get dressed."

Zane cupped her cheeks and stared directly into her eyes.

"If you mean it that you feel so much better, you might need to rest up this afternoon. We still need to be careful, but I have some ideas about how to make you feel even greater. If you're ready for it."

The pulse in her sex began to throb like a drum, and she had to squeeze her thighs together.

"I'd like that." The words came out breathlessly. "I'd like that a lot."

He lowered his mouth to hers and kissed her with such intensity, she wondered why she didn't come just standing right there. His tongue explored every inch of her mouth then licked her lips before plunging in again. They were both breathing hard when he finally drew back.

"I think I've wanted to do that from the day I met you."

"Yeah? Even in my pitiful state? You must be really hard up."

"Hard, maybe, but not hard up. But I knew what you'd been through and why I needed to get you out of town. Besides, for all I knew, you had no interest in me."

Her mouth tipped up in a little grin. "Then I guess I hid it well. I was disappointed when I couldn't even tempt you while taking off my panties."

He groaned again. "Stop. I don't need that image in my mind with people coming over here." He stepped back. "Speaking of which, do you need help with the shower controls?"

She shook her head. "I'll shower later. I want to be ready for the horses, too. Oh, and I'm not wearing the sling today."

"Lainie," he began.

"Did it look like I needed a sling? And I'll be careful. I promise."

"Okay. Go on and get ready, then."

He opened the door but as he was walking out, he swatted her lightly on her ass.

"I can't wait to kiss every inch of this."

Then he was gone to dress, leaving Lainie standing there frustrated beyond belief. How would she last the day when she knew what was waiting for her tonight? She sighed and began to get dressed.

"I've got something."

Sonny gripped his cell phone tighter at Antonio's words.

"Something good?" he asked.

"Better than we've had so far." He paused. "I know where Zane Halstead is."

Sonny's heart rate sped up. "You have his location?"

"Well, generally. I have to narrow it down specifically."

"Antonio, I'm going to punch you the next time I see you if you don't quit playing games. Do you have him or not?"

"I know the state and county he's in," Antonio told him. "All I have to do is pinpoint his specific location."

"Okay, cut out the fucking bullshit. Where is he?"

Antonio chuckled. "Montana, of all places."

Sonny frowned. "What the fuck is he doing there? And how did you find out?"

"We finally cracked his two-digit authentication."

He explained about Alex Rossi, the former SEAL and how the sheriff was reaching out to other former SEALs.

"He sent Halstead an email, and I guess they talked after that. He offered him a job and invited him to come out and look the area over," Antonio told him. "So that's where he is, and probably where Lainie Taggert is. The timing coincides."

Sonny did his best to control his racing pulse. He was close now, so close to that miserable bitch.

"Do you have someone in Montana physically who can check it out?"

"Way ahead of you. There's a guy who does some jobs for me once in a while in Billings. That's not far from where Rossi's offices are located. He's going to quietly nose around and get back to me with what he finds."

"Give me his number. I want to talk to him myself."

There was a long pause. "Okay, but don't piss him off, okay? He's good to have around."

"I'll be the soul of diplomacy," Sonny assured him.

"Yeah, yeah, yeah. Okay, but dial everything down a notch, please."

He sat there for a moment, absorbing the news then dialed the number Antonio had given him. He decided he'd offer this guy a bonus if he got the information within twenty-four hours. See if that motivated him even more. He wanted that bitch in front of him *now*. He'd get rid of that jerk Halstead then teach her what a real beating was about.

Then he'd get back to this new litigation he had to prepare for, and he was right in the mood to really put the screws to someone.

Carl Jennings had been doing "favors" for Antonio Vargas for more years than he could count. He hadn't known about his "friend's" connection to Sonny Fitzgerald, but the phone call made his mouth water. A fat bonus. Yeah, he could sure use it. But find a woman? Couldn't he get one in Florida? When he jokingly asked the question, Sonny had cut him off, told him what he needed, and abruptly asked if he could get it. For the figure the man had named, Carl figured this woman was either the greatest lay in the world or had done something to make Fitzgerald over-the-top angry. He didn't care which, as long as he got his money.

He had little to go on, except for the name of the county sheriff who was somehow connected. That meant he couldn't sit outside the sheriff's office and wait to tail him. And what the hell was Sonny doing getting involved in shady stuff? Carl knew the man had skated the law very cleverly for years, so why put himself on a collision course with it? If this woman was really hot stuff, maybe Carl could figure out a way to get a piece of it himself first. Not every woman was into his somewhat exotic tastes. He got hard imagining it and had to shift in his seat to adjust himself.

The closest town was small enough that strangers stood out and gossip ran wild. He did some research on it and was startled to discover it had been the hub of a brutal series of rapes that lasted for years, until the current sheriff ended up finally arresting everyone. That made him something of a hero. Maybe that would be a good conversation starter. He could praise the sheriff, which he was sure everyone would warm to. But he had to be careful how he did it. Too much and they'd get suspicious.

The only other option was to try and follow the sheriff himself. He was sure to show up where these people were hiding, if he'd offered the guy a job. Yeah, right. A sneaky tail on a lawman. Good luck with that.

The drive from Billings had taken less than an hour. He'd chosen to use his pickup, figuring he'd blend into the environment better, and when he pulled into the small town and saw the traffic on the main street, he knew he was right. He spotted a bar with a neon *Lunch* sign in the window and headed straight for it. These kinds of places were usually the best to pick up information and gossip.

It was almost one thirty, so the lunch crowd had thinned. Carl found a stool at the counter and grabbed a menu upright in a holder.

"Order a burger," a voice told him.

He looked up to see the bartender standing there. He grinned at Carl.

"Regular cook's out sick today, and burgers are the best thing Olive makes."

"In that case, I'll have a burger with everything." He set the menu back in its holder.

"Well done," the man added, "and with fries. She does those good, too."

Carl had to laugh. "You got it."

The bartender hollered his order through the serving window then poured Carl the soft drink he ordered.

"Still got some driving to do," he commented. "Gotta keep my head clear."

"Where you heading?"

Carl fudged his answer and took a swallow of his drink.

"I suppose no one talks about it, but didn't I read a story about this area last year? Something about some girls being raped?"

The bartender's expression turned cold. "We don't talk about that. We're just glad the sheriff, who was new at the time, dropped the hammer on it."

"Yeah. Sounds like a good guy."

"He is."

Those two words were the sound of a door being closed, so Carl shut up. His lunch came, and he ate slowly and quietly. The bartender was finished with him after the reference to the rapes, so he tried to listen to what was going on around him. He was nearly finished when two men walked in and took the stools next to him.

"Beer and burgers for both of us," one of them told the bartender. "We had a bunch of deliveries this morning, so we're late for lunch and starved."

"Yeah," the other one said. "Last one was to that house the sheriff first lived in when he took the job. You know, at the edge of the Schroeder property?"

"Oh, right, right." The bartender nodded. "Belongs to the sheriff's wife, so who's living there?"

The man next to Carl shrugged. "Strangers. Some man and a woman who pulled into town a few days ago. Those two mares that got moved are back now, and they needed feed and stuff."

"No kidding?" The bartender looked from one to the other. "Wonder who it is."

"Maybe a candidate for an open deputy slot. We only got a glimpse of the woman because she stayed in the barn most of the time. When I saw her, I could tell why. She's got a bunch of fading bruises. I wonder if he's the guy who beat the shit out of her? If so, how come she's still with him?"

"He wouldn't be if Sheriff Rossi is offering him a job," his friend said. "Alex Rossi is a stand-up dude. "

"Oh, yeah. Right. Maybe she's hiding from whoever it

was. I caught a whiff of conversation, and they've been here a few days but keep to themselves. Never even come into town."

Carl felt excitement curl in his belly. He wouldn't need to trail the sheriff after all. This had to be Zane Halstead and Lainie Taggert. How many couples could there be in a place this size where the woman had been beat all to hell? But the question was how to find the place. He finished his lunch, thanked the bartender, and slapped some bills on the counter. Then he headed out trying not to look like he was in a hurry.

The town was small enough that finding the town hall was easy enough. Long experience had taught him how to sweet-talk his way into getting documents he wanted, and before long he had everything he needed to know about the location of the Schroeder ranch and the house that sat at the edge of it.

Half an hour later, he realized he had to do some finagling to get close enough to the property. Although there was nothing on the highway to indicate the gravel road he found led to a house, the information he'd obtained told him this was it. But the road was narrow and private and, according to the maps he'd looked at, that house was the only one here.

An hour later, he had found a way to hike into a spot not far from the house on property barely beyond its boundaries. He pulled his car off the road and parked it out of sight. The abundance of trees hid the car and shielded him if anyone spotted him and he was able to climb one to survey the situation. Luck was with him today. From his perch, he could see the log cabin, the corral with two horses in it, and the barn. Beyond that, a wide prairie stretched away.

Two people stood near the corral, and, from the descriptions Sonny gave him, they were the pair he was looking for.

He took out his long-range camera and shot as many pictures as he could before climbing down and heading back to his truck. As soon as he was on the road again, he called Sonny.

"I found them."

"Already?" Sonny's tone was skeptical.

"Sonny, hardly anyone lives around here. It was easy to find two strangers. But to make sure, I shot some pictures. As soon as I get home, I'll email them to you. But I can tell you, creeping up on them won't be easy."

"If I bring enough firepower, it won't matter."

Carl snorted a laugh. "Don't kid yourself. You said this guy is a former SEAL? You might have to eat your words."

"I know what I'm doing. Stop talking and send the fucking pictures."

The line went dead. Carl stared at his phone for a minute before sticking it into the console.

Okay. Whatever.

It was Sonny Fitzgerald's funeral.

CHAPTER 13

"The best and most beautiful things in the world cannot be seen or even touched – they must be felt with the heart."
   Hellen Keller

Alex stopped by at the end of the day to check on things with Lainie and Zane.

Micki had again extended an invitation to them to come for dinner.

"Just a cookout in the backyard," Alex told them. "Nothing fancy."

"Let me see how Lainie feels about it. She's doing a little better each day, but I think today kind of tired her out. She's still getting her strength back."

"Sure. Let me know. Well, it looks like you guys are all set here, and I need to get back to my office."

"Thanks for everything. Really."

Zane watched him leave then went inside to find Lainie sitting at the kitchen table with a cup of tea.

"Tired?" he asked.

"A little." She grinned. "But it was exciting watching them bring the horses and get everything set up." Then a frown replaced the smile. "Will you be able to ride, what with your leg and all?"

He nodded. "I think so. I'll take it easy and also do my exercises every day. It might even be good for me. You hungry at all? We can talk about dinner."

She put her cup down. "To tell the truth, I think I'd like to take a shower and then maybe have a glass of wine. I'm not really hungry." She winked. "At least for food."

Despite the wink, Zane noticed that her hands holding her mug trembled the slightest bit.

He sat down at the table and closed his hands over hers.

"Lainie, whatever is going on in your mind, I don't want it to be something you're afraid of. I never want you to be afraid again. Ever. Understand?"

"I'm not afraid of you, Zane. Not even in the least bit." She took a sip of her tea. "It's so weird because even that first day I had no fear where you were concerned. I might have been looking over my shoulder for Sonny, but I knew inside that somehow you'd protect me." She sighed. "I never used to be a weakling or anything like that. Somehow, I let Sonny get into my mind until he was controlling me. And then it was the fear, an even stronger prison. But, Zane? I am really ready to move on."

He lifted her uninjured hand and kissed each finger.

"Let's take it one step at a time and see how it goes. I don't want to rush you. And, I don't want to hurt you."

When she stared directly at him, what he saw in her

eyes made hunger race through him. He saw heat and need and desire. Real desire.

Okay, Halstead. Then you'd better make it good.

"I'd like to take a shower." Then something else flashed in her eyes. "Or maybe another bath if I could have one like the last one. But this time don't treat me like a piece of fine china, okay?"

He kissed her hand. "Okay. It's a deal. Let's get to it."

Zane went to fill up the bathtub, adding bubble bath like the other night. He stripped down to his boxer briefs, leaving his clothes on the chair in the master bedroom. He wasn't sure which bedroom would serve best for what he had in mind, but he figured if she freaked out, at least she'd have her own room to retreat to.

She was in the bathroom when he walked back in, hair piled on top of her head, naked except for the towel she held in front of her. She looked up at him as if searching for something in his eyes.

"It's all good," he assured her. "I want this, too. We'll take it slow and easy, okay?"

She nodded. "Okay." Then she dimpled a smile at him. "But you do owe me one orgasm."

That broke the thread of tension, and Zane felt himself relax. He taped the plastic glove around her hand and reminded her not to put pressure on it. When the tub was full he helped Lainie climb into it. She leaned against the back, closed her eyes, and gave a sigh of contentment.

"Mmm. This feels so good."

"You have no idea how it stretched my self-control back at the motels, helping you undress and dress. I guess it's all my military discipline that helped me behave because, Lainie? I sure had a hard time keeping my hands from straying. I sure wanted to touch every inch of your body."

"You were a perfect gentleman, and you helped in what could have been a very embarrassing situation for me. It was bad enough as it was." Her mouth curved in a tiny smile. "But now, we can play."

"Damn! I should have asked Alex to pick up some wine for us. That's all that's missing."

"We don't need the wine." She studied his face. "We can get drunk on each other, right?"

"Sounds good to me."

He knelt beside the tub, being careful of his leg, dipped the washcloth into the tub, wrung it out, and began coasting it over her body. The water didn't fully cover her breasts, so he set the washcloth aside for a moment and stroked her with the tips of his fingers.

Lainie closed her eyes and hummed satisfaction.

"That feels good."

"I'm only getting started."

He continued to massage part of her breasts with his fingers before sliding his hand beneath the bubbles and cupping each one. When he brushed his thumbs over each nipple, he felt it already hard and pebbled. He stroked and pinched lightly and squeezed gently, drawing a tiny sigh of pleasure with each movement. He spent a long time on the upper part of her body, caressing her shoulders and her neck and returning again and again to her breasts. This time, when he pinched the nipples, he exerted greater pressure, watching her carefully to see if he was causing her too much discomfort. But the little moans from her were a good indication he was doing okay.

Rinsing the washcloth and squeezing it out again, he coasted it over her stomach, making sure to dip one finger into her navel and swirling it around and around. Then he slipped his hand between her thighs, paying careful attention to one before moving to the other. Lainie tried lifting her hips, silently urging him to move his hand between them, but he was determined not to rush this.

The little sounds coming from her lips had turned into a steady hum, broken by a gasp when he eased his hand between her legs.

"I won't ask you if anyone ever made you come in the bathtub," he said. "I don't want to bring up what might be an unpleasant memory, so we're going to pretend this is the first time. Okay?"

"Yes, please," she whispered.

"I love touching you, Lainie. Feeling the weight of your breasts in my hand. The hard points of your nipples. I can't wait to put them in my mouth. Maybe I can make you come just by doing that. We'll have to try it. I want to suck on them until they are so hard that every time you think about it you come wherever you are. Think you'd like that?"

She gave a strangled laugh. "I think I'd like you to make me come. That's what I think."

"But we've hardly gotten started," he teased.

She opened her eyes and looked straight into his. "I haven't had anyone care about how I feel in so long I don't know what to do about it. All I know is your touch is exactly what I imagined it to be, hard and soft at the same time. It makes me hungry for you, makes my body want to feel yours everywhere. And I want more. So, so much more. So, don't make me wait too long. Please?"

Emotion so strong it nearly shook him swept through him. He wanted to fuck her every way possible, and then when they'd finished, he wanted to start all over again. He wanted to bury himself in her so deep they wouldn't know where one of them ended and the other began. And he wanted to do it all in a way that showed her how special she was, especially to him.

Get it right, Halstead. Don't fuck this up.

"I promise you, all that will happen, but right at the moment, let's see how good I can make you feel. Close your eyes, okay?"

"Mmm. Okay. But don't take too long. Zane, I haven't been this ready in such a short time in forever."

His heart ached for what she'd been through, and tonight he was going to erase all of that.

"Bend your knees, Lainie, and separate your legs. Yes. Like that."

Nudging her thighs farther apart, he dragged the washcloth between them, teasing at the tender flesh of her sex. When her breathing accelerated slightly, he separated the lips of her sex and slipped the washcloth between them, dragging the rough material over her clit again and again. The more he did it, the faster she breathed, bracing herself on her feet and trying to lift her hips to his touch.

He wanted to slide his fingers inside her, feel that hot channel in the worst way. But first, he wanted to see if he could make her come with only what he was doing. He rubbed the washcloth against her clit faster and faster. She was panting heavily, and moaning louder, whimpering.

"More, more, more."

"Come for me, Lainie," he murmured in a low voice. "Let yourself go."

He wasn't sure if it would happen, but in the next moment, she thrust her hips up at him, clutching the side of the tub with one hand, hips bucking, and her body shook.

"Oh, oh, oh." She pushed against the cloth again and again.

Then he pulled it away and dropped it into the water.

Her eyes flew open. "No, no, no, no. Don't stop. Please don't stop."

"I'm not," he assured her, barely recognizing his own voice. "I'm gonna make you come again, and this time I want to feel it."

He slipped two fingers into her still-spasming channel then added a third, adjusting his hand so he could stroke her clit with his thumb. He drove his fingers in and out, each slide and thrust dragging his finger over that swollen little nub.

"More." She was screaming, pushing herself against his hand, riding it.

"That's it, Lainie. That's the way. Come on, baby. Let yourself go."

He pushed his fingers into her with a hard thrust and pressed his thumb on her clit, and she exploded like a steam volcano. Her inner walls gripped his fingers, milking them, as spasm after spasm ripped through her inner muscles. He kept up the rhythm until the last tremor had subsided, until her slick walls released their grip on his fingers, and she lay back in the tub, injured hand resting against the rim, the other one gripping the side. The pulse at the hollow of her throat beat rapidly, an offset to the uneven breaths she was taking.

Zane rose to his knees and leaned close enough to press his mouth to hers. It was a soft, gentle kiss, meant to convey emotion to her that he wasn't very good at expressing. When he lifted his head she was smiling.

"That was…amazing."

He chuckled. "I'm not done amazing you. Let's get you out of the tub."

He flipped the handle for the drain and lifted her out, being careful how he handled her, and stood her on the bathmat. A tiny twinge flickered in his left arm, but he ignored it. Thank god he'd been doing his exercises every day.

"Can you lean your good hand on the counter?" he asked.

She nodded.

"Good. I'll be quick."

"That's okay." Her voice was a little shaky. "You don't have to hurry."

Oh yes, I do. I need to get you in that bed before I detonate.

When she was fully dried off, he carried her into his bedroom. He had made sure everything was shipshape in there, the covers neatly turned back, the lamp on low. Placing her carefully on the sheets, he arranged a pillow so she could brace her injured arm.

"I don't think I need that," she protested. "I'm so much better."

"Lainie, it's been barely more than a week. If it feels good, I want to keep it that way." He grinned at her. "Besides, I'm in charge of the arrangements here."

Emotion swirled in her eyes. "You make me feel special."

"That's because you are."

He'd taken the two condoms from his wallet and placed them on the nightstand, praying they were still good.

Lainie touched his hand. "Just so you know, I'm on birth control."

"Good to know, but in your condition let's make sure."

Then he stripped off his boxers and tossed them to the side. When Lainie reached out to touch his cock, he moved her hand away.

"Honey, I'm so ready, if you touch me it'll be over in six seconds, and we won't even get to the main event."

Her lips curved in a tiny smile. "I like knowing I do that to you."

"I thought you'd figured that out this morning."

He moved onto the bed, taking a moment to let his eyes feast on her body. He couldn't wait to see her without those bruises and had to tamp down the murderous rage that surged through him. Never again, he told himself. No one ever will treat her that way again.

"Okay?" he asked, studying her face.

"More than."

He kissed her, tasting her lips before thrusting his tongue inside her mouth. She slid her smaller one over his, creating an erotic dance that he felt all the way to his balls. When he'd drunk his fill, he slid his lips along her jawline and down the slender column of her neck, taking gentle nips here and there.

"You lie there and don't move," he told her, stunned at the guttural tone in his voice. "This is my show."

"Okay," she whispered.

He continued his journey down her body, tracing her collarbone with his tongue, sprinkling kisses around each breast, pausing to suck each nipple and bite down with what he hoped was exactly the right amount of pressure. If her moans were any indication, he was definitely doing it right.

He kissed his way down her stomach, taking a moment to trace the swirl of her navel before continuing on down one leg and up the other. He trailed kisses down the inside of one thigh and then the other, adding a little nip here and there. Her moans increased and, when she tried to move her body from side to side, he held her in place with a gentle grip on her hipbones.

Finally, unable to wait any longer, he moved her legs apart, exposing her sex.

Holy shit!

It was a wonder he didn't come right then and there. The wet pink flesh made his mouth water and his cock flex. The auburn hair surrounding it was darker than that on her head, and her clit was a swollen, dark-pink button. He couldn't wait any longer. His self-control had already been stretched beyond its limits. Pressing her thighs wider and spreading the lips of her sex, he drove his tongue inside.

"Oh god." Her voice had a strangled sound to it.

Zane paused, frozen, wondering what he'd done wrong.

"Don't stop," she cried. "Oh god, please don't stop."

He went back to work on her, licking and sucking, stroking with his tongue and tugging on her clit with his teeth. He wanted to taste her everywhere, to fill every opening in her body, to bring her to orgasm after orgasm, but he'd settle for one more tonight. When he had her writhing beneath him, he grabbed one of the condoms and rolled it on with a hand that trembled.

"I'll be careful," he told her in a voice that shook slightly.

"I want you." Heat simmered in her eyes. "Right this minute."

Placing his hands beneath the cheeks of her ass, he lifted her to where he wanted her. Then, pressing the tip of his shaft at her opening, he eased inside a little at a time.

Holy fucking shit!

He had to close his eyes and take in a deep breath to search for some measure of control. Then he was inside her, the wet flesh clasping his cock, squeezing him.

"Do it," she begged. "Please."

Damn good thing she asked because he was almost at the end of his self-control. Taking a deep breath and letting it out slowly, he began the rhythm, in and out, slowly at first then faster and faster. He ground his teeth together to hold off until he felt her readiness. When her muscles began to squeeze him, he went into overdrive, pounding into her again and again, forcing himself to hold off until he felt the beginnings of her orgasm. The moment he felt it, he let himself go, his shaft flexing as her muscles gripping it pulsed over and over and over, flooding him.

And then it was over, leaving him breathless and stunned at the impact. His heart thundered, and his breath came in spurts. When he felt he had himself under some semblance of control, he leaned forward, catching himself on his forearms, and peppered kisses on her face, finally taking her mouth with as much emotion as he could put into it. He wasn't sure whose heart thundered harder and faster, hers or his.

He'd been with his share of women in his life, and had some of the most outrageous sex, but nothing compared to what had just happened. He not only felt it in his cock and his balls, he felt it in his heart. He prayed silently that she felt the same.

She opened her eyes and looked directly into his, and what he saw there made his heart surge and hope blossom.

"Tell me," he urged. "Say what's on your mind."

She grinned. "Wow!"

"Wow? Is that a testimonial?"

All humor left her face. "More than that. I have never felt more worshiped, more treasured, or more aroused in my life."

"Those first two? That's what's going on here. Lainie, you came into my life in circumstances I never expected would lead to this. Now? I can't imagine being without it. Without you."

She stared intently at his face. "Do you mean that?"

"I do." He pressed a light kiss to her lips. "Whatever connects us, I don't want it to stop."

"Me, either," she answered in a soft voice.

He lay there for another moment before easing from her body.

"Be right back," he told her.

In the bathroom he took care of business, washed his hands then took a moment to study himself in the mirror. For the first time since leaving the SEALs, he saw hope and pleasure in his eyes. And a future. He had to remind himself to take it slow and make sure she was on the same page, not being grateful to him for what he'd done and was doing.

When he walked back into the bedroom, she was lying exactly the way he'd left her. Her mouth was tilted in a little smile, and he did not detect any tension in her body.

"Sleep in here with me," he blurted out. "I want to feel your body next to mine all night."

"I was hoping you'd say that."

Her words were an indication of how unsure she was of their situation. He slid into bed beside her and tugged her body up next to his, being careful of her shoulder and hand.

"I don't know if it's too soon to say this, but I feel as if we've lived a year in the last week. I want you with me always, Lainie. And I've never said that to another woman."

She relaxed against him, as if she'd been holding her breath. "I want that, too. Whatever Fate sent you into my life at a critical moment, I don't want you to walk out of it."

"Good. Let's take care of Sonny Fitzgerald so you have no more worries on that score and get on with our lives."

"Amen to that. Meanwhile, we'd better get to sleep, or I might want to do this all over again."

He kissed her cheek then made sure she was snuggled against him. For the first time in a long time, he felt an unfamiliar emotion surge through him.

Hope.

CHAPTER 14

"You cannot control the behavior of others, but you can always choose how you respond to it."

Roy T. Bennett, The Light in the Heart

She's there!

Sonny stared at his phone as he scrolled through the photos Carl had sent. He could hardly believe they had actually found her. But there was no mistaking the images. It was Lainie Taggert, no question about it. And the man with her had to be Zane Halstead. Sonny only had the driver's license photo and one pulled from a government website to compare, but he was sure it was him.

Excitement coursed through him. At last the fucking bitch was within his grasp. He'd kill that asshole with her then teach her a lesson she'd never forget. He'd thought about killing her but decided that dragging her back and reinforcing that lesson every day would give him more satisfaction. But he'd better make preparations.

He speed-dialed Geoff, who was running an errand for him.

"Get back here. We've found the bitch and we have preparations to make. I want to take care of this fast. I mean really fast."

"On my way."

Fifteen minutes later, Geoff walked into Sonny's office, an expectant look on his face.

"So, is she in Montana, like we thought after Antonio hacked the email?"

"She is. Here. Take a look."

Geoff took the phone and scrolled through the photos.

"The guy with her looks tough as nails, Sonny."

"But he's only one guy. We'll have a full squad."

Geoff leaned back in his chair. "Okay, what are the plans?"

"First, call the hangar and have them get the plane ready. Then roust the pilot. He gets paid a fucking fortune for hardly any work. Tell him to get his ass out there and have everything ready to go."

"Okay. What else?"

"We need an EMP. An electromagnetic pulse machine."

"What for?"

"Because, idiot, the guy is a former SEAL. I'll bet the first thing he did was set up a tight security system, and we need something to knock it out. And get these men ready."

Sonny typed into his phone then hit Send.

When Geoff's phone signaled a message, the man read the text and nodded.

"Okay. On it."

"How long will it take you to get the EMP?"

"Thirty minutes to an hour, depending on traffic. I'll call our electronics guy. He always has at least one of everything available. I'll get it on the way to the airport."

"Good. Good. Tell those men to be at the hangar in thirty."

Geoff nodded. "See you there."

As soon as Geoff had left, Sonny buzzed his admin and asked her to come. Brenda Neiman had been with Sonny for ten years. She knew enough secrets to destroy him, but he paid her enough to squash any idea of that. She had unswerving loyalty and took care of all the little details that made his life run smoothly.

"I'm leaving for a few days. Hand off what you can and reschedule the rest."

"Of course, Mr. Fitzgerald." It was a testament to her dedication that she never even blinked. "When will you be leaving?"

"As soon as the limo service can get here. Geoff is off doing errands, and I want to allow time for traffic."

"Very good. I'm on it. The usual procedures in place while you're gone?"

Sonny nodded. "Remind me to give you a raise."

Her lips twitched with the beginning of a smile.

"You just gave me one."

"That's okay. You're worth it."

He shut down his computer and cleaned papers off his desk, locking them in a drawer. If this worked out the way he hoped, he'd be back in forty-eight hours, ready to teach Lainie Taggert a lesson she'd never forget.

LAINIE WAS SITTING on the corral fence, watching Zane get acquainted with one of the horses, when Alex Rossi's county vehicle pulled into the driveway. She waved.

"Hey, Alex. What brings you out here today?"

"I see Zane's already at work with them." The sheriff nodded at the corral as he walked toward them.

Zane heard him and turned. "Right now, getting to know them. I'm so rusty, I think I need to give myself lessons first."

"I'm sure it will come back to you."

Zane walked up to the fence. "So, what's up? I know you didn't drive all the way out here to check on my cowboy skills."

Alex shook his head. "I wish. Unfortunately, I come bearing bad news."

"Yeah?" Zane climbed out of the corral and went to stand next to Lainie, holding her uninjured hand. "About what?"

"My contact at the Montana Bureau of Justice called me. Zane, your email's been hacked."

Lainie felt as if every drop of blood suddenly drained from her body. She reached for Zane's hand, clutching it tightly.

"W-when did this happen?"

"Actually, a couple of days ago, but it took that long for

the tech guy to find it. Whoever did the hack is incredibly skilled at covering tracks."

"Fuck." A muscle ticked in Zane's jaw. "You think Sonny's already on his way here?"

"I'd say that's a good bet, but he didn't leave until today."

"Why not?" Zane demanded. "And what makes you so sure?"

"First of all, he's smart enough not to rush in here. He'd want to make sure it was really you."

"And how would he do that without coming here?" Lainie asked.

"I spent a little time easing around town this morning, asking about any strangers, of which we get few, and anyone interested in either of you. I was pretty sure he'd send someone to check it out. Sonny Fitzgerald isn't going to jump into a situation without having all the facts verified."

"And?" Zane asked.

"Some guy was in McGinnis's a couple of days ago and brought up the rapes, which no one wants to talk about. Kind of strange, out of the blue. Anyway, the guys from the feed store came in for lunch and, unfortunately, were talking about their delivery here to the new residents. That's the two of you."

Lainie clutched Zane's hand more tightly. "So he knows."

"There's more." Alex pushed his hat back. "I'm sure he wanted to know where this place was before he reported back to Sonny, so I checked at the town hall. The clerk told me some guy was in looking at the maps and plats for this area. I'm sure he drove out here to check things out and get a look."

"But if a strange car came down this road, we'd see it," Zane pointed out.

"That's right. Zane, I'd like you to take a walk with me around the area surrounding this property and see if we can find anything."

"I'm not staying here in this house alone," Lainie told them.

The two men exchanged a glance.

"Okay," Zane said with obvious reluctance. "But when we find the spot, you stay in the car. Got it?"

She nodded and climbed into the back seat. She fisted her good hand, digging her nails into her palms, to try and control her shaking. She'd thought it was too good to be true. It was a miracle that Zane had come into her life at the exact moment when she needed him. What was growing between them was another one. Was it all about to be smashed?

Alex drove along the highway shoulder, stopping when Zane pointed something out to him.

"There. You can see tire tracks heading off the road."

"Good thing it rained the other night. The ground would still have been soft. I don't guess whoever this was would care, not figuring anyone would know about him and be looking. Come on. Let's see what we find."

Lainie sat rigidly in her seat, doing her best not to have a heart attack, waiting until the men came back out of the woods.

"Well?"

Zane opened the door and crouched beside her.

"Don't freak, okay?"

Oh god. Oh god!

"He was here, right? He found us?"

Alex nodded. He could have climbed any one of a number of trees to take pictures, sending them back to Sonny for confirmation."

"So, now what? Zane, we can't stay here."

"Alex and I discussed it. If we run, he's going to find us again. We have a chance to make a good life here, Lainie."

"Not if we're dead," she pointed out.

"Have faith, please. You have two former SEALs here who have taken on worse than Sonny Fitzgerald."

"I called Sonny's office," Alex told her, "to make sure he was still in town. I can't see him not coming for this himself."

"And?" she asked.

"I was told he left town early this afternoon. Flight time is less than five hours in a private plane, which I assume is what they'll take. There are several airports where they can land. Then they'd have to drive here."

"What's the closest one?" Lainie asked. "Sonny won't want to waste any time."

"I'll pull up a map and show you. I have a feeling whoever did his research for him will pick him and whoever he brings with him up at the airport. He'd know his way around."

Zane looked at the map Alex pulled up on his tablet.

"Based on mileage and all, I'd say that brings them here around seven o'clock tonight, give or take."

Alex nodded. "But we're going to get ready for them.

Lainie, I'm going to take you to my house. Micki's expecting you. We need you out of the danger zone."

"But what if his person here comes to check things before picking them up? You know, to make sure we're still here."

Alex looked at Zane. "She's got a point but still."

"I refuse to have her in any danger." He took Lainie's uninjured hand in his. "What about this? He'd have to be gone from here at the latest by six. Maybe even a little bit earlier, depending on the exact arrival time of the plane. You stay here with me and whoever else Alex sends us until quarter after six. He'll probably do his spotting from the same place."

"I'll have my personal vehicle," Alex added, "and I can cruise down the highway and check it out. As soon as we're sure he's gone, I'll take you to my house and be back here in time to help Zane."

"Please, Lainie. I can't lose you, not after what's happening between us."

She caught Alex glancing between the two of them and trying to hide a grin. What Zane said made sense. And she'd only be a distraction for them if she were here.

"Okay. But, Alex? You'd better make damn sure nothing happens to this man."

This time his grin got the better of him. "Yes, ma'am. Word of honor." He turned back to Zane. "I put Miranda in charge of the office for the rest of the day. You and I have some prep work to do. We need to get started."

Zane nodded. "Let's do it."

"She go peacefully?" Zane asked as Alex walked back into the house.

Alex laughed. "After a fashion. I thought she'd be damn glad to be out of it, all things considered. Where'd she get all that piss and vinegar? You been feeding her something I don't know about?"

Zane swallowed a grin. "Not exactly."

"Well, whatever it is, it's nice to see it. When you first got here, I wasn't so sure about her."

"You should have seen her when I first picked her up. I was afraid she wouldn't survive the first day on the road."

Alex studied him. "So, what's brought about the change?"

Zane really didn't want to discuss it, so he just shrugged. "Stuff."

Alex laughed. "Okay, but after we get rid of the vermin tonight, I'll be asking questions again. That is, if you're still considering the job."

"I am. Now, let's go over everything and make sure we're set."

Both men had assumed Sonny would have an EMP to disrupt the security system, so they made other plans. They booby-trapped all the places Sonny and his men would have to cross to get onto the property. The biggest challenge was the prairie stretching out beyond the corral. Alex set one of his young deputies in the barn with night-vision goggles and a sniper rifle. Turned out one of his young deputies was an ace with it. His other young deputy was up in a tree where the drive to the house turned in from the highway, similarly equipped.

Zane and Alex were in the house, both dressed in dark

clothes, waiting, with rifles Alex had provided and their handguns. They had decided to leave the house lights on as a signal to Sonny that people were home. Once they used the EMP, all the electricity would be out, and they'd be in the darkness they needed. Waiting was always the hardest, but, as trained SEALs, they were used to it. Zane couldn't count the number of missions where at least half the time had been spent waiting.

Everything was quiet until Alex's cell rang about six-forty-five, and he shouted, "What? Micki, slow down. What the hell? Hang on." He pulled his radio from one of his pockets. "Miranda, get the fuck over to my house *this minute*. Make sure Micki is all right." He turned to Zane. "Don't lose your shit, but—"

"But what? What the fuck happened?"

"Whoever their contact is here apparently told them where Micki and I live. They stopped there first, figuring to take her as a hostage in case they had problems here. They must have used an EMP to kill my security system and they managed to coldcock Micki's brother. So instead of my wife, they got Lainie."

Zane wanted to scream and had to stop himself from rushing from the house, jumping into his truck, and trying to find them on the road.

"Is she alive?" He made himself ask the question.

"Micki has a big bump on her head where one of them hit her with his gun, and a bad headache. She said Sonny slapped Lainie around a little, but she's still alive."

Thank god. But they'll wish they weren't.

"I know it's hard," Alex went on, "but hold it together. Micki heard them tell Lainie they were bringing her here

237

so she could watch them kill you. Miranda's taking Micki to the office."

"I have a big fucking surprise for them," he ground out. He'd put a lid on his temper and his fear for Lainie. He was cold as ice, a SEAL on a mission, and he wouldn't fail.

At a little after seven thirty, Zane saw Alex tap his ear and heard him say, "Got it. Move to your new position."

He turned to Zane. "They're here."

And right on the heels of his words, all the electricity died. Zane and Alex took up their predetermined positions and waited. When Zane heard a car door close in the parking area, he wondered how arrogant Sonny must be to think the sound wouldn't be a signal of some kind after they lost power. Next, they heard the front door splinter at the same time someone knocked out the window with a view of the back.

Two big, heavyset men burst through the shattered front door, carrying guns that they began firing at once.

Alex shone his big tactical flashlight at the two men while Zane turned and fired a shot at someone climbing in the broken window. One of the men lifted his gun to shoot the flashlight, but Zane fired with precision and hit the man, who began screaming in pain. When the second man tried to get off a shot, Alex clipped him, too. Everything had happened in seconds.

More shots sounded outside.

All Zane could think of was, where was Lainie? Was she in the line of fire? He knew better than to go charging into unknown territory, but it killed him not to.

"Davey in the barn winged one," Alex passed along to Zane. "He's coming to cover our rear."

He kicked away the guns the downed men had been carrying and motioned to Davey, who had climbed through the broken window, to collect them.

"There's only one man left," he reported. "He's in the car with a woman."

Lainie! Now he could go after her.

Zane started toward the broken front door, gun in hand, when a man stomped up onto the porch. He had his arm around Lainie's neck, and was dragging her inside. Zane saw bright red, and he had to work to control his anger.

"Sonny Fitzgerald, I presume."

"I brought my woman here so you could watch me beat the shit out of her before I kill her." Sonny spat the words. "This is the last time she'll try to leave me."

Lainie looked terrified, but she stared directly at Zane as if trying to send hm a message.

I know you'll save me.

Zane stood there with his gun trained on Sonny's forehead. He held it in the standard, two-handed grip, bracing his right hand with his left. If his damaged left arm was bothering him, he didn't notice it. He was concentrating too hard on Lainie and the monster holding her.

Alex's other young deputy had arrived at the house and was standing behind Sonny. Alex gave an imperceptible shake of the head, and Zane knew he was sending him a message.

This one's Zane's.

"Put your gun down," Sonny told him. "You, too, Sheriff. And tell your deputies to get away from my men."

"Not happening," Zane said. "And Lainie's not your woman."

"Yeah, right," Sonny snorted. "Drop your weapon."

Steady, Zane told himself. Follow mission protocol.

Kill the bastard and save the hostage.

Lainie was still staring at Zane when, without warning, she dug her nails hard into Sonny's hand. It was enough to make the man jerk, and the gun wavered for a millisecond.

And Zane drilled him through the center of his forehead.

As the man fell backward, Zane rushed to grab Lainie and pull her away. He moved to the side with her, crushing her against his body, his arm banded tightly around her. He completely forgot he was still holding his gun until Alex gently pried it from his fingers. He kissed Lainie so hard it stole their breath then took a little step back, still holding her, to see what damage Sonny had inflicted.

"My hand," she told him, her voice laced with pain. "He broke my fingers again, the bastard. And I'll probably need to put my sling back on for a while." She looked up at him. "How bad is my face?"

He swallowed, hard. "Not as bad as when I picked you up. What did he hit you with?"

"The barrel of the gun. Just once."

"That accounts for the big cut. Thank god, he left your eye alone."

"I didn't fight him, Zane, because I didn't want him to hurt Micki any more than he did. Is she okay?"

"Yes. Miranda has her at the office."

"I think you're done with this," Alex said, amusement in his voice as he held up Zane's gun. "We'll need it for ballistics, but then you can have it back."

"Lainie needs a doctor. Do you think Sandoval would see her tonight?"

"I'll make sure of it. Let me help my deputies finish mopping up here. I called the state police. They have better facilities for these guys, and there are way more of them than there are of us. Give me a minute, and I'll call him."

Zane picked Lainie up and carried her into his bedroom so she wouldn't have to watch what was going on. He sat on the bed, crooning softly to her, one arm around her, the other hand holding her injured one. He could have lost her tonight, and the thought frightened him to death. It made him realize, though, that they had something very special going here, and he was going to hang in as long as it took for her to recover from yet another trauma and agree to marry him. He'd accept Alex's job offer, and they'd build a new life here. Finally, he saw a new purpose in his existence.

He looked up when Alex knocked on the doorframe.

"The mess is cleaned up. The staties picked up the trash and carted them off literally in chains and handcuffs. Davey's gone to get some lumber to board up your door until we can get it taken care of tomorrow. And Sandoval's waiting for you."

"Thank you." Zane had to swallow twice before he could say anything else. "Thank you very much."

"It's what SEALs do for each other, right? Listen. You obviously can't sleep here tonight. We have plenty of room at our place, and Micki insists you come over there."

"I'm not sure—"

"Just for tonight. Tomorrow you can decide what's next, but for tonight bring her someplace safe and comfortable."

"Thank you." He stood up, holding Lainie. "Come on, sugar. We're gonna get you patched up. Then I'm going to spend the rest of my life taking care of you."

EPILOGUE

"Today you are you! That is truer than true. There is no one alive who is you-er than you!

Dr. Seuss

LAINIE SAT on the top rail of the corral, watching Zane with one of the mares. Three months had passed since the horrific night when Sonny Fitzgerald had come to reclaim her and kill Zane. Three months during which she had really begun to heal. Her broken fingers were out of their cast, all her bruises had finally disappeared, and she only had a twinge every so often in her shoulder. Zane exercised his leg and arm religiously and, while they'd never be close to 100 percent again, the arm was almost like new, and his leg only bothered him when he didn't exercise. She knew that riding the horses, needing to use his thighs to guide them, had been a big incentive for him to keep it up.

The whole episode with Sonny Fitzgerald had turned

into a massive story, filling the media for days. His law offices were closed, and local, state, and federal agents were wading through documents to decide who to charge with which crimes. After the first couple of days, she and Zane had stopped watching it or reading about it. That was a closed chapter for them, and it would stay that way.

There had been many changes in their lives. Zane was working full-time as a sheriff's deputy and enjoying it. His SEAL training stood him in good stead and made him excel at his job. He was a local hero for the way he'd taken down Sonny Fitzgerald with Alex, and much in demand as a speaker at local functions, something, Lainie knew, he hated but did because he felt it was important. He and Alex often double teamed to do presentations.

Lainie had been thinking about what she'd do since she was almost back to normal. When Micki suggested she use her paralegal degree to work at the county prosecutor's office with her, she talked it over with Zane and they decided she should try it part-time at first, if they'd go for it. She started her new job in three weeks.

They'd decided to stay in the house despite what had happened there. They both loved it as well as its location. A new door replaced the damaged one, and they spent two weeks repainting and refinishing everything, making it all like new.

Drea had come to visit them for a week and was astounded at the change in both of them.

"Who knew," she told Zane, "when I made that emergency call to you all those months ago, that you'd both turn out to have a happy ending."

Zane was teaching her to ride. She hadn't been out of

the corral yet, but she decided she really liked it. She'd taken up cooking again, which she enjoyed, and reading. The simple things in life which she'd lost during the Sonny portion of her life.

Zane was doing his best to make her feel she was the most important thing in his life. If the sex was any better, she thought she might die of pleasure. And they shared pieces of themselves. He told her about growing up on the horse farm, he and Drea, and how strange it was that neither of them wanted to go into that business.

One night, lying in bed, she told him about her own life. How her father had left her mother when she was ten. How her mother went from man to man, looking for the attention she'd lost. How her own choices were influenced by a need to be cared for and cared about.

"I made a lot of stupid choices," she told him.

"Haven't we all? But that's all behind us. The future looks very good."

She agreed, but she wondered exactly what that the future would hold. He told her often how much he loved her and how special she was to him, but he never said anything beyond that. Did they really have a future together? What was in his mind?

She was still turning it over in her brain when Zane dismounted and led the horse over to her.

"I'm going to rub her down and put her in her stall then go take a shower. After that, I thought we might go sit on the back porch, have a drink, and wait for the sunset. Some quiet time. How does that sound?"

"Sounds good to me." She hopped down off the rail. "I

think I'll take a quick shower, too. Then maybe I'll fix some munchies to go with."

"See you in a few."

She was dressed in lounge pants and a soft pink top, fixing crackers and cheese in the kitchen, when Zane came in after his shower. His beard was freshly trimmed, his hair combed, and he had on clean jeans and a soft-collar shirt.

"Wow! Who's the handsome man in the kitchen?"

He grinned. "It better be me or else."

She stopped what she was doing and gave him a hug then tilted her face up for a kiss. He smelled so good from the outdoorsy cologne he used.

"It would never be anyone but you. I hope you know that."

He brushed a kiss over her lips. "That's what I like to hear."

She wondered if that was a promise of a future together. Should she say something to him? Except things were going so well, she hated to do anything to change the rhythm. And they were happy, right?

"Why don't you carry that stuff out to the back porch," he suggested, "while I pour our drinks. Wine or whiskey for you?"

"I think whiskey today. I'm feeling daring."

He winked at her. "Whiskey it is. I'm feeling a little daring myself."

His words set heat flashing through her, hardening her nipples and dampening her panties. She hoped she never got past the point where he could arouse her this easily. She loved the chemistry they had together.

She was sitting on the porch, munching a cracker with cheese, when he came out of the house. He held a bottle of his favorite bourbon in one hand and two rocks glasses with ice in them in the other.

"I think we have plenty to celebrate about, don't you? Life is good."

"Better than I thought it would be the day I left Tampa with you," she agreed.

"I had no idea what life had in store for me," he went on, "only that I hoped this job in Montana would give me some direction in life. I never expected things to turn out this good."

"You changed my life, too, Zane. You made me whole again. It's amazing that after all we've been through, we turned out to be who we really are."

He nodded. "The real us. He glanced out over their acreage. "Living a life we really want."

"I'll love you forever for that."

"Yeah? I'm sure glad to hear that. Let's drink a toast to it."

He handed her glass to her, but she noticed there was hardly any liquor in it.

"You afraid I'll get drunk or something?"

"Maybe there's something in the glass blocking the alcohol. You should take a look."

She was aware of him standing rigidly beside her as she peered into the glass.

"What's that with the ice cubes? What the heck?"

She stuck two fingers in the glass and fished around, nearly dropping the glass when she lifted out a diamond ring. She just stared at it, dumbfounded, admiring the pear-shaped diamond and the tiny stones on either side of it. She looked up at him, her hand shaking.

"Is this what I think it is?"

Zane set his glass down then put hers on the table, took the ring from her, and dropped to one knee in front of her.

"Good thing I've been doing my exercises," he joked. "Lainie Taggert, you came into my life at a dark hour when I thought I had little to look forward to. You brought me sunshine and love…" He paused. "And the best sex in my life."

Lainie felt herself blush.

"You came into my life when I had lost direction and had no idea what would be in store for me. No focus. Even when Alex offered me a job, I still felt something was missing. You made me value myself again and for that I will love you forever. I can't imagine spending any part of my life with anyone but you. I promise I will love you forever. Will you please marry me and keep the sunshine in my life?"

"Oh my god!" Tears spilled down her cheeks.

"I hope those aren't tears of sadness. I'm praying for a happy answer."

"Yes." She threw her arms around his neck. "Yes, yes, yes. I will marry you. I don't want to spend a day of my life without you. I love you, Zane Halstead. I never knew life could be this good."

He took her left hand and slid the ring on the appropriate finger.

"Whew! It fits."

"But when—How—I mean—" She had to stop babbling.

"Micki helped me. I knew if I was away from you except on the job you'd want to know where. She brought pictures of rings to the office on one of my shifts then helped me order it. I'm so glad it fits."

"It's perfect. *You're* perfect. I love you, Zane Halstead."

"And I love you, Lainie Taggert. What do you say we go inside and celebrate this special occasion?"

"I say that's a great idea."

She put the cover on the snack tray, took his hand, and walked with him into the house.

And into a better life with a better man than she'd ever thought possible. She'd be giving thanks for the rest of her life.

THANK you for reading Desperate Deception, the first book in the Heroes Rising series, part of Elle James Brotherhood Protectors World. I introduced Alex and Micki in **Unmasking Evil.** Turn the page for the prologue and first chapter in their story.

UNMASKING EVIL

DESIREE HOLT

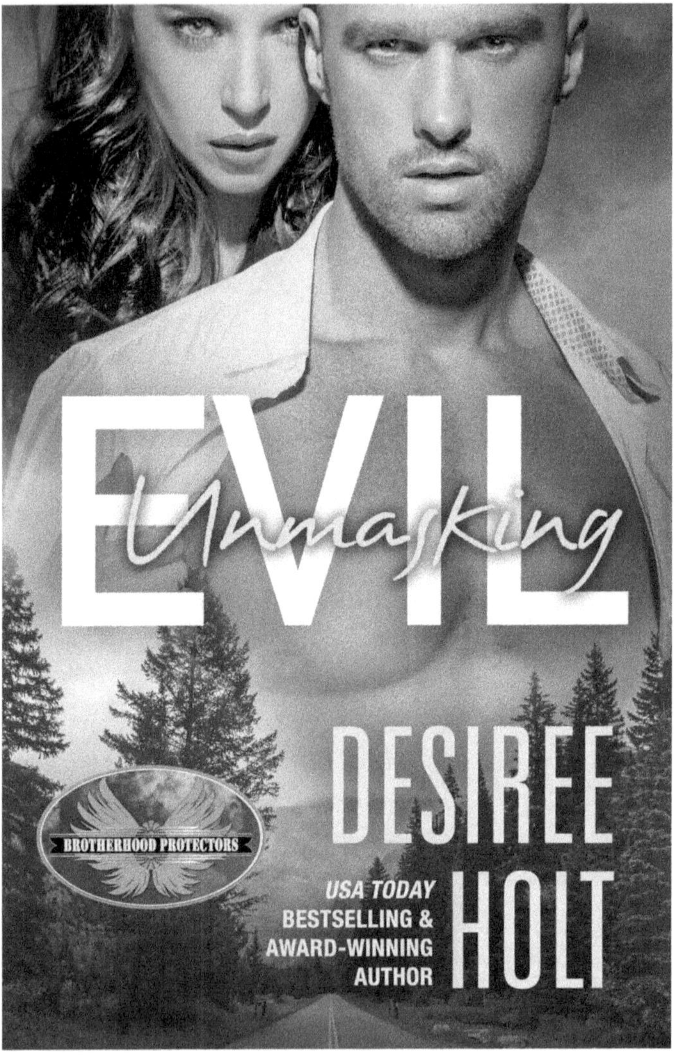
EVIL
Unmasking
DESIREE
HOLT
BROTHERHOOD PROTECTORS
USA TODAY
BESTSELLING &
AWARD-WINNING
AUTHOR

PROLOGUE

SIXTEEN YEARS ago

Micki hated the big parties her parents threw. She wasn't a big party person anyway. At fourteen, she had discovered that she relaxed the most with small groups of her friends. She liked sleepovers with four or five of them. Or riding horses. Or just hanging out. She wasn't hot for every boy in her high school as some of the girls were. Well, maybe a little lukewarm for Neil Harrison. He was, after all, super cute, with a sexy grin enhanced by the cutest dimple.

She'd come to the conclusion she was a late bloomer, but that was okay. Some of the girls were so busy learning all about sex she was sure by the time they graduated high school there'd be nothing left for them to learn. Not her. A guy had to really do it for her, really turn her on before she was ready to give him any part of her body.

Tonight's party was in full swing, at least a hundred people drinking and eating and laughing. And all trying to show everyone else they were richer and better and more important. Sometimes she wondered how her parents could stand some of them, but her father was an important person in the cattle industry and state politics, so this was part of their regular agenda.

Because it was a weekday night, she was not having a sleepover. She'd put on a dress to please her mother, done her bit by saying hello to the people she knew, and now she was going to her room to lose herself in a favorite movie.

She had reached the doorway when a thick arm banded around her waist and a hand covered her mouth, fingers pinching her nose. She heard the door slam shut and, in the next moment, she was face down on her bed, a heavy male figure pinning her in place. His fingers pinched her nose so tight she could hardly breathe. She tried to wriggle out from beneath him, but he was big, heavy, and his full weight held her in place.

"Listen to me." His voice was a raspy whisper. "Don't struggle, or I'll break your neck. Nod if you understand."

She did her best to nod her head once. What else could she do?

"I crave sweet young meat like you. The harder it is to do this, the better I like it. Sweet young virgins do it better for me."

He eased his grip on her nose but kept his hand over her mouth while he yanked up her dress, grabbed her panties, and ripped them off. She heard the rasp of a zipper and knew he was taking *it* out.

Oh sweet Jesus.

She clenched her fists and squeezed her eyes shut, trying to wish herself into a different place.

"Don't you worry," he whispered, as he kneed her legs farther apart. "I'm already wearing protection. Can't have any little schoolgirls giving birth to bastards."

The next few minutes were a concentrated nightmare. He thrust his fingers inside her, scraping her sensitive inner flesh, then shoved his thickness even deeper.

Oh god! It hurt! It hurt!

She couldn't scream, not with his big hand over her mouth. Anyway, she was sure he'd kill her if she tried to. She clenched her teeth as fiery pain shot through her and he drove himself in and out of her virgin sex. She felt the throbbing inside her as he climaxed, and then he withdrew, grunting in satisfaction.

"I'm getting off you now," he said in the same raspy whisper. "You count to a hundred before you get off this bed. And be sure you don't tell a soul, or I'll find you and break your neck." He barked a short laugh. "But you are one sweet piece of meat. You'll make a great lay one day when you grow up."

She heard the door close as he left the room, and even though he couldn't see her, she lay there counting to two hundred. Tears coursed silently down her cheeks, and it hurt to breathe. Finally, she got up and slowly headed into her bathroom. It even hurt to walk. Oh god!

It took her a while, but she managed to wash up, clean away the blood on her thighs, and pull on a nightgown. Found the housekeeper and asked her to tell her mother she was sick. Then she climbed into bed and pulled the covers up to her chin. She had no idea who the man was. He could have been any of the dozens circulating at the party. But she knew one thing.

She was staying away from parties as long as she lived at home and getting the hell out of here the minute she graduated high school. And she never, ever was going to have sex. Not with this nightmare firmly lodged in her mind.

CHAPTER 1

ALEX ROSSI STUDIED the scene in front of him, his first major crime since being appointed sheriff a little more than a month ago. As he stood at the edge of the clearing in this wooded area, looking at the body on the ground, his heart ached for the young teenage girl who would never see her next birthday. He wondered how such evil could exist in a setting with such natural beauty.

Fir trees reached to the sky, and batches of scrub punctuated the rolling land. Birds flitted through the tree-tops and brushed their wings against the scrub that grew everywhere. Above him the sky was a clear blue dusted with white clouds and, in the distance, the majestic Crazy Mountains rose with elegance from their foothills.

But, on the ground, fourteen-year-old Holly Martino lay sprawled on her stomach, arms outstretched, as if she'd been dropped there like a rag doll. Her head was tilted at an unnatural angle, due, he knew, to the fact her neck was broken. Hair as fine as spun gold was tangled, a few twigs caught in it. Her fingers were dug into the dirt as if she'd tried to claw her way up. Torn panties were wrapped around one leg, and he knew as sure as he was breathing that when the coroner did the post mortem, he'd find evidence of brutal rape. It was a signature, although one, according to the reports he'd gotten his hands on, that hadn't shown up in some time.

No one had reported her missing yet, so he could be pretty damn sure this had happened very recently. Like today. If a park ranger hadn't stumbled on the body while doing a routine tour, who knew how long it would have been until she was found. She'd been left in a remote area where days could have passed before anyone discovered her. Access to the area was all but impossible except by horseback or four-wheel drive, since most of the roads led directly to the ranches. Unluckily for the killer, a forest ranger, skirting land boundaries and checking the area, had stumbled on the body and called it in at once.

He'd seen plenty of dead bodies during his tour as a SEAL, even those of children, although they'd usually been the victims of horrific attacks on villages by the same people Alex was fighting. He'd thought those years had hardened him, but seeing the brutality visited on this young girl made him sick to his stomach.

He'd almost been waiting for this after Holly had sought him out the other night.

When Hank Patterson approached him about this job, he'd said, "For the most part, it's a snap job. Nothing goes on in the county to ruffle the surface. The biggest excitement is when everyone goes to the Fourth of July rodeo and gets obnoxiously drunk." He paused. "Except for one thing."

As head of Brotherhood Protectors, information always filtered up to him. He was pretty much plugged into everything in the county if not the state. The man had chosen to base his Brotherhood Protectors agency there and had his finger on the pulse of everything. In fact, some of the county commissioners had reached out to Hank about helping them find someone. Alex, a few months out of the SEALs after three tours of duty, had been at loose ends when fellow SEAL Scot Nolan, a member of the agency, hooked him up with Hank.

"What if they decide not to appoint me?" Alex had asked.

"Are you kidding? With your creds? Trust me, there's no one around that they'd be interested in. Besides"—he winked—"like I said, they asked me to help find someone."

So Alex had met with Hank and some of the commissioners and, before he could blink, he had a job and was renting a home on the edge of town. And what a home. It was the first place in years where he'd really felt peace.

But Hank had also clued him in about a decades-old open case.

"There's one big problem you need to know about, one that still has people looking over their shoulders. You'll have one huge fucking mess to clean up if you take this job. It's been dormant for several months, but it hasn't gone away. There are people out there who need to be identified and made to pay for their crimes."

"Yeah? What's that?"

He'd told him about the miasma of evil that clouded the county, the history of brutal rapes and murders covering two decades. The information he laid out made

Alex sick to his stomach. A series of crimes hung over the county like a black, evil cloud, brutal rapes punctuated with murder that had been ongoing for several years. Uber wealthy men raping young teenage girls, usually at a large party held at one of the sprawling ranches in the foothills of the Crazy Mountains. Either the girl lived there or attended the event with her parents. The routine was always the same. The girl would somehow be alone, separated from the rest of the party. A man would come up behind her, place his hands over her mouth, pinching the nose with thumb and forefinger, and drag the girl into a bedroom. Hold her head so she couldn't turn and see him. Press her face hard into the mattress as he attacked. All any of them knew was the man was very big and very rough, tearing their panties and raping them with brutal force.

And promising to kill them if they told.

"A few did tell," Hank told him. "And shortly after they made the report, we found their bodies. We're pretty sure Jeff Bartell was part of that group and even did the killings himself."

"Damn!" It had made Alex sick to think about it. "But if people knew who the culprits were, why weren't they arrested?"

"First of all, none of the girls who came forward could identify their rapists. And the former sheriff, now in prison, was part of that inner circle. Everyone figured he'd passed the word that a victim had filed a report and then the girl was killed. As promised."

Alex whistled. "Jesus."

Hank told him they had no idea how many had gone

unreported. Brotherhood Protectors had tried on their own to learn who the powerful men were, but the upper echelon of Crazy Mountains society was like a closed corporation. No one talked, and they resented even being questioned.

True-crime writer Jenna Donovan, born and raised in the Crazies and a victim herself at fifteen, had come home in response to an email from one of the victims and dug into the situation. She was the one who'd unmasked Bartell as a member of the ugly group, and the one who had warned the others, whoever they were, when anyone came forward.

It was unclear whether Bartell had killed all the girls himself, but he accepted responsibility and never gave up any of the other names. He was tried and convicted for the ones that could be proven. After he was sentenced, his family moved away, out of Montana. No one knew where they had gone or who had provided the funds to set them up. And no one talked about it.

A year passed 'with no more reported incidents after the sheriff's trial and conviction. It seemed that after Jenna's stories broke, all activity had died. At least no more brutal rapes had been reported. Nor had any more bodies been discovered. Alex wondered if the rapists had decided to kill their little game while they could.

The deputy who'd been serving as temporary sheriff had begged to go back to regular duty. So here Alex was, in a state he'd never even visited before, and acclimating himself to civilian life while he figured out what to do with the rest of his life. How to be something besides a SEAL, although he was pretty sure that would always be with him. He figured this was as good a place as any. Living solo suited him. History proved he sucked at relationships so, for the moment, he wasn't even looking for one. All he wanted was to get settled into the next phase of his life. And he could forego sex as long as his right hand held up. For a while, anyway.

For the past few weeks, he'd been reviewing the cold cases to give him an idea of who to look at and doing his best to quietly gather information about people in the area. He was still nowhere when, a month after he took office, Holly showed up at his place one night well after dark, frightened and desperate to ask for help. But only, she told him, if no one knew she had spoken to him. Fearful of being seen in his office, she'd come to his home to tell him what happened.

"They kill anyone who talks," Holly told him, shivering with fear, "but someone has to stop it. All my friends are afraid to leave their homes." She chewed her bottom lip as she decided what else to tell him. Then she blurted out, "Some of my friends even wonder if their fathers are involved."

That alone turned his stomach. She told him her friends tried refusing to go to the big events with their parents, only to be told that whoever was doing this was *not* someone from around there. Family friends would never do this, so whoever was spreading lies about this should just stop it.

But Alex wondered if, despite her precautions, someone had been spying on her. Or him. It was hard to keep secrets most of time in this county, and he knew word had gotten out that, as the new sheriff, he'd received copies of the crime reports from the Montana Department of Law Enforcement. While no one had been named, the girls who had been brave enough to come to the sheriff were killed within a week of meeting with him.

The. murder of Holly Martino was the first incident since Bartell had been arrested. Alec kept the report locked in his safe at home, so all he could think was someone had been watching Holly Martino. Now, looking at the body of the pretty young girl on the ground, he wanted to hit something. Or someone.

"It's a damn fucking shame." Miranda Golden, his senior deputy, walked up to stand beside him. It hadn't taken him long to discover Miranda knew everything there was to know about the area and about Montana law enforcement. That she was respected by almost everyone in the county. And that if he got on her bad side, he'd better quit his job. Getting on her bad side wasn't even on his list.

"A fucking shame indeed," he agreed. "And I can't help feeling that somehow it's my fault."

She stared at him. "How is that possible? I'm pretty sure you didn't do this."

He shook his head. "She came to me, terrified, but determined to report it anyway. I should have found a way to put her in protective custody."

"And how would you have managed that?" Miranda demanded. "What would you use as an excuse to her parents? And where would you have set her up, anyway?"

He knew she was right. In a sparsely populated county, with a small town for the county seat, there were no secrets, no matter how you tried to hide things. But that meant someone had been keeping an eye on the young girl, since he had arranged to meet her away from his office at a distant location. Either that or his house was bugged. If that was the case, he had bigger problems than he thought.

So here he was, barely five weeks into the job, doing his best to transition from the high-pressure life of a SEAL to a supposedly quiet job as a county sheriff, with a murder on his hands tied to an evil that continued to grip the area. He did have one thing, however, that no one knew, and he planned to keep it that way. Holly had given him a small paper sack containing her torn panties. When the rapist had pulled out of her, the condom had torn, and although he had taken it with him, there was enough semen spilled on the inside of her thigh to scoop it up with her underwear. Alex had taken it home with him and locked it in his private safe. Not yet knowing if he could trust everyone on his staff, he was keeping that sucker under wraps until hopefully it could be used.

"Well." Miranda sighed. "The coroner's here, and Chad Jenkins has finished taking pictures. Do you want to preserve the crime scene for any reason? I can't imagine that there are traces of anything with all the dirt and leaves."

Chad served as the crime-scene photographer for the office, along with some other duties.

"Let's do it anyway. I want to come back out here with the pictures Chad shot and go over everything myself. There's probably nothing, but I want to satisfy myself that's the case."

"Got it. Let me know if there's anything I can do. Oh,

and Jenna Donovan is still around here." She chuckled. "Married that hunky bodyguard of hers. Hell, I'd stay around for him, too. Ask Hank Patterson to hook you up with them. Scot Nolan still works for Brotherhood Protectors." She studied him for a moment. "Bet you thought it would be a little dull here after the SEALs."

Alex barked a short laugh. "Actually, a little dull wouldn't be bad after all those years in one conflict after another."

"Hope it works out. We, uh, sort of like having you here." She grinned.

"Thanks." He glanced over to where the body still lay. "I see the coroner is getting ready to bag her and take her to his lab. Let's walk over there. I want Chad to get pictures of the site without the body."

The coroner gently moved the body into a black bag for transport before moving it into his van.

"I'm pretty sure nothing new will turn up," he told Alex, "but I'll move it up to the top of my list. Expect something preliminary by tomorrow."

Alex nodded. "Appreciate it."

Then he watched Miranda and another deputy string yellow tape around the perimeter of the area where the body was found and waited while Chad grabbed a bunch of shots of the area without the corpse.

"Keep a lid on this until I get back to the office," he told Miranda. "Find out where her parents are, so I can do the notification. You know stuff before anyone else does."

"I don't know if Gavin Martino will be home," she told him. "He's some big deal in the state cattlemen's association and is always flying that plane of his back and forth to Butte and Helena, or Great Falls or someplace."

"Check on it for me, will you? Without giving away why I want to know? And see where his wife is."

"That's easy. It's Tuesday. Celeste Martino will be at The Promenade, the ritziest place in town. She's chairing the upcoming fashion show to raise money for an addition to the local clinic."

"So they're both pretty big on the political scene?"

Miranda snorted a laugh. "If it gets them publicity, they manage to be part of it."

"Do me a favor," he said. "I'm sure you know who her friends are. Get hold of one of them, let them know what happened, and have them bring Celeste to my office. Let me know when she's on her way. And check on her husband's whereabouts."

"Got it." She strode off toward her SUV.

Alex hung back as everyone else left. He wanted to get the feel of the area without another human being around.

If anyone wanted to commit a murder, he thought, this was the place to do it. The Crazy Mountains as a range were forty miles long and almost completely surrounded by private land. That limited the access of strangers to the area, which meant any crime committed was usually laid at the feet of some resident. It also meant that the people living in the Crazy foothills were sharp enough to be careful and not get caught.

And rich. It had to be some of the obnoxiously wealthy assholes who were used to buying their way out of anything and controlling their environment and anything that happened in it. He'd seen enough people like that in his lifetime, once to his great sorrow. They were the wealthy and privileged who thought they could get away with anything because rules did not apply to them. Because power was what it was all about. Plus, their money could cover up anything.

When everyone had left the scene, he walked over to Holly's body and studied it carefully. They hadn't found the tire tracks of any kind of vehicle, not even the four wheelers so many of the ranchers used to get around. So, how the hell had whoever it was brought her up here? On horseback? Always a possibility. God knew this wasn't what you'd call an area of heavy traffic. Or any traffic, for that matter.

It was someone's land, without a doubt. Most of the area around the Crazies was. Although a good bit of it was fenced, the rough terrain made it difficult for people not used to it to get around and so could be accessible only if you knew what you were doing. He'd have to check and see who owned this particular parcel, although he was sure whoever had killed Holly Martino hadn't dumped her on his own land.

Shit!

Still, it wasn't as if he had anything else to do. Since it seemed he sucked at relationships, he lived a pretty solitary existence. Except for the few times he hung out with Hank and his wife, Sadie, and some of the other Brotherhood Protectors, his social life was a big fat zero. But that was good, he told himself. No chance to screw up again and all the time in the world to find the answers to this terrifying puzzle.

Tomorrow, he had to stop by the Schroeder Ranch and

see what Tom Schroeder wanted regarding the big party they had coming up this weekend. Miranda had told him that after Jeff Bartell was arrested, when anyone threw a party, they wanted law enforcement there, as if to let the world know they weren't involved in the nasty business. Not, he knew, that it would stop someone if they were bent on rape. Apparently, over the span of two decades, these men had perfected their technique, even where timing and circumstance were concerned.

His thought process was interrupted by the ringing of his cell.

"Yeah?"

"Sheriff, it's me. Miranda. I'm calling you on your cell rather than having dispatch put through the message so we can keep it on the downlow." Her voice dropped even more. "I have Celeste Martino in the office, and she's demanding to know what the hell is going on."

"Okay. I'm on my way."

He wasn't looking forward to the next hour at all.

ABOUT DESIREE HOLT

USA Today best-selling and award-winning author **Desiree Holt** writes everything from romantic suspense and contemporary on a variety of heat levels up to erotic, a genre in which she is the oldest living author. She has been referred to by *USA Today* as the Nora Roberts of erotic romance, and is a winner of the EPIC E-Book Award, the Holt Medallion and a Romantic Times Reviewers Choice nominee. She has been featured on *CBS Sunday Morning* and in *The Village Voice, The Daily Beast, USA Today, The (London) Daily Mail, The New Delhi Times* and numerous other national and international publications.

Desiree loves to hear from readers.

www.facebook.com/desireeholtauthor
www.facebook.com/desiree01holt
Twitter @desireeholt
Pinterest: desiree02holt
Google: https://g.co/kgs/6vgLUu
www.desireeholt.com
www.desiremeonly.com

Follow Her On:

Amazon

https://www.amazon.com/Desiree-Holt/e/
B003LD2Q3M/ref=sr_tc_2_0?qid=1505488204&
sr=1-2-ent

Signup for her newsletter
http://eepurl.com/ce7DeE

 facebook.com/desiree01holt

 twitter.com/desireeholt

ORIGINAL BROTHERHOOD PROTECTORS SERIES

BY ELLE JAMES

Brotherhood Protectors Series

Montana SEAL (#1)

Bride Protector SEAL (#2)

Montana D-Force (#3)

Cowboy D-Force (#4)

Montana Ranger (#5)

Montana Dog Soldier (#6)

Montana SEAL Daddy (#7)

Montana Ranger's Wedding Vow (#8)

Montana SEAL Undercover Daddy (#9)

Cape Cod SEAL Rescue (#10)

Montana SEAL Friendly Fire (#11)

Montana SEAL's Mail-Order Bride (#12)

Montana Rescue (Sleeper SEAL)

Hot SEAL Salty Dog (SEALs in Paradise)

Brotherhood Protectors Vol 1

ABOUT ELLE JAMES

ELLE JAMES also writing as MYLA JACKSON is a *New York Times* and *USA Today* Bestselling author of books including cowboys, intrigues and paranormal adventures that keep her readers on the edges of their seats. With over eighty works in a variety of sub-genres and lengths she has published with Harlequin, Samhain, Ellora's Cave, Kensington, Cleis Press, and Avon. When she's not at her computer, she's traveling, snow skiing, boating, or riding her ATV, dreaming up new stories. Learn more about Elle James at www.ellejames.com

Website | Facebook | Twitter | GoodReads | Newsletter | BookBub | Amazon

Follow Elle!
www.ellejames.com
ellejames@ellejames.com

facebook.com/ellejamesauthor
twitter.com/ElleJamesAuthor

www.ingramcontent.com/pod-product-compliance
Lightning Source LLC
Chambersburg PA
CBHW071309200626
46813CB00015B/725